Old Friends and New Enemies

Owen Mullen

They dragged him from the boot of the car, down an embankment to the shore; gagged, bound and blindfolded. His feet scraped grass and stones; a shoe came off and was left behind. At the jetty, Kevin Rafferty waited in the boat. In a long career of violent persuasion this guy had been the hardest to break. But it wouldn't last. When the blindfold came off he'd realise the loch was to be his grave. Then the begging would begin because pain and death weren't the same. And he'd tell. Everything. It never failed. Plastic ties fastened the victim's wrists to hooks hammered into either side of the gun-wale, holding him upright. His head moved, blindly drawn to every sound. With what he'd been through – the beating, the burns, the loss of blood – it was a miracle he was still breathing.

Rafferty turned up his collar, dipped the oars in the water and started to row.

After a while he stopped. Late afternoon drizzle falling from a grey sky stippled the calm surface, they would drift, but not much. He released the blindfold. They stared at each other. Rafferty broke the spell. He opened a canvas bag that lay across his knees, slowly, so the man could see the knives, the screwdrivers, the pliers: his tools. On top he placed a bolt cutter and patted it as he would a faithful dog. The thief moaned and fought against the restraints, wild terror in his eyes. The cutter trapped the first finger of his right hand between the blades. He began to cry.

'Last chance,' Rafferty said.

The blades tightened, a muffled wail came from behind the gag.

'Sure? Okay.'

A thin red line appeared at the joint. Rafferty sighed fake regret.

'This little piggy went to market…'

An opal moon hung above the loch, it had stopped raining and the night sky was clear. The thief was slumped forward, passed out. They'd been at it for hours - or five fingers - he should be pleading for his life. Better yet he should be dead. In Glasgow, Rafferty understood it wasn't going to be easy. Something wasn't right about this guy. He didn't get it. Kevin's job was to make him get it.

He peeled the sock from the shoeless foot, bleached like a corpse in the moonlight, and lifted it into position. For the moment the gag was unnecessary, he ripped it away and waited for his victim to come round; when he did it would continue. A noise took him by surprise. He tensed. At the other end of the boat the head came up, eyes blazed in the gloom and the madman grinned at him through broken teeth.

'I'm starving,' he said.

'What…what?'

'Could murder a curry.'

Rafferty's voice cracked with desperation. 'What did you do with the money?'

'Chicken Tikka.'

This was insane.

'The money! Where is it?'

The thief spat blood and sniggered. 'Fuck off.'

Rafferty snapped. He grabbed a knife and buried it in the crazy bastard's heart.

No,' he said, 'you fuck off.'

The body rolled over the side and disappeared into the dark water, Rafferty gathered the severed fingers and threw them after it; food for the fish. At the jetty, he got out and stood for a long time watching the untethered boat float away. He had been so confident, so sure. But it hadn't worked out. He was going back with nothing. The thought of telling his father made Rafferty sick with fear — more afraid than the man he had just killed had ever been.

Jimmy would go mental.

Glasgow 2006

He was standing inside the door, watching me. The cheeky grin came naturally. He had been using it all his life. The trade mark *fuck-you* confidence was harder to fake but he tried. So why was I surprised? On a Friday night in Glasgow you might meet anybody; it's that kind of place. The girl I was flirting with laughed and floated past; she was too good looking to go home by herself and knew it. She was playing a game. Later we'd play a different game.

He came towards me. 'Get in touch with your emotions, Charlie,' he said and gave me a hug. When he let go I caught something in his eyes; a trace of anxiety.

'Ian! What the hell are you doing here? What're you drinking?'

I shouted my question over the noise of the band. He waved the offer away. 'Off it,' he said, then changed his mind, put a hand on my shoulder and drew me to him. 'Tell you what, seeing it's you, a large glass of your father's finest. Just to be sociable.'

He made it sound like he was doing me a favour.

My father's finest was Cameron's whisky, world famous. Archibald Cameron was the CEO. I hadn't followed the path he'd taken and he never let me forget what a disappointment I was. Unfortunately for both of us, for the last couple of years I'd been proving him right. But my days as a waster were numbered. The money my grandmother left was almost gone. Beyond that I had no idea. All I could be certain of was that returning south with my tail between my legs to a job in the family business was a non-starter. Not happening.

Ian took the amber liquid from the bartender, swallowed half and wiped his mouth.

'The bad penny, eh?

'What a coincidence running into you. Where's Fiona?'

'In Spain. Doesn't know I'm here. Forgot this was your local.'

No he hadn't.

'This was where we met a year ago.'

'So it was.'

The club was busy. Under my feet the floor vibrated. The weekend had started. I led him to a corner where there was a chance of hearing ourselves think and signalled for another round. Across the table I watched, waiting for him to get to the point. With Ian Selkirk there was always a point. He was one of those people who sailed through at the expense of whoever was handy. For as long as I'd known him he'd been charming and funny and selfish. We'd had some good times together. Except I wasn't a nineteen-year-old student anymore. Those Friday and Saturday nights at the Moti Mahal and our Thailand adventure, when I asked Fiona to marry me, were long gone.

He raised his glass in a toast. 'To old friends. The best friends.' Fiona's words.

'Old friends,' I said.

He grinned. So much of what he came away with was bullshit. That hadn't altered. He wasn't off it, he was drunk. 'What're you up to these days?'

I avoided answering. 'This and that, you know.'

He drummed his fingers on the side of the table and let it go, laughing his nervous laugh at a joke he was getting round to telling. 'Got myself into some trouble. Wondered if you could help.'

'What kind of trouble?'

'Nothing I can't handle. I need money. Not a gift, Charlie. Not something for nothing.'

I asked how much and he told me. It was a lot. 'I don't have it, Ian.'

'Not even for an old pal?'

'Why do you need it? What's happened? You and Fiona were doing great out there.'

He smiled his disbelief and stood.

'If you don't have it you don't have it, Charlie. Thanks for the drink.'

Old friend or not, I hadn't been his first choice, more like his last. Bumping into me wasn't a coincidence. God knows how many times he'd been in here until he eventually tracked me down. And suddenly I understood. He'd remembered my grandmother had included me in her will, put two and two together and come up with five. It wasn't anxiety in his eyes, it was desperation.

'Sorry, Ian, I really am.'

'Me too,' he said. 'Me too.'

I never saw him alive again.

Chapter 1

Those who know don't speak. Those who speak don't know.

Jimmy Rafferty was in his twenties when he heard that scrap of ancient wisdom. It appealed to him. He quoted it often without understanding. Or perhaps he did. The mafia had Omerta, in the east end of Glasgow, Rafferty had the Tao. It was enough. The boy from Bridgeton climbed the mountain and for over forty years his empire was held in place by the unsaid. No one discussed him or his business.

All his life Rafferty had been strong, physically and mentally, depending only on himself. Few were brave enough to go up against him. Those who had regretted it. The stroke and the stick that came with it represented what he despised most. Weakness. He had lost weight, a lot of weight; clothes hung on him like hand-me-downs, and his eyes were watery hollows that could no longer intimidate. Illness had aged him. Before, he'd stood ramrod straight, now he stooped and when he walked he shuffled. More and more he found himself thinking of the past. And it wasn't just his body that had suffered; something at the very centre of his being was missing: the iron will of old was gone. His concentration wandered. At times he wasn't really there.

That left a question: who would take over?

The trouble the family faced cried out for a leader but his sons didn't have the stuff. Kevin was thick and Sean was a non-event. In a year what he had achieved would be gone. Between them they would lose it all.

It should've been easy. Steal from the thief and bury him where he'd never be found. Jimmy had let Kevin handle it. A mistake.

1

Rage built in the old man like an approaching train; a murmur on the air, a quiver in the rail, until the monster roared and thundered, unstoppable. His hands trembled, the stick danced. He screamed. 'You moron! Fucked us right up, haven't you, boy?'

At the end of a lawn shaded by trees and set back from the road the house held its secrets. Nobody would hear. Kevin fingered the scar running from his ear to his chin and braced himself against the expected tirade. It didn't come. Instead the tone was gentle; it terrified his eldest son.

"Come on. C'mon, Kevin. Convince me. Tell me it wasn't your fault.'

Sean watched his brother's humiliation. Kevin was still scared of his father – maybe understandable in the past – not now. For all his noise Jimmy was spent and knew it. He'd been decisive. A force of nature. Once. With his hold slipping, anger replaced action. The old man's power was gone; he was impotent.

Jimmy said, 'How does a guy end up dead before he gives us what we want? I mean, how can that be? We needed him breathin' in and out. Didn't even capture his mobile. A bastard monkey could figure it. But not you.'

Kevin's excuse was worse than feeble. 'He laughed at me.'

'So you knifed him. That would take the smile off his face. Taken the smile off mine. Pity you didn't remember why we lifted him in the first place.'

Kevin blurted out his defence. 'That guy was a nutter. I pumped him full of shit. It didn't matter, he was never going to tell. He just kept laughing. I lost it.'

Rafferty's face was inches from his son's. Kevin could smell his breath, sour with cigarettes. 'You never had it to lose,' his father said. 'Your brother got the brains.'

Sean knew he wasn't talking about him.

'We're out because a junkie you were working on laughed at you. He thought you were a clown and so do I. Our friend in the sun is expecting results.'

'He was waiting to make contact. We know he was waiting.'

'Hear that Sean? Your brother said something that wasn't stupid. That's what we have to do. Wait. Sounds like the kind of thing you'd be good at, Kevin. Maybe I should put you in charge. Head of Fucking Waiting.'

The son had endured taunts and jibes and worse from his father all his life. This time it was deserved so he took it but, then, he always did. Getting people to talk was Kevin's speciality and he enjoyed his job; it shouldn't have been a problem. Except the thief wasn't right in the head. He didn't care. Even with his injuries the bastard was mocking him. With the last "fuck you!" Kevin snapped. The knife felt heavy against his palm. He heard the thud and sensed the blade twist into the heart.

Jimmy Rafferty turned to his sons. The effort had drained him; his chest rose and fell. 'We've still got a chance. Sean, keep an eye on your idiot brother. Make sure he doesn't screw up.' He sighed and leaned on the stick. 'I wish Paul was here. He was young but he was a doer. And he was smart.'

Sean flinched. Paul. Always Paul. Should he tell the deluded old bastard the apple of his eye was a reckless fool who died an unnecessary death proving it? Wouldn't the great Jimmy be surprised to discover that sainted Paul had mocked him behind his back? Talked about replacing him. Not yet, this wasn't the moment.

Those who know don't speak

But soon.

Chapter 2

I was late. The visitor pulled herself tight and held the cup Jackie had given her in both hands. I laid the blame on road works at Charing Cross, hung the coat I had on behind the door and went into my busy act. Papers got shuffled that hadn't been shuffled since yesterday. When I'd made enough of a fuss I said, 'Right. How can I help you?'

A small mouth in a pleasant face voiced her uncertainty. 'I haven't done anything like this before.' She drew a nervous hand through light-coloured hair that may have been blonde in her youth. 'I'm not sure how to begin.'

'Then I'll begin. I'm Charlie Cameron. Anything you say will stay here. If I feel you'd be better off without me I'll tell you. You can hire me by the hour or daily, depending. At the end of my enquiry I'll give a written or a verbal report, whatever suits. And I don't have a team of highly trained operatives. I'm it. Sometimes I'm successful, sometimes not. All I guarantee is to give it my best.'

I'd used that little speech before. Charlie Cameron, honest injun. As near to a mission statement as I would ever get. 'So how can I help you?'

'I want you to find my husband. Two weeks ago I buried my son; my husband walked out the day before the funeral.'

'What's his name?'

'Stephen. Stephen McNeil. I'm Cecelia McNeil. I'm worried sick about him.'

She lifted her teacup and gave me an insight into what she was going through. Her fingers were the most slender I'd ever seen: long and delicate, porcelain-white and china-fine; beautiful, spoiled by unpainted nails bitten to the quick.

'I'm a tea person, always have been. Earl Grey is my favourite. Coffee doesn't agree with me.'

Nonsense chatter.

She tried a smile that didn't fit and touched the black mark on her forehead. Burnt palm. I recognised what it was.

'Which mass did you go to?'

'St Andrew's on Clyde Street. The eight o'clock service. My own parish is the Immaculate Conception, Maryhill. Do you know it?'

I shook my head.

'Since Christopher did what he did, God and I aren't speaking. That's hard for me. Without faith I'm lost. Today starts the forty days Our Lord spent in the desert. Forty six days actually. Sundays don't count.'

Talking to a stranger is supposed to be easier than talking to a friend. Not always. I said, 'Take your time, Mrs McNeil.'

She drew strength from a private well and spoke. 'Christopher took his own life. I found him in the garage. He had locked the doors and turned on the ignition. His father drove non-stop from Dover to get home. He was devastated. I told him it wasn't his fault. The circumstances meant a sudden death inquiry. The funeral was held back. Stephen retreated further and further into himself. He couldn't get over it. The suicide verdict was more than he could bear. The day before we buried our boy, Stephen disappeared. I haven't seen or heard from him since. His employer says he's quit; they don't know where he is.'

'Have you reported him missing?'

'He isn't missing, he's running away.'

'Why?'

'Because he thinks he's to blame. And he took his guns.'

'Guns?'

'That's why I'm here. I'm afraid he'll do something stupid. My husband's a long distance driver. After a week stuck behind the wheel he needs air. Shooting and fishing help him relax.'

'What makes him believe he's responsible for his son's death?'

'Things haven't been easy at home. Christopher argued with his father night and day.'

Fathers and sons. I got it.

'When he was younger they were so close. Stephen's a Celtic fan. Even before Christopher was old enough he had season tickets bought. Beside the corner flag. When the TV cameras were there Christopher would wave to me. I tried to see him. I did too, sometimes. Apart from Rangers, they never missed a game. Christopher detested the atmosphere at Old Firm matches, so full of hate. Stephen went. Christopher stayed away. Taking his son to the football – being a part of his life – was something to be proud of. His own childhood hadn't been happy; his father was a brute. I loved seeing them set off together wearing their green and white scarves.'

Cecelia McNeil dwelt on the memory.

'So what happened?'

'Christopher took up with the wrong crowd. Overnight he became a stranger. His father tried talking to him. I tried too. All we got were tantrums and tears and silence. Out of the blue he announced he didn't want to go anymore.'

'Stephen was hurt. I put it down to the terrible teens. Christopher's grades dropped. My boy was always near the top of the class: his teachers were concerned because the slump was so dramatic. One even came to the house to discuss it with us. Other parents told me to wait it out, that it would pass. Par for the course they said. Be thankful I didn't have a girl.'

'What age would he be?'

She thought about it.

'Fifteen.'

'A tough time.'

'Though we often had words, his father got the worst of it. Stephen couldn't do right for doing wrong. It affected him, even more than me. He lost weight and there was a tension in him that hadn't been there before.'

'Teenagers like to give parents a hard time.'

'Through the storm, the door-slamming, the backchat, the lack of respect, Stephen kept his temper. He once told me his greatest fear was of turning out like his father. I never met that man and I'm glad. The crunch came when Christopher stole the car. He just took it. He crashed – of course – into another vehicle.'

'Was he injured?'

'He was lucky, there wasn't much damage but Stephen was angry. If somebody had got the registration it wouldn't be long until the police arrived. Next day they did. My husband told them he was driving and showed them the marks, scuffed paint mostly. He claimed the other driver was at fault; they didn't disagree. Problem was, Christopher had left the scene. Fled they called it. That was their main concern. And it threw up another problem. Stephen was a long distance driver. My tuition didn't bring in enough, our livelihood depended on his license. The police accepted his story, Christopher was in the clear, but they charged Stephen.'

She looked away and back again.

'I don't know why I'm telling you this. It isn't important.'

'Right now we can't be sure what's important and what isn't. Go on. When was this?'

'About eighteen months back. In the end it came to a fine and a lecture from the judge. Unfortunately, Christopher forgot the part he played and the risk his father had taken to protect him. The attitude returned, if anything more hostile. Stephen took a firmer line. Maybe too firm. They argued. Every weekend started and ended with a shouting match.'

She trembled. 'Am I taking too long? There must be lots of people waiting.'

'They'll have to wait,' I said. 'Go on.'

'It got bad, really bad. One night they actually fought. Christopher locked himself in his room, Stephen went out to calm down. Our home had become a battlefield.'

She touched the ash on her forehead and returned to the present. 'I'm talking too much, sorry.'

Cecelia McNeil placed her palms together. 'Please find Stephen, Mr Cameron, he's out of his mind with grief. His father failed him. He thinks he failed Christopher. If there's any hope of getting him back it isn't the police. We need to heal, together, by ourselves. This morning at St Andrew's I let God in again. And I was none too easy with him either. I told him straight.'

'Let's hope he was listening.'

'I'm sure he was,' she said. 'He sent me to you, didn't he?'

**

She answered my questions about her husband and son, let me have her contact details, and pushed a couple of photographs across the desk. Neither was recent. In the first the boy wouldn't have been more than ten; his father's arm drew them together. There were fishing rods in the shot, they'd been on the water somewhere. No fish to boast about, just smiles and blood ties. The other was outside a football stadium. The scarves draped round their shoulders told which one. The boy was older, the pose was the same and set together the pictures suggested a bond the man had worked at building.

The snaps were a beginning but a visit to the house would tell me more. Christopher McNeil had taken his looks from his mother: fair hair, the shape of his young face; the tapered fingers gripping the team colours said his father's genes had lost out. The adult beside him was dark and well-built, swarthy, his jowls overlaid with shadow.

'Christopher's like you.'

'Yes, but in those days he was his daddy's boy.'

We went downstairs, to the door. Jackie Mallon worked at a table nearby. When we shook hands Cecelia McNeil's felt soft and fragile.

'Stephen lived for his boy, Mr Cameron. It made me so sad to watch him going to the game by himself. It had been such a great thing to share. A father and son, supporting their team.

My husband kept telling Christopher what he was missing, encouraging him along. He wouldn't join in.'

'Why did his father still take two tickets? Football isn't cheap.'

'I suppose he hoped Christopher would change his mind.'

'He never did?'

'No, he said he wasn't interested. Stephen paid a lot of money for those seats.'

'What did your son do instead?'

'I'm ashamed to say I'm not sure. What kind of parent does that make me?'

'The normal kind. Young people like their secrets; it's how they cope with experiences their folks would rather they didn't have. They aren't good at criticism.'

'There was his music, of course.' She laughed. 'His father's a rock 'n' roll man, Christopher played classical.'

'What did he play?'

'Piano. Like me.'

'Did you teach him?'

'Oh, when he was a wee boy I helped him find his way round the keyboard. After that he went to lessons. When we met, Stephen was a huge Hendrix fan but Georg Frideric Handel was my superstar. His *Messiah* is a masterpiece. They lived next door to each other in London, did you know that? A couple of hundred years apart mind, but still.'

Cecelia McNeil was easy to like. Behind the old fashioned religious intensity was a nice lady.

'Find my husband, Mr Cameron, he isn't well. Tell me where he is so I can go to him. I take my vows seriously. In sickness and in health aren't just words to me. They're a sacred promise.'

'I understand. I'll do my best.'

'God will be with you.'

I smiled. 'Then it's a done deal.'

Chapter 3

The city of Glasgow is well served by hospitals. I tried six. No one matching Stephen McNeil's description had been admitted in the previous weeks. He wasn't in jail either. If he'd gone to Central Station and jumped the Euston train, London would swallow him. I went downstairs to NYB and ordered a latte. Andrew Geddes was in his seat by the window, suit stretched tight against his stocky frame. That style would come back again someday.

Andrew was a DS in Police Scotland CID and my mate, a moody guy with an unshakeable concept of right and wrong; divorce had given him a singular view of the world. Now and then he helped me so I regularly paid his tab. It never altered, no matter what shift he was working; sweet black coffee and a bagel, used in a fascinating ritual that wasn't pretty to watch.

He buttered the bagel and dipped it in the cup. With wet pastry floating on the surface, he bent forward, slurping and snaffling like a truffle hound. People stared, he didn't mind. I waited for him to resurface and wipe flakes of cooked dough from his mouth.

'This is how it's done in the Big Apple,' he said.

'I'll take your word for it, Andrew.'

I'd had that explanation a hundred times.

'I'm looking for somebody.'

'Who isn't?' He stopped mid-dunk. 'Couldn't you take a boring old surveillance job, or snap some dirty pictures for a divorce lawyer for a change?'

'This one isn't missing exactly, more like AWOL. The hospitals don't have him, he isn't in the cells.'

'Could be in the Big House on remand. Or the morgue.'

The Big House was Barlinnie. The Bar-L.

'I don't think he's dead.'

'Try the morgue anyway. I start in twenty minutes. I'll call them. See what they've got.'

An hour later my phone rang. 'Unidentified male washed ashore four days ago at Luss. Two canoeists found the body. Worth a look. I'll tell them you're coming.'

On my way out, Pat Logue gave me an empty glass salute. His father had lost to cancer the previous week; his mother was already dead. He was still wearing a black tie although the funeral had been on Friday. It clashed with the polo shirt.

'Charlie! Want to buy an orphan a drink?'

He slid off the barstool and fell into step. 'Where're we going?'

'We're not going.'

'No harm in a wee walk.'

The gaunt guy on the corner let us pass without offering the magazine. His eyes were heavy, lowered so he didn't have to look at me. When we passed he shouted after us.

'"The rank is but the guinea's stamp, the man's the gowd for a' that!"'

Pat Logue clocked it. 'Hear that? He blanked you. Now he's givin' it Rabbie Burns. What've you done to him?'

'Last couple of times I'd no change. Elephants and Big Issue sellers never forget, Patrick.'

'Probably doolally. Christ knows when he last had something to eat.'

'Didn't notice you making a contribution.'

'Can't,' he said. 'Haven't a razoo. Where're we off to?'

'Pat, I'll let you know if I need you.'

He got to the point. 'I'm looking for a sponsor, Charlie. Things aren't the best with me and Gail. I got a bit out of order after the funeral so she's given me a red card. Have to stay clear of the house.'

I took out a ten pound note. He eyed it with dismay. 'What's that?'

'A donation.'

'Noticed the prices in there? A bigger photo of the queen would help, take it off my money. Call it a retainer.' I gave him a twenty. He said, 'Keep it in your trousers, Charlie,' and walked away with a spring in his step.

Where I was going wasn't far, through Candleriggs towards the Green, to a squat stone box building topped with a band of red brick. The sun came out; it would take more than a splash of warm light to improve the look of the mortuary. Inside a man in a white coat asked my name and showed me to a room on the left, empty except for a few chairs and a television built into the wall. The sign on the door read Visitors Room. It wasn't a welcoming place – it didn't need to be – nobody would stay overlong.

'You won't see the body,' the attendant said, 'just the face.'

The next few moments could break Cecelia McNeil's already broken heart and make this the shortest case I had ever been on. I wondered if her god had heard, or if the faith of a decent woman would be tested again. I took another look at the photograph of the football supporters. One of them was already dead. The TV picture flickered in black and white, the image grey on grey. A face filled the screen, bloated and waxy, unlined, neutral in death. It wasn't Stephen McNeil. But it wasn't a stranger.

I hadn't seen Ian Selkirk in a long time, not since the night he asked me for money. The night I turned him down.

Got myself into some trouble. Wondered if you could help

He had laughed that nervous laugh of his.

Not a gift, Charlie. Not something for nothing

For Patrick Logue a big photo of the queen was enough. Ian had needed a lot more. And he wouldn't explain.

It was just another day down on the farm for the mortuary attendant. He wasn't the right person to speak to but he was the only one there.

'What did the autopsy show?'

He straightened chairs; the smell of old tobacco followed him around. My question held no interest. 'Hasn't been done yet,' he said. 'They're running behind. Be Friday at the earliest. Next week more likely.'

I couldn't take my eyes from the television. Ian's water-blown features filled my mind. He had been one of the most alive people I'd ever known. We had been mates. That summer in Thailand, Ian was the one who got the three of us jobs at the diving school in Koh Tao. They hired Fiona and me because they needed him.

I felt cold. I spoke to myself. 'He couldn't have drowned. He was a great swimmer. How could he drown? He was too good. Far too good.'

The attendant shepherded me to the street; he'd seen the same reaction scores of times. His priority was to clear the place ready for the next one. In daylight his complexion wasn't much better than Ian Selkirk's; he needed to get out more, and not just for a cigarette.

I babbled. 'He was ace in the water, how could he drown?'

'What's your relationship to the deceased?'

'Friend. A close friend.'

He looked at the sky and the Tron clock at the top of Saltmarket and nodded as if my reply explained something he hadn't understood. The words escaped from the side of his mouth in a smoky whisper. 'Off the record. Your pal didn't drown.'

I took a step back. He shied away from qualifying his statement.

'He didn't drown. Believe me.'

The door closed.

I believed him.

Chapter 4

I didn't go back to the office. I went to High Street where my car was parked. Andrew Geddes said the body washed ashore at Luss on Sunday; the scene would still be intact.

Great Western Road took me north, out of the city. Normally the mix of Persian and Greek restaurants, West Indian greengrocers, Pakistani take-aways and Halal butchers appealed to me. I liked the colour and chaos. Today it seemed drab.

At Anniesland Cross, a silver Volkswagen Passat pulled in behind me as the sun broke through the clouds. The day was brightening, I was blind to it. Beyond Dumbarton strange names, difficult to pronounce, appeared on road signs. The turn-off for Duck Bay Marina and Cameron House Hotel came and went then, through the trees over on the right, there it was: Loch Lomond. Impressive enough to merit its own song. Flat calm stretching into the distance flanked by Ben Lomond; over three thousand feet high, patched with snow, the most southerly Munro. Out on the loch a speed boat skimmed the surface drawing a foaming line, white against dark blue. Scotland saw too few days like this; opportunities to play with such expensive toys were rare.

My mood was sour. Seeing him, cold and swollen and empty of life had left me unfit to be with people. I hadn't thought of Ian Selkirk in more than a dozen years, now I could think of nothing else. Memories came in numbers, I didn't resist them. At a rock gig in the QM it was Fiona who caught my attention; slim and dark and smiling, watching Ian push his way to the bar, apologising when he squeezed into space where there was no space. Jumping the queue of thirsty students. The band was trying to be Talking Heads. I'd given up on them after the third number and taken a strategic position at the bar, an arm's length from the taps. The place was mobbed, eight deep, everyone harassing the over-worked staff for service. Ian struggled like a salmon against the tide, determined to get where he needed to go. Whenever someone complained about his cheek he grinned and said something I couldn't hear. It must have been funny because they laughed.

He used that trick more than once, edging closer, until the last row lay between him and his objective. He tried to manoeuvre himself one more time but the serious drinkers held their ground, immune to his jokey asides. Every arm was raised to attract attention. Fingers flicked fivers and tenners and twenties, all claiming to be first. I looked through the crowd to his girlfriend and saw her face. It was a lovely face. That made up my mind. I stretched a hand towards him; he took it and I pulled him home.

He said, 'Thanks mate. What you having?'

And that was how we met.

I gave my spot at the bar to some sweaty guy in an Iron Maiden t-shirt and joined them. We clinked glasses and introduced ourselves. They were at Glasgow Uni. Ian put an arm round his companion, a signal she was taken. Fiona seemed content to let him do most of the talking. He would ask a question and answer it himself. Witty observations collided with fragments of trivia, his eyes dancing with mischief. I thought it was a performance for my benefit. If it was, his girlfriend enjoyed it as much as I did. The bond between them was undeniable. My strongest recollection is of laughing. After a while I fell about every time he opened his mouth, even before he said anything. We all did. By the end I was hoarse and exhausted.

I sneaked a look at the girl. She was very attractive; they both were. One dark, the other fair, with even white teeth and skin that glowed beneath clothes worn with stylish indifference. Her hair was shoulder length, in long black curls. When she spoke she shrugged it back. I thought she was wonderful and ached to kiss her. I envied him. They had something, something I hadn't come across before. An energy. A synergy. He was a cool guy and I fancied her. When it was time to go our separate ways I was sorry.

Ian clapped my shoulder. 'Thanks for helping me out,' he said. 'I'd still be stuck with the plebs with my tongue hanging out.'

'No problem, you were doing all right on your own.'

'We come here most weekends, maybe we'll see you again.'

They did. I made sure they did. We met often, drank too much lager and talked and talked. Many nights ended at the Moti Mahal, stuffing ourselves with traditional Glasgow fare, Ian's name for tandoori chicken drumsticks and – if he was really bladdered – lamb vindaloo. The people who owned the Moti were from Kerala: Mr Rani Das; his wife Anjali; sons Salman and Videk, and their daughter Geeta. Everyone worked in the restaurant. They became friends. Mr Rani would sit with us, running a hand through his bushy black hair. If he wasn't too busy and we weren't too drunk he'd tell stories about his boyhood in India: exotic tales of train journeys at night across the vast sub-continent. Dawn arrivals with mynahs and parrots circling in the first golden light of a new day, and vendors on the platform shouting "Chai garam, chai garam" [hot tea, hot tea].

We hung on his descriptions of places beyond our experience. Videk would take Ian through to the kitchen to have a word with the chefs. Sometimes he wandered in on his own and helped himself to vegetable pakora, fresh from the hot fat.

'These are unbelievable. Try one.'

And when we passed he'd put on an Indian/Scottish accent, say 'Pure dead fucking brilliant', and make Mr Rani laugh. No one thought it out of the ordinary. That was how it was. He would put his arm round Ian Selkirk. 'This is my third son,' he'd tell us, and, to Fiona, 'this is my second daughter.'

With me he just smiled. When her father didn't see, Geeta smiled too. The sons fell under Ian's spell. They huddled with him at the end of the night, grinning and giggling at his patter.

Ian and Fiona never discussed their relationship though every time I called his flat she answered. It hadn't been an act in the

QM; Ian pushed his luck with everybody. He was outrageous, irreverent and amusing. And he always had good dope. On an odd occasion when he went too far I saw Fiona shake her head, or take him aside and speak to him. Then he would behave – for a while.

Vanity wasn't one of my weaknesses. Girls had told me I was handsome though I hadn't given it too much thought. At five eleven, with brown hair, blue eyes and no obvious flaws I supposed I was acceptable enough. Still, I got why she was attracted to him and considered myself dull by comparison.

During the second semester I made half-hearted attempts at classes without taking much in. A law degree was my father's idea, not mine. The exam results were due. I feared the worst – with good reason. I hadn't done enough to even scrape a pass. I felt trapped and depressed. A failure. Almost twenty, stuck on a path I didn't give a damn about and bombing; if anyone had asked what I wanted to do with my life I couldn't have told them.

All that kept me sane was my friendship with Ian Selkirk and Fiona Ramsay.

Family was a no-go subject; uni was the same. I had known them five months and still wasn't sure what courses they were on. They weren't secretive; that kind of stuff just wasn't important to them. Everything was about the moment. Everything was about now.

One night we left the pub, bought some wine and went back to Ian's flat on Hyndland Road. He put on music and rolled a joint. Fiona got glasses. The wine was cheap German plonk, ideal for the undiscerning young people we were. I understood, later, they were sounding me out. At the time I thought it was him, at it as usual, having a laugh.

They were side by side on a faded sofa. I was on an orange beanbag on the floor. He lit up and put his arm round her. 'We're leaving Glasgow,' he said. 'It isn't right for us anymore.'

I scoffed through the alcohol. 'What're you talking about? You can't just leave.'

'Yeah we can. We've discussed it, it's happening.'

They waited for my reaction. 'Fiona,' I said, 'he's winding me up, isn't he?'

'No, we're leaving, Charlie.'

'Uni?'

'Everything.'

I sat forward. 'To go where?'

He gave the spliff to her and answered for them. 'Thailand.'

She pulled on it, closed her eyes and handed it to me. Dope smoke burned my throat.

'What's brought this on? What about your careers, your future?'

'Fuck the future. I'm telling you the future. We're going to Thailand.'

My head swam; fear churned inside me more acid than the wine. I was losing my best friends. 'What'll you do in Thailand, for Christ's sake?'

A look passed between them. Fiona's lips parted in a slow smile, her eyelids, made lazy by the drug, fluttered in half time. It was the most sensual thing I'd ever seen.

'Have fun,' she said. 'Want to come?'

***

Remembering distracted me. Traffic on the A82 thinned. The crowded central belt disappeared, replaced by the scenic route north and Tourist Board Scotland. On a straight piece of road before the turn off to Aldochlay a car appeared from nowhere, accelerated effortlessly ahead and startled me back into the present. It was silver. I was sure it was the VW I'd noticed at Anniesland; it must have been behind me all the way from Glasgow and I didn't see it because my mind was in another place.

The passenger stared at me as they glided past; a hard stare and a hard face, scarred on the left side from ear to chin.

I made the turn and entered a world asleep and at peace. Yards from the road a dozen small boats at anchor on the loch waited for an artist to capture the scene in watercolours. Tranquil would be selling it short; serene was nearer the mark. Late afternoon sunshine fell across nearby fields. It would soon be gone; the mountains stole two hours of light every day – the price of their inspiring presence. Luss was deserted. I pulled into the car park of the Loch Lomond Arms Hotel and got out. Pier Road ran in a straight line to the water. On both sides, brown stone cottages with slate roofs stood as they had since eighteen hundred, owned no doubt by retired Sassenachs, delighted with the little piece of heaven that was theirs.

These days, English accents, clipped and rounded like my parents', were common in the beautiful parts of the country. In the city they were few and far between. Mine was a mongrel, my childhood in Edinburgh stripped away by a decade of money-no-object private schools in the south; four years at Willington, six at Bonnerhill. I could claim to have been born on the right side of Hadrian's Wall even if I didn't sound much like it. The source of the Cameron family fortune was distilled and matured here; the single malt was famous all over the world. I never drank it, a rebellion that went unrecorded.

Strathclyde University was an academic failure for me. In every other respect it was a success. It was my way back home, to Scotland. Without it I wouldn't have met Ian Selkirk and Fiona Ramsay. And life would've been very different.

A man in his seventies dipped a paintbrush in a tin and dabbed the fence outside one of the cottages in bright blue. He stuck to his task even when my shadow darkened the wood at his hand. Visitors were all too common in Luss. Ignoring them was a necessary response. I headed for the church then cut down to the shore. I saw the officer before he saw me; he was young, gazing into the distance, pausing on his patrol. Blue and white tape stretched between metal stakes along the sandy beach where Ian's body had been found. I knew the form: until the crime scene manager was satisfied the area would remain cordoned. The constable nodded to me and started walking. I must have looked like a ghoul, the kind who charges after ambulances for reasons of their own.

Of course there was nothing. I hadn't expected there would be. The sand was wet and unmarked; further along, stumps of wood grew out of the water. I imagined the shock to the canoeists who discovered him and hoped they were all right.

The policeman paced the distance in measured steps that left deep indents in the tan earth. When he reached the end he stopped. A sense of unease made me glance along the path to the church; a tall man was standing in the cemetery, staring at me. Our eyes met. He folded his arms across his chest in a deliberate gesture and didn't look away. It was too far to be certain but, for a moment, I thought I was seeing the scarred angry face of the guy in the silver car.

Nonsense of course. Ian Selkirk's dead body and the mortuary attendant's whispered dramatics had spooked me. I was rattled.

Above my head a gull made a noisy pass, chased by another, bringing me back to reality as the sun disappeared behind the hills. I'd come here with a woman once. She wanted to talk things through. It was summer; a group of teenage girls giggled and goaded each other into jumping off the pier. When they surfaced, their faces said it hadn't been worth it. They didn't learn. Soon they were squealing and shrieking again, the memory of the cold water forgotten.

The woman and I had our chat, but it was still over.

That night in Ian's flat I became one of them. Fiona's smile, her lips, the words; as much a dare as an invitation. No different from the kids on the pier.

Have fun. Want to come?

We arrived at Bangkok airport in darkness, collected our luggage and sat around until flights to the coast started in the morning. If my companions had a specific destination in mind they didn't share it with me. University, my father and Glasgow were far away. This was another world, where soldiers with guns cradled in their arms eyed travellers queuing to check in, and

Alsatian dogs straining at the leash sniffed bags and cases. If they found what they were looking for, signs posted where their chilling message couldn't be missed made clear what to expect.

THE PUNISHMENT FOR DRUG

TRAFFICKING IS DEATH

Fiona seemed relaxed but the atmosphere made me uneasy. Ian felt the same. He tapped his feet and played with his fingers. No jokes now and when he spoke it was a whisper.

At one point he got so freaked she took him to a corner beyond a fast food outlet. He stood in front of her like a naughty child, head lowered, chin on his chest while she laid into him. I had never seen her angry before, her teeth bared in a silent snarl, a finger admonishing our over-anxious friend. A different Fiona. She put her hands on his shoulders, their heads almost touched. The intimacy of the pose provoked a feeling I had never lost. Envy.

Whatever she said worked, Ian returned, sheepish but calm. At the ticket desk Fiona insisted on going to Koh Tao; she'd read about it in a magazine. Apparently it was paradise.

It was. We got accommodation within an hour: chalet-style huts, more functional than anything, so close to the beach you drifted to sleep to the sound of the sea. In Koh Tao Ian and Fiona had separate rooms. Whatever had happened at the airport still lay between them.

Now we were settled on the coast, Ian was back to normal. By day two he was on first name terms with everyone. I spotted him on the beach, deep in conversation with a tall sunburned guy. Later he burst through the door, breathless and excited. It was sorted, he said. All fixed. We had jobs, starting the next day. How easy was that? The guy was hiring; he needed someone who could dive. That didn't let me out – Ian had told him I could drive the boat. I hated boats and avoided them; a detail, not a problem. Fiona would serve in the shop. Ian signed on as an instructor; he persuaded his new friend he had a PADI qualification. Maybe he did but it was the first I'd heard about it.

Owen Mullen

Driving the boat turned out to be steering the small craft the diving school owned, and it wasn't difficult. After a while I actually enjoyed it. The weather was humid and cloudy. Most days we would have two or three people out with us. I had to admit, Ian did seem to know what he was doing. He had a gift for gaining people's confidence and put it to good use.

A week after the scene at Bangkok airport Fiona and Ian still hadn't made up. He took to cruising the bars that sprawled for miles along the coast. He didn't invite her or me, where he went and what he did never got discussed. We found ourselves in each other's company and, of course, the talk turned to him. I took a leaf out of his book and asked straight out. 'What's wrong with you two?'

She didn't understand. 'Nothing. What do you mean?'

The cheap Thai beer made me bold. 'He's out alone every night. Separate rooms. You were so close in Glasgow.'

She laughed and shook her head, her eyes a mix of amusement and affection. 'You're sweet, Charlie, do you know that?'

'So I've been told.'

'You are. Really. We aren't involved. How could you think that?'

'Because you're always together, you sit next to each other, hold hands. Whenever I called his flat you answered. What else was there to think?'

She leaned towards me and squeezed my hand. 'Charlie,' she said, 'how can you not have noticed? Ian's gay.'

'Gay!'

'Absolutely. He's especially partial to blonde guys. I'm the sister he never had, that's all. We haven't had a fight. He gets emotional sometimes. I talk to him. There's nothing wrong.'

'So?'

'Young, free and single. It was me who asked if you wanted to come. Now why would I do that?'

***

Our bodies bronzed in the months that followed. We walked on the beach as the sun went down. And I fell in love with Fiona Ramsay. I may already have been in love with her. That summer was the happiest time of my life.

One afternoon there were no tourists booked. I hung round what passed for the town, browsing for things I didn't need. I had learned to filter the noise of the street, drift with the crowd and keep my hand on my wallet.

They were sitting in a cafe under a yellow awning drinking coffee; their body language told me all was not well. It reminded me of the airport, except this time Ian was giving as good as he got; his face contorted, going at it hard. Flecks of spit flew from his mouth in a fine spray. Fiona stared, paralysed, unable to control him. He got up, towering above her, still raving. In his final gesture he struck the table with enough force to make the cups dance and stormed off. She stayed where she was. My instinct was to go to her but something held me back. Minutes later she put down money and left.

Although my own opinion of him wasn't as high as before – I'd caught him screaming at my girlfriend after all – Ian was well thought of by the small community of booze-cruise sailors and diving instructors. They drank beer and swapped stories. They had a code, and support for each other was unconditional. We were on our way out with a German party when a returning boat warned us to be careful. An Australian, in cut-off trousers and a tattered shirt, balanced on the prow and hailed us.

'Snakes. Sea snakes. Lots of them. Must be something driving them in. We've packed up for the day. Be careful, mate.'

The Germans hadn't understood. I glanced across to Ian, his expression didn't alter. I dropped anchor at our usual spot, fifteen feet above some orange and purple coral. The tourists suited-up. Ian did a final check and over the side they went. For a while everything was fine. I was thinking about Fiona, coming to a decision, when one of the tourists crashed to the surface, tearing at his mask. He got it off and started yelling. His friends came up beside him with Ian close behind. They shouted to each other; I don't know what was said. They were thrashing the water, panicking, making a hell of a racket. I dragged them on board and turned to Ian. 'What's wrong with them, they're terrified?'

He answered with a petulance I hadn't noticed in Glasgow, 'Fucked if I know.'

'Was it the snakes?'

His reply came with a sneer. 'There weren't any snakes. Just drive the fucking boat, will you?'

The lesson was over. We got word the Germans had cancelled next morning. Ian banged around in a temper, cursing under his breath. Early in the afternoon a boat landed near us and hauled a figure over the side onto the sand. One of the crew knelt beside the body pressing hard on the chest, bending to the mouth. A crowd gathered. Where we were was close enough for me. A man staggered away; he was crying. It was the big Aussie. He shook his blonde head at us. 'Those bloody snakes,' he said. 'They were in the coral. Those bloody snakes.'

**

Ian didn't speak about it though I knew we'd been lucky. In Glasgow I'd enjoyed the crazy side of Ian Selkirk, but he wasn't funny anymore. I saw him as an irresponsible risk taker. Sea snakes are amongst the most poisonous creatures on earth. Attacks were rare because the reptiles are docile. Nevertheless we'd been told something unusual was going on and ignored it. A dead man on the sand reminded us that rare didn't mean never. Ian had forgotten we were winging it. I hadn't. Thailand was supposed to be about escaping, having fun. Suddenly it wasn't for me. That made my mind up.

Ian didn't go out that night; he got drunk and talked about moving on. India was mentioned. The stories of Mr Rani recalled. Fiona seemed keen. If she wanted to go then I would go too, although I had other plans.

Judging the moment wasn't easy – there was always someone in the way. When I couldn't hold back any longer it just sort of came out. We were on the beach with the sun a flaming ball dipping below the horizon and stopped to watch the dying rays. I took her hands in mine.

I said, 'This is wonderful but it can't go on forever. Let's make a real life. Let's get married, Fiona.'

As soon as I spoke I knew what her answer would be. She ran a finger down my cheek. 'Charlie,' she said, 'why spoil it? It's fine just as it is, isn't it?'

And that was that. The affair and the adventure ended together.

Two days later word came. My grandmother was dead. I flew back for the funeral. My father avoided me. Even my mother was distant: I'd let them down, I understood that well enough. I was their only son and, of course, they were entitled to their expectations.

A pity they weren't the same as mine.

Chapter 5

Except my feelings for Fiona Ramsay remained unaltered.

One morning, a particularly vicious hangover and a female in my bed I couldn't remember meeting, brought my attention to the mess I was making. I was proving my father correct, I couldn't have that. A woman had turned me down. So what? I lacked purpose, I needed responsibility. I needed to get a grip. Catch myself on, as they say in Glasgow. Decisions got taken, even the odd good one, but I was still aimless.

Twelve months later the ghosts showed up to haunt me.

I was at the bar in the club, on stage a group of long-haired rockers were doing their thing. A blonde with the world's longest eyelashes had me in her sights. I smiled, just enough to keep it friendly.

He was pushing his way to the bar, apologising when he squeezed into space where there was no space. A salmon swimming against the tide, determined to get where he needed to go, grinning and joking his way to the front. I looked through the crowd and saw her face. It was a lovely face. I stretched a hand towards him. 'Ian! Here!'

He took it and I pulled him home. He said, 'Thanks mate. What you having?' and the present melted away.

I paid for their drinks. Fiona threw her arms round me and held on. When she let go he took over. 'Get in touch with your emotions,' he said and gave me a hug.

'How's Thailand?'

'Spain now,' she said. 'We left not long after you.'

'Thought you were there for keeps?'

The idea amused her. 'Keeps is a long time, Charlie.'

She was talking about my proposal. In the semi-darkness I blushed.

'So what're you doing here? Rainy old Glasgow pulling you back?'

Ian answered. 'We're in real estate. The UK is the primary market. Thousands of Britons own houses there, more are keen to buy. We want to create links with existing agencies and represent them on the ground. It's Fiona's idea.'

He didn't sound like the crazy loon I'd known. Ian said, 'What about you?'

'Nothing much. Working my way through what my grandmother left. Real estate's a bit dull for you guys. What happened to having fun?'

Fiona said, 'Making money is fun. Great fun.' Her eyes travelled round the club.

I said, 'How long are you in town?'

'We're leaving tomorrow. Flying visit.'

'How can I reach you?'

She dug a pen and a scrap of paper from her bag and wrote down a number.

'My mobile if you ever want me.'

If I ever wanted her.

Fiona raised her glass. 'A toast. To friendship.' We echoed the sentiment. She took my hand and squeezed. 'Old friends are the best friends.'

Ian interrupted. 'One for the road, Fi?'

She spoke to him though her eyes never left mine. 'Can't. We're already late.'

To hell with pride. I was still in love with Fiona Ramsay. Not what I told her.

'Maybe next time,' I said. 'Let me know you're coming and we'll do the Moti again.'

She tossed her hair over her shoulder. 'That would be nice.'

I thought about them, pictured them; in a taxi going to the airport, waiting at the gate, sitting on the plane, leaving me behind. I studied her mobile number; the ragged scribble was all I had to hold on to.

Ian and Fiona had unsettled me; they still had the ability to make what they were about sound more interesting than everybody else. I felt flat.

A year after they left, Ian was back asking for help. Not Jack the Lad Ian – the one who conned his way to the bar – this Ian Selkirk was on the edge of pleading.

Not even for an old pal?

I didn't realise he was frightened.

Then I got the call, the words rushing from the phone, breathless and unqualified. No introductions. None needed. I was in love with that voice; and the mouth, and the eyes.

'He's disappeared, Charlie. Ian's disappeared.'

'I saw him last week.'

'Where?'

'Here, in Glasgow. He needed money.'

She hesitated. 'Did you give it to him?'

'No, I didn't have it. What's gone wrong, Fiona? When we met I thought everything was great.'

'Everything was.'

I heard her sigh. 'A property developer gave us exclusive rights to market a beach front complex. The units sold like hot cakes. There was only a handful left. We had had a hectic few days. Too much money to keep in the safe. Ian was on his way to the bank.'

'With cash? Doesn't it get transferred electronically?'

'This is Spain we're talking about, Charlie, cash is king. Nobody declares the true amount. Business is done under the counter, brown envelopes all over the place.'

'So what happened?'

'He never got there.'

'Have you called the police?'

'Of course, I told them he was missing. I kept quiet about the money.'

'You think he stole it?'

She didn't answer.

'How can I help? What can I do?'

'Look for him. Find him and get him to come back. I'll come over if I have to. Whatever mess he's in can be sorted. I should've known the bloody idiot would go to Glasgow.'

That conversation was the first inkling things weren't as rosy as Ian and Fiona painted them. The force field round them had been breached.

I decided to trust Andrew Geddes. I told him about Ian. He listened without judging and pointed me in the right direction. Days were taken up with telephone calls to hospitals and visits to hostels. I tracked down some of his class from Glasgow University. Andrew worked his contacts. We found nothing. I even tried a couple of gay bars hoping to see him.

One young man, a pale, thin boy barely old enough to be allowed over the door, said he had met an Ian who lived in Spain. I gave him my number and asked him to contact me if he saw him again. A few nights later he did - Ian was at the bar, drinking alone. I drove like a lunatic across the city. When I arrived he wasn't there. I'd missed him by ten minutes.

It was the Fiona of old who rang the second time. Confident. Unfazed. The everything's-wonderful girl. 'Panic over. He's here. It's all been a misunderstanding. I over reacted, I'm sorry.'

No mention of the money, no explanation of why Ian Selkirk had been in Scotland, or why he approached me. 'And thanks, Charlie. Stay in touch.'

No mention of us.

I told Andrew. He made a face. 'You were having fun for a while, tracking down your friend, weren't you? Found him too.'

It hadn't occurred to me. 'I suppose I was, Andrew.'

'Fancy trying it again?'

That was the start.

***

The city lights blinked in the late evening gloom. I parked and headed for an Italian restaurant near Kelvin Bridge, a haunt when I was at Strathclyde. Tonight the food had no taste; my fault not theirs. Ash Wednesday was drawing to a close. Cecelia McNeil and her God, Luss and the old man painting the fence were already a dream. Then Ian Selkirk's grey dead face and the certainty of the mortuary attendant.

Off the record. Your pal didn't drown

Yeah. It had been a strange day.

Chapter 6

Donnie Fulton watched Eddie Tumelty slap a shovelful of earth on the dark brown mound they'd created; some of it trickled down the side and dropped over the edge. In the hole, water collected around Eddie's boots in a muddy pool.

'Clay,' he said. 'Less than two feet and already we've hit clay.'

Donnie didn't respond. It could've been concrete for the difference it made. They had their orders, what was there to say?

Fulton didn't much like his partner. Tumelty was lazy and a complainer; all the way from Glasgow he'd moaned. Eventually Donnie got tired listening to him whine and made a suggestion, 'Want me to tell Kevin you're not happy? Sure he'd sort something cushy for you if you asked him.'

Kevin would sort him all right.

Donnie rested his elbow on the spade and rolled a fag with the dexterity of a magician. He scanned the empty horizon. His boss had been very clear about where they were to go. Mamba country. Miles and miles of bugger all. It was certainly that.

'Make it deep,' Rafferty had said.

They arrived in the middle of the afternoon and, at first, the two men worked together until there wasn't enough room for both. Now they took turns. This was Eddie's turn and he didn't like it. Not what he'd signed on for. He saw the fag between Fulton's fingers. 'Do one for me, will you?'

Donnie ignored him.

'Come on, don't be a tight arse, do one for me.'

'Do your own.'

Donnie had no interest in anything beyond finishing and getting back to Glasgow. They'd been at it for over an hour with at least another hour ahead; heavy work, slow work; a job they'd done more than once. And Eddie was right, it was crap. Donnie hated it every bit as much he did. He stared into the excavated ground and thanked god it wasn't for him.

They were digging some unlucky bastard's grave.

***

In the east end of the city Alexandra Parade was quiet, unrecognisable from the bumper to bumper traffic jam it was during the day. The Parade began where the New Edinburgh Road ended and ran as far as the Necropolis overlooking the city. On the whole stretch there was only one pub – unusual for Glasgow. Inside the Gables the landlord chivvied stragglers to do their talking walking.

Ambrose Reid, Ambie to his friends, stood at the kerb whistling a tuneless melody and waited for a taxi. The Cheltenham Gold Cup had been good to him. His lucky race he called it, and it had been again; under his jacket a wedge of notes pressed against his shirt. Reid wasn't a boozer – he preferred women – but tonight he wanted to celebrate. He had called Isobel and told her to get some wine. Laughter and loud voices drew his attention to the pub and the manager shepherding the last of the diehards into the street. When the door closed the laughter ended. Denied sanctuary the drinkers seemed lost. Reid shook his head. Losers. He couldn't know time had been called on him as well.

Across the street Kevin Rafferty watched from the front of a white Vauxhall. Ambie Reid was no stranger to him. Occasionally he'd used the pretty boy when charm was more effective than muscle; in his business those kinds of jobs were few and far between. Reid was a gambler, a handsome nobody who lived by his wits, with a well-earned reputation as a ladies' man. Something Kevin would never be.

The guy behind the wheel said, 'Yes?'

Rafferty answered. 'Yeah. Take him.'

The driver flashed the lights. Further down the Parade a black cab coughed to life and moved through the junction towards Reid with its hire sign lit. The window rolled down.

'Where to, mate?'

Reid told him and got in the back. Without warning the doors opened, two men appeared and slid in either side of him. Ten minutes later they stopped outside Sandro's fish and chip shop in Baillieston. The blinds were drawn. The sallow skinned owner and his wife weren't there. Kevin Rafferty was. Reid's affair with his mother was known to everyone but him. When his father told him, he wanted to be sick. Jimmy was cold. He could have ended the relationship with a word – the affair had been going less than a week when he heard about it. Instinct told him to let it mature so the hurt, when it came, would be greater.

Reid thought he was fucking Isobel Rafferty; instead he was fucking Jimmy.

They huckled him out of the car into the shop. Kevin was behind the counter wearing one of Sandro's white coats. He smiled. 'Single fish or supper, Ambrose? What do you fancy?'

Reid struggled to break free. 'Kevin. What the…Let me speak to Jimmy.'

'Pie then? Or a pudding, maybe? Sandro does a very nice pizza.'

A terrified Ambie was dragged to the range. Rafferty turned the thermostat all the way to the top. Isobel's lover started to cry. 'Please. Please. Please!'

Hands grabbed his hair, he saw himself in the mirror above the gantry.

Kevin said, 'Take a last look, pretty boy' and dipped Ambrose Reid's face in the hot fat. He held it under. Reid's days as a ladies' man were over.

***

As soon as Isobel Rafferty saw her son standing in the doorway she knew.

Unless Kevin was here to tell her Jimmy was dead this visit wasn't about anything good. Since the divorce, Kevin and Sean hadn't come near her, they'd taken their father's side. She didn't understand why.

Kevin looked his mother up and down, taking in the lipstick and the length of the skirt. Disapproval mixed with contempt in his eyes. He said, 'Don't bother waiting up, he won't be coming. Shame you've gone to so much trouble.'

'What?'

'Lover boy can't make it tonight.' He grinned. 'Or any night.'

'Ambrose?'

'The very same.'

From the beginning of the affair, Isobel was aware she was putting herself between a vicious thug and a smooth talking user. But she was a single woman, now, with the paper to prove it. Reid wasn't the answer to anybody's dreams. Already he owed her more money than he could ever repay. That didn't matter. He listened when she spoke and lifted his eyes when she came into the room.

Her voice faltered, afraid to ask. 'What've you done to him?'

'What he deserved.'

Kevin walked to the car idling at the kerb.

'Jimmy says hello by the way.'

Isobel shut the door and pressed her back against its cool surface. Ambrose was dead, murdered because of her. Reality hit, her eyes closed against it; she was a prisoner, the divorce was a sham, meaningless legal waffle Jimmy hadn't bothered to challenge because he knew what she was only realising: it changed nothing.

Her legs gave way and she collapsed on the floor sobbing quietly. Mascara worn for her lover ran in black lines down her face. There would be no fresh start, no freedom, no new life.

Her ex- husband wouldn't let her go. Not now. Not ever.

Nobody quit on Jimmy Rafferty.

***

'Is it done?'

'It's done,' Kevin said and told his tale, teasing out the details.

The old man leaned on his stick, feeling nothing in his left leg and close to nothing in his arm. The body he'd relied on had let him down, betrayed him after a lifetime. The mother of his sons was another example of the same truth. In the end everything, everyone, let you down.

He allowed himself a grim smile and savoured the graphic descriptions of pretty boy Reid's demise, enjoying the irony. Ambrose must have been an even bigger fool than he had seemed, to imagine he could mess with Jimmy Rafferty's property and go unpunished. Ex-wife or no, Isobel would always belong to him.

He wouldn't tell him but, for once, Kevin had done well.

Sean heard his brother speaking and switched off. A nobody had died an agonising death. How did that help them? Where was the advantage? They only had so much energy; they shouldn't be wasting it settling scores. His mother had got herself a new man – so what? Jimmy and Kevin couldn't see it. Clowns, both of them.

Kevin knew he'd pleased his father; his mood was bright. 'We've got a break,' he said, as if it had slipped his mind. 'Somebody's interested in the thief's body.'

'Who?'

'Nobody we know. Guess where he went when he left the mortuary.'

Sean wasn't interested in games. 'No idea?'

'Loch Lomond.'

'What did he do?'

Kevin shook his head.

'Did he meet anybody?'

'No, he walked on the pier and stared at the water.'

'Any sign of the woman?'

'None, though it can't be a coincidence. Maybe he was trying to pick up the money trail?'

Jimmy broke in. 'Find out who this character is.'

Sean said, 'If he laughs at you, count to ten.'

Kevin balled a hand into a fist. 'Don't push it, Sean. Christ, I took his fingers off. He was never going to break.'

Sean was unimpressed. 'They always break. You pressed the wrong buttons. At the very least you should've hidden the body. And how did you lose his mobile?'

Jimmy listened to the exchange. Kevin he understood. Sean had always been a mystery. Neither resembled him. Kevin was six foot one, dark and fiery; handsome if he didn't have the scar. The Ambie Reids of the world were meat and drink to him. Not a talent to be underestimated, he had inherited that gift from him. Sean was fair like his mother, not as tall as his brother. And the boy was deep, always had been.

Sometimes Jimmy wondered if he'd fathered a ponce.

Chapter 7

I woke on Thursday morning to find a stone where my heart should have been. During Ash Wednesday my life had slipped its moorings and left me adrift. My watch told me it was twenty past seven; memories jostling with doubts about my choices overwhelmed me. If I'd said this, if only I'd done that. It was a mistake to leave Thailand when I did. I ought to have gone back after my grandmother's funeral; how different it might have been. Fiona and I would be together. Why couldn't that have been enough? And Ian would be alive, conning somebody and making them feel good about it.

Blue thoughts on a blue day. Getting out of bed wasn't easy.

The sky threatened rain. Yesterday's sunshine had been a fortunate fluke; the Scottish weather assumed its default setting, overcast and chilly. It suited my mood. I waited an hour before calling. Andrew Geddes was at home. Noises in the background said Sandra might be with him. It wasn't the right moment to give him the whole story so I asked if he could chase the autopsy report and let it go at that. I pushed what I had to do to the back of my mind; it wouldn't go away.

Someone would have to tell Fiona. I would have to tell Fiona.

I dragged myself under the shower and let the water cleanse me, until I felt good enough to cancel the day, then I called Jackie and let her know I wasn't coming in. She didn't ask why.

'If anybody wants me urgently, tell them to go fuck themselves.'

I wasn't joking. She didn't laugh.

I hung round the flat, walking in and out of rooms, going over what I would say and how; pretending I wasn't sure where Fiona's number was, all the while knowing it was in my phone.

A dozen times I dialled and killed the call, inventing one excuse after another; it was too early, although Spain was only an hour ahead; she might be busy, might be at lunch or with someone. Be married, have kids. Wouldn't it be better to wait until evening? The number I had was old, almost ten years old. There was every chance it was no longer in use. In the end I punched the button and heard the tone ring a thousand miles away.

'Hello?' It was her. She sounded sleepy.

'Fiona? Did I wake you? It's Charlie.'

'Charlie? Charlie? What a lovely surprise. No I wasn't asleep. Are you calling from Glasgow? I was just thinking about you.'

People always said that. I never believed them. 'How are you?'

'Fiona this isn't a catch-up call, I've got bad news, very bad news I'm afraid. It's Ian.'

'Ian? What about Ian?'

'He's dead, Fiona. I found out by accident. Ian's dead.'

Seconds of silence then she hung up.

I wanted to hear her voice, share our pain. Fiona had been closer to Ian than me, closer than anyone; she deserved time to herself. At nine o'clock that night my mobile vibrated on the glass coffee table. It was her. The conversation took up where it left off.

'What happened?'

I told the little I knew, leaving out the mortuary attendant's dramatic aside. She said, 'I'm coming over,' and rang off. Midnight she was back again. 'I've got a flight tomorrow afternoon getting into Glasgow around six.'

'I'll meet you.'

'No need, I'll hire a car at the airport. Where will you be?'

I gave her directions to NYB.

'Okay. See you around seven thirty.' She must have heard the concern in my voice. 'And Charlie, don't worry about me, I'm fine.'

Friday was another strange one. Jackie was in her office under the stairs, working her way through a plate of Danish pastries, looking the way I felt. Man trouble, had to be. I would've helped but didn't know how. I was shocked about Ian and nervous about Fiona. His death was a landmark in my own life, a realisation that the Moti Mahal era – ten pints of lager and a vindaloo, cheap wine, good blow, laughing at his mad antics 'til I was sore – was over. I would never be young again.

Cecelia McNeil added to my woes. Her note took me by surprise; she must have written and posted it hours after our meeting. This was a lady expecting miracles.

Dear Mr Cameron,

Excuse me for being over-anxious. I'm aware it hasn't been long, but I just had to thank you for listening so sympathetically. Please let me know as soon as you have news. These last weeks I've lived in despair. Now, at last, I can believe again. Be assured you are in my prayers. God is at your shoulder.

Yours, Cecelia McNeil.

In NYB, Andrew Geddes waved to me and shook his head. It would be next week before the pathologist pronounced on the cause of death. I tried to reserve a table in case Fiona was hungry. There wasn't one; the restaurant was fully booked. I pulled Jackie aside.

'Stick something together for tonight, will you? It's important.'

'It's Friday. We're chocka.'

'Then give me the table you give Brad Pitt when he comes in on a Friday and you're chocka.'

'I'll sort it out.'

I should've left it there. So should she. Neither of us did.

'Good of you, Jackie. Considering I'm your best customer.'

She bit back. 'And that entitles you to what exactly?'

It was banter, our usual thing, except for different reasons we were both too fragile for humour. A flash of annoyance washed over me. 'Seven thirty. If you really don't have space we'll go somewhere else.'

'You're your father's son, Charlie.'

That small exchange warned me, if I needed warning, where I was emotionally. Discovering Ian had hit me hard. Fiona's world must be rocking.

At seven I was waiting, more nervous than I would've believed possible. Every few minutes I glanced to the door; seven thirty became eight o'clock then quarter past. Jackie Mallon breezed by. Busy improved her mood but not her timing.

'Been stood up?'

I might have killed her with my bare hands.

The first thing I noticed was the cigarette; Fiona hadn't been a smoker when I knew her. The City Fathers had banned smoking in public places; this wasn't the moment to mention it. She ran to me. I took her in my arms and held her until she pulled away. Rain lay on her coat. 'The flight was delayed. I got here as fast as I could.'

'Are you all right?'

She shivered. Her voice was a monotone. 'I don't know what I am, Charlie. I don't know anything right now.'

I searched her face for the girl I'd known, hoping she'd be there, unchanged. Selfish, yet I did. I didn't find her. On another day perhaps, not today. Her skin was dry, her eyes red from crying. Her hair wasn't the colour I remembered; it wasn't any colour really, and it was short. I doubted she'd even remembered to run a comb through it. Grief sapped her spirit. All the women in my life had been measured against this woman and found wanting. I'd told myself they didn't suspect they were being judged. Of course they had, they must have felt her, always close. No face, no name, no number; a ghost. The perfect girl. The one that got away. Fiona.

'Let's sit down. Are you hungry?'

'Not really, I haven't eaten much since you called.'

I led her to our table. She said, 'What happened to Ian?'

There wasn't anything new to tell. 'His body was found in Loch Lomond. God knows what he was doing there. Cause of death won't be established until the autopsy report. We're expecting it at the beginning of the week.'

A waiter approached – I waved him away. She said, 'He's dead. I can't believe it.'

'Neither can I. When did you last see him?'

'I've been trying to remember. It must be three years.'

'You weren't working together?'

'No, not for ages. Ian got restless. You know how he was, always itching to be somewhere else.'

'He left you?'

I couldn't imagine it, Ian Selkirk had needed Fiona more than I did.

'I asked him to go.' That admission came at a price. She drew in on herself, became smaller. She didn't look at me. 'Could I have a drink?'

I clicked my fingers in the air. My father did that sometimes, and I detested him for it. Wine would have been inappropriate. I ordered brandies, large ones. We sat in silence until they came. No toasts. No cheers! The alcohol was medicinal. An antidote to sorrow.

'You remember the time he disappeared and turned up here asking for money? I didn't tell you the truth. He was robbed. In Spain he did what he did in Koh Tao, went off by himself every night. Ian wasn't particular about who his friends were. Probably met some pretty rough characters. Of course he never could keep his mouth shut. He must have told one of them. They rolled him and took the cash he was supposed to pay into the bank. It wasn't ours – it belonged to the construction company we worked with.'

'Thought you were in real estate?'

'I am. Re-sales and new builds. Our office deals with the clients, organises viewings, collects deposits. The buyers come through us. The whole sector's flat, no one's spending. The financial meltdown has made people cautious. Back then it was a different story; the amount of money passing over my desk was unreal. When he got mugged he panicked. Typical Ian. That's when he asked you.'

'But you sorted it?'

'Don't ask me how, Charlie. The builder wanted nothing more to do with him. My savings went, and the car. We worked for nothing for eighteen months. All our nice commissions put towards repaying what had been lost. That wasn't enough. I had to guarantee his conduct.'

'Sounds tough.'

'He promised to behave, meant it too, and he managed it. But you know, Ian. In the end he forgot what he'd got us…me…into. Six years ago he started using. A bit of blow once in a while never hurt anybody. I wouldn't have minded if that was all. He was on it twenty-four-seven. Lord knows what else. Eventually I told him he was finished.'

Her eyes darted over my face looking for reproach; she wouldn't find any.

'I couldn't take the chance. He was a liability, paranoid, obsessed, unreasonable.'

Her hand closed round my wrist, urging me to understand.

'He wasn't how you remember him, Charlie. Good-time Ian, always joking, taking the piss. That wasn't him. He was different. When he was wasted he didn't care about anything; when he wasn't he was freaked. I'd done it once. I couldn't cover for him again.'

'What did he say?'

'Not much, tried to brass it out, said he'd been thinking of moving on. He had some money coming, not enough to last, especially with his habits. He said, "Take it easy, Fiona" closed the door and that was that.'

Her shoulders shuddered. I signalled for another couple of brandies, without the clicking fingers routine. 'Since you telephoned I keep asking if I could've done more, got him help, something. I don't know.'

'Ian was always a headstrong guy – he danced to his own drum. Behind the smile he was complex. I realised that in Thailand. You saved him the first time; after that it was up to him.'

Brandy wasn't my drink but tonight I welcomed it.

Fiona said, 'I don't get Loch Lomond, I mean, what was he doing there, or in Scotland for that matter? And Ian was a great swimmer. In Koh Tao he swam all the time. How could he drown? Him of all people, how could he drown?'

How indeed?

Questions poured from her. 'Was he by himself? What about his things? What about...'

I took her hand. 'Let's see what the autopsy says. Drugs and deep water don't go together. Speculating won't help – we need information. And I think you should try to eat; they do the best burger in Glasgow here. I recommend the mozzarella and pesto combo.'

We attempted conversation, the normal kind. Tell me about this? Are you still doing that? It lacked conviction. Ian Selkirk's death never left our thoughts. Time had made strangers of us. Around half past ten I asked where she was staying, half hoping the answer would be 'With you.'

'The Millennium. I told the office they'd see me when they see me. I'll have to organise the funeral, after that...'

'I'll walk there with you.'

The hotel, down one side of George Square, had been the scene of a tragedy. A few days before Christmas, a lorry driver collapsed at the wheel and crashed through the traffic lights into the building. Six people died that day. Like many in the city, I remembered what had happened every time I passed.

The rain had stopped. We strolled to the corner and crossed near the cenotaph. The benches where office workers ate lunch on sunny days were empty now. In an hour or two the party would spill out of the pubs, kids pretending to be grown up by acting like kids. We hadn't been part of that scene. The gang of three's evenings ended at the Moti; South Indian garlic chicken, Mr Rani's stories and Geeta's secret smiles. Above, on the central column, Sir Walter Scott gazed over the Dear Green Place as he had for one hundred and eighty years. Old Walter must have seen some sights.

'We won't know anything until Monday at the earliest. How will you spend tomorrow and Sunday?'

'I don't have a plan. I don't want one. I'm tired, still reeling. I expect I'll stay in bed. Call me when the autopsy report arrives.'

Fiona was friendly, but her meaning was clear, she intended to keep her distance. There would be no grief inspired reunion. I felt disappointed yet strangely relieved. She kissed me on the cheek.

'Goodnight, Charlie.'

If there was anything else to say we didn't find it. I was almost asleep when my mobile told me it had something for me. I fumbled in the dark; the screen came alive in my hand. Reading brought back everything I was unsure about.

NITE NITE SLEEP TIGHT

DONT LET THE BED BUGS BITE FI x

Chapter 8

The next forty-eight hours crawled by. My mother left a message on the ansaphone. She hadn't heard from me in a while. Was I okay? Wasn't it about time I called?

Yes it was, but I wasn't going to, not today. I couldn't deal with the inevitable interrogation about girlfriends, especially the nice one, what was her name again, the singer, the one that played in a band? She meant Kate Calder.

On Sunday night I ran into Andrew and his new partner, holding hands and whispering to each other in the diner at NYB. Sometimes she laughed. I leaned against the juke box and watched them, wishing it was me and Fiona. Sandra was a quiet brunette with a good figure. When she went to the ladies I said, 'Nice, you're doing all right there, Andrew.'

He let the compliment pass. 'And you're trying too hard, Charlie. What do you need? Spit it out.'

I didn't waste time with denials. 'A car reg. No felony, far as I know.'

The number was in my pocket, written on a piece of paper. He took it. 'See what I can do. About time you got yourself a girlfriend. Plenty of fish in the sea.'

He sounded like my mother. That kind of chat was guaranteed to send me running for cover.

Danny Galbraith finished his set to a sprinkling of applause. The Great American Songbook fitted with the theme. He patted my shoulder on his way to the bar. 'Piano's out of tune, Charlie. Feel like slitting my wrists when it's like that.'

It sounded all right to me. 'Tell Jackie. She'll sort it.'

I should have been well refreshed – up for the cup Pat Logue called it – on Monday. Not so. My head felt heavy and my joints ached. Maybe I was coming down with something; more likely it was emotional backlash.

Andrew contacted me mid-morning about the autopsy. 'We'll have the report this afternoon. We'll know how your friend died. Expect my call. And they'll need you to formally identify him.'

'All right.'

All right was as far as it went, I doubted Fiona would be keen. I called her. No reply. I tried the Millennium. 'I'm sorry, sir, Miss Ramsay checked out.'

'Are you certain?'

'Absolutely.'

I wasn't ready for that. Later when Fiona called me the first thing she said was 'I'm not at the Millennium, I didn't like it.'

Mystery solved.

'So where are you?'

'The Artto. Much better, and they've got an Indian restaurant. Any word?'

'This afternoon. Someone will have to ID the body. Want me to do it?'

'I don't think I could, Charlie. Seeing him lying there…'

'I'll do it.'

'Thanks.'

Thirty seconds later my mobile rang: Cecelia McNeil. She launched straight into it.

'He's taken money from our account, Mr Cameron. Quite a lot of money.'

'How much?'

'Fifteen thousand pounds.'

It was the kind of detail I should have checked. Finding Ian Selkirk at the city mortuary had distracted me. No excuse. Mrs McNeil was doing my work for me. But what she'd said cast doubt on her assumption that her husband was a danger to himself: a man who intended to end his life didn't need money.

Though I didn't feel like working I tried to put myself in Stephen McNeil's shoes. He had the car and fifteen thousand pounds from their bank account, a sizeable sum, enough to see him over a weekend or two. His wife had requested credit card statements. Visa would tell us where he had been even if he wasn't there now. His only son committed suicide; he blamed himself and ran away unable to face the boy's mother or his loss. Where would he go? Where would I go? There wasn't enough information. The police might turn-up a parking ticket. If we were very lucky he could've been pulled over and charged with drink driving and we would have an address. Unless he did something to draw our attention it wasn't going to be easy to trace Christopher's father.

McNeil was a trucker with Newlands, a firm of carriers in Whiteinch. I drove to a flat patch of gravel behind a metal fence. To one side was a warehouse fronted by a loading bay and a series of roller doors. In the early hours I imagined it would be a busy place. Now it was closed. One driverless vehicle stood alone. Cecelia McNeil said her husband's employer hadn't seen him. Maybe this was his rig. I went to a single-room building tacked on to the store where a man wearing a jacket on top of overalls sat behind a desk covered in paperwork. Pre-season posters of Celtic and two bare-breasted females pouting at the camera gave clues to the male-dominated workplace. A blown-up photograph of five men in matching t-shirts took pride of place. Their beer bellies said darts. The guy in front of me was one of them. Stephen McNeil was another. A calendar a month out of date clung to the wall at an angle; Miss March encouraged us to believe summer was round the corner. She didn't have any clothes on.

The guy looked up, already annoyed. 'Yeah?' Newlands wasn't big on visitors.

'Hi. Is Stephen McNeil around?'

His reply set the tone. 'Who wants to know?'

'His wife's trying to contact him.'

'I wish her well,' he said, and went back to whatever he'd been doing.

I was expected to leave. It took him a full minute to notice I was still there. The place smelled of cigarettes and oil, a layer of dust filmed every surface and a bare bulb hanging from the ceiling cast weak light in the middle of the afternoon. Earth trailed from the door to the desk and the single-bar electric heater at Mr Friendly's elbow. Displeasure darkened his eyes, our initial conversation might never have happened.

'Something I can help you with?'

I asked my question again knowing he was going to be upset whatever I did.

'Is Stephen McNeil around?'

His grip tightened on the pen in his hand. 'Who wants to know?'

The old line about déjà vu all over again jumped into my head. His angry eyes dared me to keep the routine going. I cut it short. 'His wife.'

'He's not here. He asked for his cards a couple of weeks back.'

'Why?'

He shrugged and started writing.

'Any idea where he went?'

'Nope?'

'No forwarding address?'

'Nope?'

'Was he a friend of yours?'

He gave me his attention one last time. 'McNeil worked here,' he said. 'Now he doesn't. Anything else?'

I chanced my arm a little further. 'You play darts with him?'

He didn't answer. He was done with me.

Newlands was an unpleasant place to earn your corn, unless you were one of the gang, in with the bricks. In the darts team.

I should've brought Pat Logue with me. He would've got more. When I arrived at NYB, Patrick was at the bar nursing the dregs of his drink. He smiled when he saw me, though not his 100% chancer smile. He gave me his pleased-to-see-you-how-can-you-help-me expression; a grin on the edge of defeat. I smelled continued domestic disharmony.

'You look like you could use another likeness of Her Majesty.'

A light came on behind his eyes. 'Who d'you want me to kill?'

I laid it out. 'A boy takes his own life. The father can't handle it and leaves the mother the day before the funeral. According to her he blamed himself because their relationship soured. Christopher was the apple of his eye. They went to Celtic Park together.' I handed him the photograph Mrs McNeil had given me. 'Sometimes they fished. One day the boy announced he didn't want to go with his father anymore. Maybe he outgrew the arrangement. He was a teenager; it happens. Things became difficult and the mother got caught in the middle. Two males butting heads, a familiar story. Then Christopher snapped.

'The day before the funeral the husband packed in his job, took the car, lifted money and disappeared. His wife's worried he's having a breakdown and wants him found. He's big on sports, all kinds. He liked to hunt, took his guns with him. She thinks he might do something stupid. Straightforward. Except it isn't. McNeil doesn't want to be found. He travelled light. A few clothes. No mobile phone. It isn't a crime to quit your marriage or your job. He's done nothing to interest the authorities. This was two weeks ago. Any thoughts?'

'Did the boy leave a note?'

'No.'

'All right. Juice. Maybe the guy stopped for petrol. We could try the nearest stations, somebody might remember him. We have the car reg, that's a link. You've got connections who could keep an eye out.'

He meant DS Geddes. Patrick and Andrew had been coming to NYB since the beginning. They were from different sides of the fence, spoke only when it couldn't be avoided and gave each other a wide berth the rest of the time.

Patrick was warming up. 'His last conversation with his wife, what did he say?'

'She doesn't recall any final conversation, they were about to bury their son, they were in shock. But well done, you've got the scent. We need to know more about the suicide.'

'I threaten to put my boys out of the house every other day, ungrateful young tykes. Liam especially. It's the age they're at. How serious does it have to be for a teenager to top himself?'

Good question.

Chapter 9

For once he didn't do his trick with the bagel; he ate it like a normal human being. Today he was DS Geddes, not my pal Andrew. And he wasn't enjoying himself. It was the middle of the afternoon, we were in NYB, Andrew stirred three spoonfuls of sugar into the cup of black liquid. 'The autopsy,' he said. 'I've read the report.'

I waited.

'Good news and bad news.'

'What's the good news?'

Andrew sipped his coffee. 'Your friend was out of it. Heroin. Did you know he was a junkie?'

'No.'

'As high as the moon.'

'What's the bad news?'

'He didn't drown. No water in the lungs. He was dead when he went into the loch. Somebody stabbed him. Just once, through the heart. The body was dumped in the drink. No attempt to hide it. Tortured. A professional job. Cigarette burns on the torso and genitals and five fingers missing from the right hand.'

'Christ.'

'The officer in charge is DI Nigel Platt, haven't run into him, transferred from the Met, rubbed a few people up the wrong way already. Word is he's a bastard. Keep your guard high, he doesn't like civilians.'

'Not much I can tell. I hadn't seen Ian Selkirk in years.'

'Then tell him that.' He drained his cup and stood. 'Double shift for me, the divorce is costing a bomb. Next incarnation I'm coming back as a lawyer.'

'A scum-sucking bottom-feeder.'

He laughed. 'DS in the CID, I'm halfway there. I gave Platt your number, expect his call.'

'Will do, Andrew, I appreciate you taking the time. Nothing on the car reg yet?'

'Not so far.' He towered above me and put a hand on my shoulder. I thought he was about to commiserate about Ian. Not so. Andrew Geddes was as wrapped up in himself as everyone else, even when he was telling me a friend had been murdered.

He said, 'Do yourself a favour, Charlie, never get married. It's a mugs game.'

'I'll take your word for it.'

'Do that.'

From then on I was in big demand: DI Platt called to say he was on his way. I guessed he was a policeman before he spoke or showed his card. Not as tall as Andrew or as well built, nevertheless he carried himself like a man used to being listened to. His eyes were grey, alert and disapproving, the intelligence behind them clear. He introduced himself and his colleague and sat down. 'It's in connection with a suspicious death. DS Geddes tells me you're aware of the case. At the moment we have nothing to go on. Can I ask you a few questions?'

One of those requests that wasn't.

'The man you recognised at the city morgue, what was his name?'

'Ian Selkirk.'

'How did you know him?'

'We were friends from university.'

'When was that?'

'The nineties.'

'When did you see him last?'

'A dozen years, easy. We lost touch.'

'I thought you were friends?'

'We were. For a while.'

'Any idea what he'd been doing since then?'

'None, last I heard he was abroad. It was a shock to see him like that.'

'Is there anybody else, friends, family, business associates who may be able to tell us more?'

I shook my head. 'Sorry. We hadn't spoken in a long time.'

'I'll need you to identify the body, this afternoon if possible.'

'I can be there at four.'

'Fine,' he said, 'my colleague will meet you.'

The moment the door closed behind them Pat Logue was at my shoulder. 'Haven't got in over your head, have you, Charlie?'

'That's you you're thinking about, Patrick. Beat it back to the bar will you?'

The procession ended with Fiona.

What I had to tell her stuck in my throat, and there was no easy way. Tension pulled at her features, black smudges darkened the skin at the corners of her eyes. She took the chair opposite, the one DI Platt had occupied. I tried to be light. 'How's the new digs?'

'Better. Have they released the report yet?'

This was the hard part. 'Unfortunately they have. It isn't what we want to hear, Fiona.' She leaned towards me, braced against the pain that was surely coming. 'Ian was murdered.'

She gasped and slumped forward. What blood was in her cheeks drained away. She buried her face in her hands. 'Oh God! Oh God! Poor Ian.' Then tears came, quiet sobs rocking her shoulders in a silent rhythm. I didn't interfere; crying would be good for her. Better than any words of mine. Her voice was hoarse with sorrow. 'How? How did he die?'

'His killer doped him up, enough to leave him helpless, and stabbed him. We were right, he was too good a swimmer to drown.'

She used a tissue on her eyes. 'He was crazy, a mad fool, but he didn't deserve that.'

She hesitated, on the point of saying she'd come with me to identify the body. I cut in.

'Stay here 'til I get back. Jackie will look after you.' There was no need for Fiona to know all of it. It wouldn't enrich her life.

On form Jackie Mallon was hard to beat: she could manage staff, had an eye for detail and she understood people. That Jackie hadn't been around lately. Now she was at my elbow, zeroed in on the problem, ready to be a friend. I left them together and headed for the morgue.

DI Platt's colleague was waiting for me. No sign of the attendant. Everything was as before: the waiting room with its un-used chairs and hospital smell, the television in the wall and the feeling of being witness to something unhappy. When the screen came on, Ian Selkirk's eyes were still closed in death. I nodded without having to be prompted and confirmed his identity. The detective thanked me.

I had a question. 'When will you release the body?'

'Procurator Fiscal's decision. I expect we've got all we need.'

Saltmarket was busy; people hurrying on their way to who knew where. A man with a boozy face bustled out of the Empire bar deep in conversation with himself while vehicles collected at the traffic lights, raced to the Albert Bridge and across the river Clyde to the south side. Tomorrow would be no different. Or the day after. For our friend, Ian, it was over. But for the rest of us life went on.

Fiona was calm; she didn't ask how I had got on. Jackie gave a nod that told me things were better. I was glad she'd been around. We sat for a while not talking, uncertain what should happen next. Sadness dominated every sigh, every gesture, every lonely glance. In the awful reality words were inadequate.

Fiona said, 'I'll organise the funeral.'

'Sure you're up to it?'

'What else is there to do? I owe it to him.'

That statement was a clue. Fiona Ramsay was blaming herself for events beyond her control. Emotion twisted reason into guilt. I'd been there. 'I can't recall him ever mentioning family, can you?'

'No, Ian was on his own in the world. We were closer to him than anyone.'

I corrected her. 'You were closer. It was you he leaned on.'

It was a foolish comment, bad timing, she broke down again. 'Well that was his mistake. I pushed him away.' Her eyes were wild with remorse. 'He didn't want to go, he needed help. I was afraid Sebastian would see the state he'd got into. Ian's welfare never crossed my mind.'

'Who's Sebastian?'

'The contractor. We depend on his business.'

'So he's a client?'

'More like a partner. The money Ian lost belonged to him. That time he let us pay it back. There wouldn't be a second chance. You don't know him. He isn't a guy to cross. We're talking big money. Big money. It was only a matter of time before Ian messed up again, so I sacked him.'

Fiona was in pain. 'You should've seen his face, Charlie, like a child who doesn't understand why everyone's angry with him. I almost changed my mind.'

She grabbed my wrist. 'Don't you see? I was supposed to be his friend but when it mattered, when it really mattered, I let him down.'

Ian Selkirk had come to me too. I said, 'It wasn't just you, we both let him down. It wouldn't have mattered how much help he got, he was always going to need more.'

She drew away, exhausted. 'I'll organise the funeral.'

'I'll help.'

She lifted her head and stared into the past. 'No, Charlie, I'll do it, I'd feel better.'

Arguing wasn't an option. 'I'll find out when they'll release the body.'

She got up. 'Call me when you know.'

We shook hands; in a strange day nothing was stranger than that.

'I don't mean to brush you aside,' she said. 'This is the last thing I'll ever do for him, can you understand?'

'Of course. He meant a lot to you. Old friends are the best friends. You told me that.'

'Did I? I'd forgotten.'

Cecelia McNeil telephoned again. I hadn't thought much about her or her husband since my first visit to the city mortuary. We'd spoken that morning when she told me about the fifteen grand. I asked her about Stephen McNeil's friends, maybe he'd talked about changing jobs, and cut the connection with a promise to myself to give her the attention she deserved.

I'd seen the cost of dereliction, real or imagined, in Fiona Ramsay's haunted expression. It was a price I couldn't meet.

Chapter 10

The house was off Maryhill Road, a neat 1930's building with a well-kept garden in front. I guessed Cecelia McNeil was responsible. The garage where Christopher died was closed.

She was waiting for us, peeking from behind net curtains like a nosy neighbour. I brought Patrick along; he had two teenage sons and might spot something. He was quiet on the way over, not his jaunty self. I assumed his weekend hadn't gone well. When she saw him she smiled and offered her hand. I introduced them. He raised his game and went into his Everyman act.

The room had the feel of ordered clutter, ornaments crowded on top of the fireplace beside furniture you might inherit from your parents when they passed on. We sat on a sofa that had seen better days. Mrs McNeil poured tea into china cups that could have belonged to her grandmother and probably had. A plate of biscuits went untouched.

She was smaller than I remembered, as fragile as the crockery.

'I didn't expect to hear from you so soon,' she said. 'You're very efficient.'

'We haven't located your husband yet I'm afraid. That's why we're here. I asked you about friends or mention of a new job. Has anything come to you?'

She shook her head.

'We need to understand more about Stephen. There's a photograph on the wall at Newlands. Darts, isn't it?'

'Stephen started the team not long after he went to work there.'

'When do they play?'

'Tuesday nights at the El Cid.'

'Christopher ever go?'

'No, darts was Stephen's thing. Christopher wouldn't have been interested, it was…'

She pulled a handkerchief from her sleeve and blew her nose. 'I'm thinking of moving. In fact I've made the decision. This house. Too many memories. I don't think I can ever be happy here.'

The tragedy had stolen her resolve; she was resigned to losing her son and her husband. I tried to give her hope. 'It's early days, wait 'til we locate Stephen or he gets in touch. We won't give up.'

A tear trickled down her cheek. She said, 'He's not coming back.'

Husband or son? I couldn't tell which one she was talking about.

'You don't know, he could be on his way right now.'

Empty words. All I had.

'He won't, Mr Cameron.' Her sadness weighed her down. Patrick made eye contact with me. Cecelia McNeil's lip trembled. She cried, more like whimpered. If it had happened to me I'd cry too.

An old upright piano stood against one wall. The green leaves of a plant drooped from a pot with a strange design, half stone, half tin, a memento of a trip, flanked by statues of the Child of Prague on one side and Christ the Redeemer on the other. Above them a crucifix leaned into the room. And a memory of my childhood, a display cabinet; dolls from around the world dressed in national costume, plates and saucers, a fan from Spain, a couple of yellowing spoons, and a tiny sack of earth from the Holy Land; the kind of stuff it took a lifetime to gather, priceless to the collector, meaningless to anyone else.

With the exception of a flat screen TV in the corner, incongruent as an alien craft, nothing was even close to being new. Mrs McNeil read my mind. 'Stephen bought it,' she said. 'I told him it was too big, he wouldn't listen.'

Someone else might have described the decor as busy. The adjective in my head was less kind. It was a strange scene, out of time, at odds with the modern world. No sign a teenager had lived here.

'It would be helpful to understand more about your son. Can Patrick take a look at his room? The garage too, if you don't mind.'

'I don't see why.'

I reassured her. 'It's about building a picture, trying to understand. It's how we work.'

She wasn't convinced. 'I suppose so. I've left it exactly the way it was.'

Patrick took that as a yes and got up.

'The door to the right at the top of the stairs. Just don't touch anything.'

Cecelia McNeil picked up where she'd left off, 'I don't watch television, too much violence. Can't they find nice things to put on?'

'Nice doesn't sell, Mrs McNeil.'

Then something I hadn't noticed. Although the room was full of personal touches there wasn't a single photograph. The son was close to his father, the apple of his eye she'd said, sharing a musical talent with his mother. Why was there nothing of him?

'Do you have a more recent picture of your husband? In the one you gave me Christopher's only nine or ten.'

She lowered her eyes. 'I'm sorry, no. We hardly ever took photographs. Such a bother.'

I didn't believe her. In most families an only child is the centre of the universe, every occasion, every achievement marked and celebrated. And photographed.

'Where did you and your husband go on holiday? Did he have a favourite place?'

'Stephen wouldn't go abroad. He didn't like planes and he couldn't be sure what he was eating in a foreign country. We stuck to Scotland. Fife. He liked the east coast. Pittenweem.'

'Beautiful part of the world. Has he got relations he might go to?'

'No, there's no one. Just me.'

'No friends, other truckers he met on the road?'

'Stephen didn't make friends very easily. Too shy.'

Though not too shy to start a darts team.

'Tell me about the guns.'

'Stephen is a sportsman. Shooting is one of his hobbies. Been doing it since before I met him. He was always cleaning those guns, getting oil on the carpet. I went with him a couple of times in the early days. He tried to teach me.' She shook her head. 'I didn't like it. Hated it really. He wasn't pleased.'

Patrick came back and she saw us to the door.

She said, 'I appreciate what you're doing, Mr Cameron, I really do. Finding Stephen is all that's keeping me going.'

We were crossing the Kingston Bridge before I asked. High above the Clyde the city skyline was etched in grey. 'What did you make of it?'

Pat Logue gazed at the river. 'Wouldn't want to go through it every day. Couldn't handle it. Absolutely no way. Losing your only son's bad enough, losing your partner as well…'

'What about Christopher's bedroom?'

'A couple of boy band posters. No books. Didn't come across any porn. CDs, classical stuff. All his clothes on hangers, socks and pants in separate drawers. Very tidy for a young guy. When I was that age my room was like the bottom of a river. Gail goes mental at our two. Makes no difference. They wait her out. She cracks before they do 'cause they don't care. Eventually she can't stand it any longer and guts the place, then they complain they can't find things. Every once in a while I hear her laying down the law: "while you're under this roof… this isn't a hotel…" all that crap. Nothing changes, nothing will until some girl comes on the scene. Then they'll set up camp in the bathroom, we'll be choking on aftershave, and their mother won't know how to iron a shirt. Apart from gardening stuff and a couple of fishing rods, the garage was empty.'

Nelson Mandela Place brought us to the Square. I said, 'Took his guns, left the fishing tackle. Not good news. It felt weird being in that house.'

'So what now, Charlie?'
'Fancy a game of darts?'

***

Patrick showed the photograph of Stephen McNeil at garages near the house. I thought it was a long shot. It was. We hung around the office the rest of the day. He didn't say much. At five I suggested we go for a drink and something to keep us from falling down dead. What I had in mind was coffee and toasted cheese sandwiches. Patrick downed three pints and crunched his way through two packets of crisps. Smoky bacon. The alcohol did its work. He stared into the bottom of his glass. 'Gail's leaving me,' he said.

'What's the problem?'

He drew himself together. 'We've been together for twenty-two years. Gail gets the credit for that. If it had been down to me the marriage wouldn't have survived. But she's changed, she's not the same woman. The boys are growing up; they don't need her the way they did. And there's a clash of cultures, Charlie. She believes there's more to life than enjoying yourself.'

He finished his drink and let the subject drop. 'What do I have to do?'

'You're on point. Check it out. See if Stephen McNeil keeps his regular date. The guy I spoke to at Newlands will be there. I'll stay in the car.'

I passed the photograph to him. 'Taken seven or eight years ago. Think you can recognise him?'

He looked at it hard. 'I'll recognise him.'

'There should be a gang of them, Newlands finest.'

'Stephen McNeil's a broken man. Is it likely he'll be throwing for double tops?' Patrick was back to being a detective. 'He might not be in Glasgow, or even Scotland. A truck driver can get a job anywhere.'

All true.

'Got a better idea? It's a line of enquiry. We don't have too many.'

At the weekend the El Cid would be packed with teenagers, Tuesday's crowd was older. I waited in the car park, Patrick went inside. Ten minutes later the door opened and he slipped into the passenger seat. He said, 'It's pretty busy. Local teams playing each other. There's a guy in the corner, don't think it's McNeil.'

He handed me the photograph of Christopher and his father. I put it in my pocket and got out. I hadn't been in a pub on a darts night in a long time. A crowd of over-weight men hogged one corner. The marker called the scores and chalked them on a board, adding and deducting with a speed that was way ahead of me. A man in a checked t-shirt and faded denims steadied himself and leaned forward, head still, eyes fixed, lining up the shot. The darts left his hand, true and straight - single twenty, treble eighteen; the last one landed in double twelve. His friends whooped their congratulations. I knew the face if not the expression. There had been no smile in the office at Newlands' yard. The others were strangers and Patrick was right, Stephen McNeil wasn't with them.

Chapter 11

We arranged to have dinner on Wednesday. Nothing fancy, just pasta, and for that Fatzi's in Bath Street was as good as any. Fiona was there when I arrived, beautiful as usual in white jeans and a cropped top. I kissed her cheek and smelled roses.

'Hungry?'

'Famished.'

The lasagne comforted the way only Italian food can. Sharing a panna cotta brought intimacy that had once been second nature. Fiona waited until coffee to tell me her news.

'The funeral's organised. Monday at eleven, Daldowie crematorium.'

'Good. Whatever it costs I'll pay.'

'No need, it's taken care of.'

I was excluded, as if grief belonged to her alone.

'Five days, a long time to hang around, why don't we go away? There's nothing more to do in Glasgow. The police are handling the investigation. I kept your name out of it, by the way.'

She toyed with her spoon. 'I don't know, somehow it seems… disrespectful.'

'Fiona, we're talking about Ian. Ian Selkirk was the most disrespectful guy I've ever known. Nothing was sacred with him. Remember when we went to the Scotia bar to listen to some left wing poet?'

'It was full of social workers and English teachers.'

'Ian went on all night about the dignity of man. When we came out he ran across to Paddy's market; a line of down and outs were asleep in cardboard boxes.'

'Yes, yes.'

'He woke them up, every one of them. We tried to stop him. Remember what he kept saying.'

She was giggling, so was I. "CID. Get to fuck! CID. Get to fuck!"

A stout woman at the next table gave me a sour look. I was too far gone.

'The dignity of man my arse.'

We were almost hysterical. I noticed the restaurant manager coming towards us. It was time to go. Out on the street we laughed so hard my stomach hurt: shades of times past. I said, "CID. Get to fuck!" and we were off again.

Across from the King's Theatre we fell through the doors of the Griffin. The barman must've thought we were on something but he served us anyway. This was Glasgow.

Fiona said, 'It was outrageous. And cruel. Those poor people.'

'So don't tell me about disrespectful, not in the same breath as Ian Selkirk.'

'You're right, why don't we go away? What were you thinking?'

The truth was I hadn't been thinking. There was no plan. I said, 'Skye. Let's go to Skye. Drive up, stay a couple of days and back for Monday.'

She was interested. 'When?'

'Tomorrow. Lunch in Fort William, dinner in Portree.'

'Don't you have a business to run?'

Mrs McNeil would have to wait.

'Alright, you're on.'

'Pick you up around eight thirty?'

'Fine. At the airport hotel.'

'The airport? Thought it was Artto?'

'I changed my mind, I'm not in the mood for people.'

On the pavement she turned to me. 'We haven't really talked... you know...about what we're going to do.'

I did know. I'd put it out of my mind. Ian had been murdered; the police were on it. Fiona was asking a question I hadn't had the courage to ask myself. Was that enough? Perhaps a better question was why I was hesitating. An old friend had met a violent death; shouldn't my response be to get involved? I found people who were missing, finding Ian Selkirk's killer wasn't much different. Yet I held back, maybe because I hadn't forgotten how headstrong Ian could be. And how reckless.

The taxi pulled in to the kerb. Fiona kissed my cheek, maybe for just a little longer than before. Imagination was a wonderful thing. 'See you in the morning,' she said.

'Bright and early.'

'Lunch in Fort William, dinner in Portree.'

'Sheep and Highland cattle, hardly any people.'

She waved through the window. I stopped myself from blowing a kiss. I was falling all over again, and there was nothing I could do about it.

The next morning, from the moment Fiona settled into the passenger seat, I sensed it was going to be a good day. We were visitors in our own country. I loved it and having her beside me made it perfect.

I'd spent two hours on the net gathering information for the journey. At Glencoe I got my chance to shine. The sky was overcast, the dark history of the place heavy in the air.

'Easy to imagine what happened here, isn't it?'

Fiona was unsympathetic. 'Jacobite propaganda.'

'You can't be serious. Thirty-eight men were murdered, forty women and children died of exposure after their homes were burned down.'

'I thought the soldiers helped the MacDonalds to safety.'

'Some did, but it was a heinous crime. Murder Under Trust. The worst crime you could commit in the Highlands. The massacre was part of...'

Fiona interrupted me. 'Can we stop for a bit, I'm stiff?'

The whitewashed Clachaig Inn near the site of the original village had a fine selection of real ales and malt whiskies. A notice at the door for the benefit of strangers said "No Hawkers or Campbells". We ordered tea. Twenty minutes later we were heading for Fort William. This part of the world was mountains and glens, rivers and lochs. We went to Inverlochy Castle, a luxury hotel and gastronomic jewel in manicured grounds. Well-heeled foreigners made it their touring base. In the middle of the day we had the dining room to ourselves.

It was too good to last. Fiona articulated what was in our minds. 'Don't you think we should be doing more? I do.'

'More?'

'About Ian, shouldn't we be trying to discover why he was in Scotland? Why he ended in the loch.'

'The police are on it, Fiona.' I'd had my fingers burned on the edge of a police investigation before. 'And to be honest, it's a bit out of my league.'

'I'm saying a friend has been killed and asking what that means to us. Would it be so different from what you usually do? Haven't you ever had a murder?'

'A couple of cases turned out to be foul-play. I didn't know that at the start.'

'Otherwise?'

'It would be a police matter.'

She went quiet, then said, 'There's a difference, Ian was your friend.'

'So I'm emotionally the wrong person. It matters too much, I couldn't be objective.'

'Objective's over-rated. Making a wrong thing right is what counts.'

A part of me didn't disagree. I took her hand; it was trembling. 'Look,' I said, 'we're here to get away from everything. Let's leave it for now, there'll be plenty of time to decide after the funeral. I'm not against getting into it but I need to be sure it's wise. Somebody stabbed him for a reason. I don't want to rush into anything. That isn't wrong, is it?'

She pulled her fingers from mine. 'No, Charlie, that isn't wrong.' Her voice was flat, dismissive, she was angry with me.

On the surface we were in agreement, underneath the mood had changed. Ian Selkirk lay between us. I had hoped we could leave the ugly stuff behind, even for a few days, and of course I was keen to have Fiona to myself. It would be easy for me to agree to anything she wanted to make her happy. I would too. The reluctance inside me was hard to explain, but it was there and it wouldn't go away. Fiona's displeasure was a surprise. Whoever put a knife through Ian's heart would do the same to me. I suppose I wanted her to show more concern. Instead she sulked.

Our destination was in the north of the island. The volcanic landscape distracted us; heather hills, dark purple in the evening light, and the deep clefts of the Cuillin twin peaks helped repair our differences. Skye was casting its spell.

Fiona said, 'It's magnificent, just magnificent. Where shall we stay?'

'All arranged. The House Over-by.'

'What a lovely name.'

She caught her enthusiasm and smiled. 'I'm sorry for being ratty. Ian's death was a shock. Guilty conscience. We parted on bad terms. Didn't mean to take it out on you.'

'Forget it. It upsets you, of course it does. Let's see what the police come up with. If we aren't satisfied we'll consider our options. Fair enough?'

She didn't answer.

The House Over-by was five star accommodation, split-level luxury suites on the banks of Loch Dunvegan, The last thing I'd done that morning before leaving was make a reservation. For two rooms. It was arguably the most romantic location in the Highlands; yards from shore, and next door to The Three Chimneys, one of the top places in Scotland to eat. Fiona was impressed. Tomorrow Skye would be waiting to entrance her, and put distance, albeit temporarily, between us and the mystery of how Ian Selkirk met his death. Tonight was about Fiona Ramsay and me or at least I wanted it to be.

We walked the short distance to the restaurant with the sound of the Atlantic Ocean lapping the rocks; across the water the island climbed in silhouette into the darkening heavens. 'Who would've thought people would come here?' she said.

'Somebody thought it.'

'They were right. It's wonderful.'

Out of nowhere Fiona said, 'I'm sorry.'

'What's to be sorry about?'

'Thailand. I let you slip away.'

'Ancient history. We're here, nothing else is important.'

'But I was wrong. I loved you, I just wasn't ready. I suppose I was scared.'

I reached for her hand, this time she didn't pull back. 'I'm sorry too, I gave up too easily. I should've tried harder. Fought for you. You were so happy with life as it was. Talking about India. I made my own contribution to the way it ended. And regretted it ever since.'

She said, 'I'd forgotten about India. Maybe Ian would still be alive?'

I rushed to stop the conversation going down that path. 'You weren't to blame, Fiona, neither was I. Each of us has to be responsible for ourselves. Whatever we talk about we won't talk about Ian.' I poured wine for us and raised my glass. 'To new beginnings.'

She joined in the toast. 'Old friends and new beginnings.'

In my bed she cried out, whispered words I'd longed to hear, and for a few hours Ian Selkirk was forgotten.

My eyes blinked open to strange shapes and moonlight. I lay still. Where was I? Then I remembered and my fingers reached for Fiona.

I was alone.

Panic gripped me, for a second I thought it had all been a dream, a blissful illusion and now my brain demanded I face the painful truth: I had lost Fiona, lost her forever on the beach at Koh Tao. Then I realised I was in the House Over-by and we were together again. I found her on the shore, gazing at the black water, thinking thoughts no one could share. She shivered in the pre dawn chill. I held her. Tears marked her cheeks and I knew our time, all too short, had run down.

Before she spoke I knew what she was going to say, just as I knew my answer. A second chance was a gift from God. Cecelia McNeil understood. That's why she'd knocked on my door. I pushed the thought of Christopher's mother from me and resolved to do better. So far it hadn't been my finest hour.

Fiona crushed against me. 'I can't get him out of my mind, Charlie. I'm sorry, I just can't.'

'Then don't try.'

Her voice cracked. 'I need it to end. I need to know what happened to him. I need to know.'

We hadn't left Ian Selkirk's violent murder in the south, it was with us still. Skye wasn't far enough away. Nowhere would be. We carried him in our minds and in our hearts, in the past and in the present. There could be no escape. My futile attempt to outrun my responsibility ended as it always had to end, with a return to the city and my duty to a friend. Fiona was my conscience, the link to the part of me I would rather deny. And I was glad.

We turned our backs on the loch and picked our way through the stones to the road and the House Over-by. Making love was a quiet joy. I paid the bill, apologised for having to rush off, and thanked them for everything. We'd only had a day but for as long as it lasted it had been a sweet, sweet thing.

***

It was early and still dark. Tumelty was driving. From the passenger seat Fulton glanced at his bald head, a silhouette in the early light, and wanted to cave it in. Tumelty was fresh; he'd slept most of the night. Fulton had let him, an easy decision; hearing him snore was preferable to listening to him speak. Anything was better than that. And if it meant landing himself with the whole watch, well, on balance no bad deal. Tumelty hadn't even thanked him; the man was a moron. But the moron wasn't sleeping now and every few minutes he whistled the same tuneless snatch of melody. Fulton turned away and swallowed his anger.

Outside, Skye slipped behind them. Ahead the car carrying Cameron and the woman drifted through a deserted Broadfoot and on towards the bridge connecting the island to the Kyle of Lochalsh and the mainland. Fulton's tired mind wandered to what he had witnessed.

Sometime around four he'd seen the female walk to the shore and stand, looking out to sea. After a while her boyfriend joined her. They talked. He held her close. Maybe they'd had a falling out though judging by the kiss she gave him it didn't seem like it. Fulton kept his eyes on them until they went back to their room, and at that moment he envied Cameron. They reappeared with their cases and got into the car. That was when he'd wakened Tumelty.

Tumelty asked Fulton to drive. Fulton gave him a mouthful. The useless bastard had slept all night. Now he expected a ride home. Thirty minutes beyond Fort William, Fulton took out his mobile and dialled. Sean Rafferty answered.

'They're on their way back.'

'Already, they only just got there? What happened?'

'Christ knows. Cleared out in a helluva hurry.'

Fulton recounted the strange scene on the shore in the middle of the night and the hasty departure. Sean said, 'What was that about?'

'No idea.'

'Did they meet anybody up there?'

'Nobody. Only time they went out was to the restaurant next door. I took a chance and asked reception if there had been any messages for them, a letter or a package maybe. The girl didn't know what I was talking about.'

'All right. Keep on their tail. Let's see where they go from here.'

Fulton held back from complaining about Tumelty; it wasn't the right time. Sean wasn't happy, he sounded uptight. He was reckoned to be the quiet one, not crazy like Kevin or as hard as his old man, but it was worth remembering, at the end of the day he was a Rafferty.

Chapter 12

We made good time to Glasgow. The anxiety of the wee small hours faded with the night and the talk was about tomorrow, the future: us. I drove straight to the airport.

'From now on you're staying with me. No more hotels.'

'Assertive. I love it.'

We bought fish and chips in Byres Road and wine from Oddbins. Fiona tried to drag me round a supermarket for 'essentials'. I held my ground. My only concession was a butcher where the sausages were so outstanding they won awards. We loaded up with them and other good things. At the flat she unpacked and settled next to me. 'I'm happy,' she said. 'Really happy.'

'Me too.'

'Thanks, Charlie, without you I'd be out there by myself.'

'Then that would make two of us.'

I waited for her to bring Ian into the conversation. She didn't. Not that night.

She came to me naked and I was ready. I cupped her buttocks, she moved under me, matching every thrust with one of her own until her breathing pounded in my ear like waves breaking against the shore and we were in Thailand again, on the beach. The years apart, the wasted years, melted away. Loving her was the easiest thing I had ever done.

My cleaner arrived around ten. Fiona stayed in the bedroom, I pretended a hangover. We didn't fool anybody. Mrs McCall knew what was going on. It was afternoon when we got out of bed. Fiona went to the shops and came back with more wine, prawns, peppers and onions, noodles and a jar of sweet and sour sauce. Later we curled on the sofa and watched some old horror movie, relishing every corny second. She lifted my mobile and fiddled with it.

'What you doing?'

'Setting a ringtone so when I text you'll know it's me.'

She chose an upbeat snatch of bubblegum pop. 'Like it?'

'My favourite. How have I survived without it? Do you text a lot?'

'All the time. It's a girl thing.'

On Sunday we made love again, slowly, and I cooked a fry up: the works; sausage, bacon, black pudding and egg; tomato, mushrooms and tattie scones.

'Of all the things to miss about Scotland tattie scones is a definite top five.'

'Along with Iron Bru, square sausage, Gregg's pies and…'

'…tandoori chicken drumsticks?'

From nowhere Ian Selkirk burst in. 'Sorry,' Fiona said, 'I didn't mean to…'

'That's all right, you're allowed to remember; we both are.'

'Yes but I have to let it be. This is an important point for us, I don't want always to be spoiling it the way I did in Skye.'

'You didn't. Skye was wonderful, and so are you. How are you about the funeral?'

'I just want it over.'

'Let's just enjoy each other.'

'Sure. I over-reacted. There's so much to decide, it freaks me out. First big decision. What will we do today, any suggestions?'

'Why don't we do what millions of people do?'

She grinned. 'Thought we'd done that?'

'I mean go to Kelvingrove.'

'I haven't been there for years. Old Masters and stuffed animals. A perfect combination.'

At Kelvingrove the Old Masters were there, so were the stuffed animals. We wandered, Fiona put her arm in mine, I acted as if it was the most normal thing in the world and pretended not to notice. On the first floor, Dali's Christ of St John of the Cross was smaller than I remembered. A middle-aged female guide gave its controversial history to a group of earnest Japanese. Fiona and I tagged on.

'Painted in 1951 the picture was inspired by a dream Dali had. It was bought in the early fifties for eight thousand two hundred pounds...'

I said, 'It was vandalised, wasn't it?'

She sniffed and gave me a look. I'd stolen her thunder. 'Yes, dear,' she said. 'I'm coming to that.' I'd been admonished. 'A man threw a brick at the canvas in 1961 because he objected to the interpretation. Spain is rumoured to have offered one hundred and twenty million for it. The offer was rejected and it remains here in Glasgow.'

We left her - not sorry to see me go - and sat in the cafe discussing what was around us. I said, 'Museums have a hard time in the modern world. Objects in glass cases don't impress youngsters used to electronic magic in their own homes.'

'True, except what museums offer is unique. The real thing. The Magna Carta, the death mask of Tutankhamen, the Mona Lisa. Not some facsimile. Not Hollywood special effects.'

'Had enough of the real thing yet?'

'Almost. Another ten minutes. We ought to get an early night, be fresh for tomorrow.' Fiona always was practical, one of the reasons Ian had clung to her.

'And listen,' I said, 'it'll soon be over.'

'Will it, Charlie, will it really?'

I held her close. 'Yes. Soon. Very soon.'

***

Daldowie Crematorium had the aesthetics of a concentration camp; down a winding road with the hum of the motorway in our ears, through gates and along a country lane until the trees gave way to car parks and grass. Off to the right a collection of stone buildings, stark and unlovely, waited for us. Signs advised which chapel those paying their respects should go to. The sky was cloudy, rain wasn't far away and a cold wind coloured our faces.

Fiona was subdued at the flat. I hadn't expected anything else and respected her mood. We arrived at eight minutes to eleven. A service had just ended; another would follow ours in a parade of tears and regret. Mourners gathered outside in groups, talking, shaking hands with the principals, ready for the next part of the ritual, the funeral meal in a local hotel. We wouldn't be needing hospitality; the only people present at Ian Selkirk's funeral were Fiona Ramsay and me.

Fiona cried when the curtains closed and the casket was drawn behind it to the flames. I put an arm round her. A small man with a bald head crouched at the organ, glancing at the music, playing the same tune in an endless cycle. Beautiful Dreamer. Over and over. It was the most soulless occasion I ever attended.

Outside a smell hung in the air, an unpleasant reminder of what we'd witnessed. Another party arrived; no doubt their service would be more personal than ours. With the coming and going I almost missed the silver VW at the far end of the car park. I was sure the man behind the wheel hadn't been in the first group; he made no move to join those arriving for the next cremation, and he hadn't been with us.

'It's sad,' Fiona said. 'Ian was so popular, yet no one was here. He wasn't bad, Charlie, whatever went wrong he wasn't that.'

I wasn't listening, my eyes were on the stranger.

'Fiona, I lost touch with him years ago. I couldn't tell you who he was.'

She bridled. 'He was a good guy. A great guy.'

Her memory was selective. It left out his character defects. Saint Ian was being created.

'He'd do anything to help, always willing…'

I interrupted. 'Don't turn round. Somebody's watching us.'

She tensed. 'Who is it?'

'Nobody I recognise.'

The Volkswagen came alive, reversed and swept away, too far to get the registration or a description of the driver.

Fiona stepped closer. 'Who was that, Charlie?'

'Whoever it was he took a good long look.'

Fiona shivered. I guessed it had nothing to do with the weather. The rain arrived to complete a rotten morning, a drizzle that would last into the night. As we headed off more vehicles were arriving. Death was a good business to be in. I loosened my black tie.

Fiona said, 'Who do you think that was?'

'Probably one of Platt's men. It's common practice for the police to check out the funeral. Apparently some crazies like to be there. It wasn't anybody you know, was it?'

She shrugged rain from her hair. 'Scotland's a foreign country to me now. I'm a stranger here.'

It was an answer, just not to my question. She sighed. 'Well that's that. What now?'

'Back to NYB and coffee.'

Pat Logue was at the bar, where else? He said, 'Funeral? Got a good day for it' and grinned. But he was faking, Patrick wasn't a happy bunny. 'Anything in yet, Charlie? The fans are askin'.'

I was getting good at ignoring him, he was giving me plenty of practice. Jackie Mallon had had a renaissance; I heard her chirping away with customers. When she came to us she asked what people always ask. 'How did it go?'

'All right. Glad it's behind us. Just coffee I think, Jackie. We're not hungry.'

Fiona pulled off her gloves. 'What's your relationship with her?'

'We're friends.'

'Apart from that.'

'Apart from that we're friends.'

'That all?'

'Absolutely. I'm not her type.'

Fiona was sinking, the strain was getting to her and I was the nearest target. 'Because if I found out you were at it I'd cut your balls off. I'm not joking, Charlie. Don't mess me about.'

Her face was lined and hard; the Fiona I'd seen at Bangkok airport.

'Fiona, I've waited long enough. I'm hardly going to blow it, am I?'

She changed the subject, not for the better. 'What're we going to do about Ian?'

'Tomorrow I have to catch up. After that I'll start working on it.'

'Then I'll take the first flight I can get.'

'You're leaving? What about us?'

'I'm coming back. Give me four weeks to sort things over there. Wind up the business. Speak to Sebastian. Put my villa on the market and say goodbye to people.'

'Okay, four weeks, no longer. Then it's me and you. This time I'm holding on. Is there anyone you know who might have a clue what Ian was doing for the past three years?'

'I doubt it, I'll ask. He could've been in Glasgow. There's nothing to say he wasn't.'

'There's nothing full stop. DI Platt might have had some luck.' I tugged her sleeve. 'The guy at the table in the window. He look familiar?'

A minute passed before she let her eyes go to him. 'No. Why?'

'He reminds me of someone, that's all. Excuse me.'

I walked over to Patrick and told him what I needed without saying why. The fans could stop asking.

Fiona said, 'Is everything okay?'

'You're keen to get started on Ian, well I've started.'

That night when we made love neither of us wanted it to end. We were two halves of the same being. We fitted. And there was a lot to discuss. Fiona couldn't just quit her life in Spain. It didn't suit me but she had to put her affairs in order.

She was fortunate. She got a seat on an early flight. I offered to run her to the airport; she refused. Of course it wasn't necessary; she had her hire car to return. I had a premonition I'd never see her again. She put her arms round me and kissed my lips.

'Next time I'll be here to stay.'

'Promise.'

'Cross my heart and hope to die.'

'Don't say that, Fiona.'

She laughed. 'I'll call you tonight. Nine o'clock your time.'

'Text or call?'

'Both. Find out who killed Ian. Do that for us, Charlie. Old friends and new beginnings, remember?'

How could I forget?

***

I didn't feel good about Cecelia McNeil; she hadn't had a fair shake. It wasn't the Enigma Code she was asking me to crack. All she wanted was somebody who cared enough to find her husband. Usually that would be me. Ian Selkirk had got in the way. No excuses, her case deserved more of a priority than I'd given it. At least it had roots; discovering who killed my old friend was a long shot.

Andrew called to tell me the car hadn't been involved in any traffic violations. My last line petered out. In my honest injun speech I'd promised to tell her if I felt she was better off without me. That time was now.

She answered after the first ring. I got the impression she was sitting beside the phone, waiting to hear from me. I said, 'I have to see you.'

Her response was breathless. 'Have you found him?'

'That's what I want to talk about.'

Jackie and I had changed roles: she was animated, bright and cheerful today. Almost girlish. I was under a cloud. Pat Logue caught it and kept his distance; he buried his face in the Daily Record. I was on my own.

Cecelia McNeil was in her garden. She waved to me and peeled off her gloves. 'I'm too old for this,' she said. 'I'd be better off in a flat. Come inside, Mr Cameron. It isn't good news, is it?'

'No it's not I'm afraid.'

The room was the same suffocating collection of nothing very much. As it had been, with one exception: the plant was gone. A photograph sat in its place. Christopher McNeil was eleven or twelve when the camera captured him squinting into the sun, older than the boy with the fishing rod, and even more his mother's child.

'That's new, when was it taken?'

'A school trip six years ago. One of the teachers gave it to me. It was a good day, Christopher came home happy. I'll get some tea.'

Tea was the last thing I wanted but she needed to be busy and I needed to let her, the least I could do. I studied the room again. On my previous visit the lack of family pictures struck a dissonant chord. Now, even with the image of young Christopher McNeil on top of the piano, I sensed I was missing something. The kettle rumbled to the boil; moments later she joined me. No china this time, two mugs, no biscuits either. The facade of normality was fading. I marvelled it had lasted so long.

She repeated her question. 'It isn't good news, is it, Mr Cameron?'

'Mrs McNeil, it isn't any news. Your husband hasn't left a trail. I'm assuming no purchases have been made on his credit card and there have been no more bank withdrawals.' Her silence told me I was right. 'The usual avenues have dead ended. No trace on the car. If Newlands have information on where Stephen is they're keeping it to themselves. We went to the El Cid last night; his friends were there, your husband wasn't.'

Her eyes gave her away.

'But you knew that, didn't you?'

She straightened her skirt, guilt on her face. 'Yes,' she said, 'the first week I tried to find him myself. Newlands were...unhelpful. I went to the Cid and saw the others. They didn't see me. They were laughing as if nothing had changed. Of course for them nothing had. It wasn't their son who'd killed himself. It wasn't their...'

A knock at the door broke into her confession. She got up to answer it. Muffled voices filtered through. Cecelia McNeil returned with a man I hadn't met. The set of her shoulders and her lips drawn tight said she was less than pleased to see him. I stood. She introduced us. 'George Lang, Charlie Cameron. George was Christopher's piano tutor.'

Lang nodded, we didn't shake hands. He was mid-thirties, slightly built, not tall. His features were too fine to be handsome, against pale skin. The black three piece suit hadn't been in vogue recently; neither the cloth nor the cut were expensive, and the colour wasn't right for him. There was a reserve. I might have guessed he was a piano teacher. My presence may have thrown him off balance because he had only just arrived yet seemed anxious to leave. He spoke to Cecelia McNeil, his voice a quiet well-articulated sound.

'I said I'd keep in touch. If there's anything…you know…'

'Very good of you, George. I'm fine.'

It sounded hostile.

'I'll be moving soon. I was just saying, wasn't I, Mr Cameron?'

She took me by surprise. I hadn't expected to be included. 'Yes you were.'

The conversation, what I'd heard of it, had been short. Now it was over. George Lang backed towards the door. 'All right,' he said. 'So long as you're sure.'

She handed him an envelope and didn't escort him out. When the door closed she faced me. 'Nobody writes letters anymore. I always do. I would've been at home with the Victorians. Texting, email and the like are beyond me. I haven't the first idea how to scan the net.'

I didn't correct her. I said, 'You don't like him, do you?'

'Is it that obvious?'

'Do you blame him in some way?'

She folded her arms round herself and stared past me. 'No, I don't blame George. I'd rather not see him that's all. He reminds me of things I'm trying to forget.'

'Was he close to Christopher?'

'He taught my son for two years. Christopher was neglecting his practice. I thought it would be good for him. There never seemed to be enough time; he was always going somewhere. Music takes commitment, Mr Cameron. Talent by itself won't do.'

The mugs of tea were props, thanks to George they were unnecessary. I returned to the reason for my visit. 'I'm sorry to say my efforts at tracing your husband haven't been successful.'

'But it's only been days, please don't give up so soon. Please.'

I winced at her desperation and hoped she'd understand. 'There's nothing to go on. Stephen covered his tracks. I can't take your money. It wouldn't be right to make positive noises with what we've got. On the other hand he doesn't appear to have come to harm. Maybe he just needs space.'

She took my hands in hers, near to tears. 'Please, please Mr Cameron, I have to find him, it's all that's left. Keep on. In my heart of hearts I believe God sent you, you will succeed. Don't stop, you're my last hope.'

Letting go is never easy, especially when someone is pleading. It took a strong character, stronger than I would ever be.

'How about this? I'll keep looking. Off the clock. When I get a break I'll follow it. If your husband comes back let me know. No promises, except I won't walk away.'

She broke down and cried. I'd told Cecelia McNeil what she wanted to hear, her reprieve was temporary, her gratitude misplaced. When days became weeks and then months she would realise as I already realised. And I'd be kept at the door like George, not blamed, but no longer welcome.

The case was closed.

Chapter 13

The Raffertys had messed up big time. Stealing from the thief had been Kevin's idea, he'd seen a chance to make easy money. Stupid. There was no such thing. "Our friend in the sun", as Jimmy called him, was more powerful than the Glasgow family would ever be. Kevin paced the floor like his father had in the years before the stroke. Sean wanted to laugh. It was a performance for Jimmy, meant to impress. But only one son impressed the old man and he was in the ground.

'She turned up over a week ago, they met at a bar. Used three hotels in a few days, and she looks different from her photograph, short hair.'

'Did she go out?'

'Only when she changed hotels. The guy is Charlie Cameron. Father's a big shot. Cameron's whisky? And get this, chairman of the Conservative Party. Hasn't done anything out of the ordinary, but a detective inspector paid him a visit, so the cops must think he's involved. It was Cameron who ID'd the body. Then him and her went to Skye, one night and back again.'

'Skye? What's that about?'

'No idea. Could be they spotted us and got out of the city. On Saturday she moved in to his flat. Sunday they went to Kelvingrove.'

'The museum? What're they up to?'

'Yesterday we followed them from the crematorium to the Italian Centre where Cameron has his office.'

The information was presented as Kevin's work. No mention of his brother's contribution although it was Sean who had done most of it. Jimmy Rafferty leaned on his stick; his skin had a grey tinge, he looked ill. 'We know about her, where does he fit? Could be they intended to cut the thief out.'

'They're very pally. If he's with her...' Kevin let his father draw his own conclusion and searched his face for the approval that never came.

'They still together?'

'They were shacked up at his place until this morning. Now they've split, she's on the move.'

Jimmy said, 'Tell me we know where she is.'

Sean answered. 'We know. We've got them both.'

Kevin resented the interruption. He fingered the scar on his face. Thanks to his mother he'd survived a childhood under the same roof as a monster, but at a cost. He was beaten, many times, often without knowing what he'd done wrong. His father admired intelligence and the eldest Rafferty boy wasn't bright. As he grew, violence, often beyond his control, was his default response. It was all he'd ever known. At Loch Lomond it got away from him. He'd been terrified to report the thief was dead and that they were no wiser.

Jimmy Rafferty was a cruel complicated father, incapable of love. He despised his eldest son for reasons even he didn't understand. Sean he ignored, too much of his mother in him for Jimmy's liking. Paul, the youngest brother, was the exception. His death affected Rafferty like nothing ever had. He drifted into depression. His interests needed a strong leader but for months they didn't have one. Rivals on the south side saw the vacuum and seized the opportunity to launch a series of attacks to test the strength of the east end team: a late night drinking den owned by the Raffertys was wrecked, two bag men were clubbed and robbed in broad daylight, and every trader in Dennistoun was put on notice that the area would soon be under new management.

The opening shots in what those behind the grab expected would be a brief struggle, for without the figurehead who would oppose them?

They expected wrong. Jimmy Rafferty was far from finished. Every week for a month bodies were dragged from the Clyde.

Then it was over.

Kevin would have kept on killing – why he could never be trusted to lead. His old man knew better. The point had been made.

This time it was different. Emil Rocha, "our friend in the sun", played in a higher league. He was immensely wealthy; forty percent of the cocaine that found its way into Europe came through Spain, much of it supplied by him. His Latin mentality would demand he wage war and he had the resources to do it. Sean had seen them with his own eyes.

***

The aircraft banked and made its decent. Sean Rafferty gazed at the whitewashed buildings crowded along the shore and the Mediterranean, sparkling blue and inviting in the brilliant sunshine. His father sat beside him staring straight ahead. Jimmy Rafferty didn't like flying. Sean was surprised when he found out he was on the trip – he had assumed Kevin would go. Of course Paul would have been their father's first choice. But Paul was dead.

Sean watched Jimmy grip the armrest so tightly his knuckles stretched the skin. Few things would have induced him to make the journey. He had no choice: there was too much at stake. They were on their way to meet their future partner and if it went well, they would be the most powerful underworld family in Scotland. And the richest.

Their host didn't deal with strangers. He insisted on meeting everyone he supplied, partly to assess them, partly to intimidate them. There would be no contracts, nothing written down, a handshake would seal it, honour would do the rest. The Spaniard chose his associates carefully. He could work with whoever he wished because he had what everyone wanted.

Outside the airport a chauffeur stood beside a limousine. The Raffertys got in. They had no bags; they wouldn't be staying.

The drive into the hills above Marbella took almost an hour. At the end of it they were frisked before being allowed to enter the compound. On the other side Emil Rocha was waiting. He smiled. The men behind him were expressionless. They weren't there to smile. Sean saw them, at the gate, in the courtyard, high on the terraces, and realised he was looking at an army. The villa was a fortress.

Rocha greeted them like long lost friends. 'I apologise,' he said. 'A necessary formality. You understand.'

He was closer to Sean's age than Jimmy's, lean and tanned, but his eyes were old. He led them to a courtyard in the shade of an orange tree, offered iced tea and flattered his guests, claiming to have heard how well ordered things were in Scotland's second city, congratulating them on their operation. He sounded sincere.

The Spaniard did most of the talking. Jimmy lacked his social skills; he had never needed them. Emil Rocha's came easily. He was polished; courteous and charming. After a while they went to the library to discuss the deal. Sean was left alone. He walked in the garden between palm trees and jacaranda until he came to the swimming pool, deserted except for a dark haired female sunbathing topless on a lounger, her body slicked with oil, face hidden behind out-sized shades. Sean Rafferty knew she'd be a looker. And there would be plenty like her. He felt aroused. And envious. This was what real money could buy. Emil Rocha was a fortunate man.

At the villa Jimmy and the Spaniard were back; it hadn't taken long.

'Your father drives a hard bargain,' Rocha said.

'Always.'

Jimmy didn't speak.

They toasted in Champagne. His guests could have whatever they wished, Rocha told them. They only had to ask and it was theirs. Sean wondered if that included the woman. He would have been happy to stay on but his father wouldn't hear of it; he preferred to get home. Rocha had been a gentleman, though charm hadn't got him where he was. The sophisticated veneer disguised a man no one dared displease.

Their plane touched down in Scotland under a sky heavy with rain. When they were in the car Jimmy said, 'What did you think of him?'

His son's answer was accurate and honest. 'Dangerous.'

For a day or two Kevin sulked because Jimmy had taken his brother instead of him. He believed he'd missed out and he was right. Not going to Spain meant he'd failed to appreciate what they were up against. None of the family met or even spoke with Emil Rocha again. He kept his distance, others acted on his behalf, but Sean remembered him.

***

Kevin Rafferty acted as if he had uncovered the information. 'And something else about Charlie boy, he's a private investigator.'

Sean said, 'This guy isn't short of a few bob. His family is loaded, he doesn't need the money.'

'Yeah, but he isn't loaded. Besides, everybody needs the money, especially if it's five mil.'

'So why don't they just take it and run?'

Kevin felt his grip on the meeting slipping away. 'You're wrong, Sean, he's waiting for things to cool down.'

Jimmy said, 'Is he any good?'

Sean answered. 'He's particular about what he takes on. No divorce evidence, nothing like that. Concentrates on missing persons.'

'Just the guy we need. He can find what we're looking for.'

Kevin wouldn't give up. 'They're both involved.'

'Then he'll lead us to it, or she will.'

'What's the woman up to?'

'Good question. Either she knows what the thief did with the money and she's keeping her head down, or she's using this guy to get it for her. Something doesn't…'

Kevin sensed his brother was taking over again and cut him off.

'Why wait? I say we do her, Jimmy.'

Sean couldn't disguise his impatience. Thanks to Kevin their problem had doubled. He cursed him under his breath for dropping them in the crap. And the way he sucked up to his father made him sick. He was a walking liability. Jimmy was an impotent semi-invalid, thundering away, pretending to still be the man he'd been. Between them they'd get them all killed.

Jimmy said, 'Don't let them out of your sight. And Kevin, first they talk then they die, got it?'

Chapter 14

Give Jackie her due, she shared joy and misery in equal measure. Right now joy was on a roll. I got a big hello. 'Your friend not with you today?'

'She was only here for the funeral.'

'You two seemed pretty tight.' She was fishing.

'Old friends.'

'The best friends, so they say. Pat Logue was looking for you.'

The perfume she was wearing drifted my way, cool and green and feminine. The scent, the smiles, the friendly enquiries? Of course, Jackie had a new man. The last one had been the drummer in Big River, NYB's resident band. I'd liked him a lot and was surprised when it ended. Impossible to guess which relationships would survive and which wouldn't. My affair with Kate Calder proved it. We'd lived together, even talked about marriage, but it didn't go the distance.

I said, 'Don't see much of you in the morning, how come?'

'Alex lets me go to the gym before I start.'

This was a development. 'You into all that workout stuff?'

'Gary says looking after your body is an investment for the future, just like pensions and savings.'

And there it was: "Gary says".

From experience I could expect to be hearing a lot more of what Gary said. Jackie was an independent lady but every time a new guy came into her life she morphed into a likeness of them. By the sounds of it Gary was a fitness fanatic.

'Is he good looking?'

'Great body.'

Too much information.

The conversation was off in the wrong direction. Patrick Logue strolled through the door at the right moment. He sat down across from me, waited for his drink to arrive, took a sip and gave an appreciative sigh. 'First today,' he said. 'You're attracting the attention of the wrong people, Charlie. Might have to change my boozer.'

'How so?'

'The guy you asked me to find out about is Sean Rafferty, one of Jimmy Rafferty's sons. What's the connection?'

'No idea.'

He was unconvinced. 'Turns up at the funeral, then here. That's an awful lot of interest for you to be in the dark. Don't want people like him in your universe.'

I had never met Jimmy Rafferty and never wanted to. He'd been at the centre of two high-profile trials, I recalled television pictures of him on the steps of the High Court. In the first case he was accused of ordering the execution of Joseph Doland, a small-time crook who worked for him. Rafferty hired the finest lawyer dirty money could buy. Frank Rossi had an awesome reputation and a long history of successfully defending the guilty. His tactic was always the same. Establish an alibi. Rossi called two men and three women who straight-faced told the jury they were ten miles away having dinner with Rafferty in the Bothwell Bridge Hotel at the time it was believed Doland was murdered. Nobody could remember the gangster ever speak badly about the dead man, let alone sanction his demise, although it was common knowledge Doland was skimming off the top; supplementing his wages he called it and boasted about it in the pub when he'd had a few too many. Stupid of him. The prosecution's hopes rested with the testimony of their star witness, Robert Small, Doland's brother-in-law. Whatever Small told the police in the days after the murder changed on the stand. Under oath he swore Rafferty had treated Joe like a member of the family and revealed the accused had paid for Doland's funeral out of his own pocket.

Rossi milked that admission dry and although it was a fairy story, it wasn't easily disproved. The jury was back in less than an hour. The verdict surprised no one.

It was a bad day for the police, the procurator fiscal's office and for justice. But it underlined the power of Jimmy Rafferty in the city.

The second trial was even harder to credit. Rafferty appeared for the prosecution when one of his sons was gunned down in Shettleston Road. His role on this occasion was the grieving father, unable to understand or explain how Paul, described as a quiet lad who hadn't an enemy in the world, came by a bullet in his head.

Paul Rafferty had been a thug. Rossi did a breathtaking job of turning him into a saint. Billy Lyle got twenty years. He should've been so lucky; four months into his sentence he bled to death in the showers at Barlinnie.

What the hell had Ian got mixed up in?

At Loch Lomond, according to Andrew Geddes, there was no attempt to conceal the crime; the killer had left the body to drift ashore. It was a message, a warning to others not to cross whatever line Ian Selkirk had crossed. So why wait in the car park at Daldowie and follow us back to NYB? They were after something they thought we had. Drugs, money, it didn't matter. Our old pal Ian had landed us in deep shit. Rafferty wouldn't give up until he got what he wanted. For Fiona, Spain was safer. In Glasgow she was in danger; we both were. Ian paid with his life for whatever he had. I needed to find it and give it back.

Patrick watched my reaction. 'You know what I'm sayin', Charlie? I'm talkin' serious bad guys. Don't get in their way.'

'Seems like I've got some more work for you, Patrick.'

He raised his hands. 'Hold that result. Leave me on the bench, the boys have a father, Gail's got a husband, that's how it has to stay.'

'Gail's chucking you out, you told me yourself.'

He dismissed my reminder. 'She'll come round. Good men are hard to find.'

I assumed he was kidding.

'Feel rotten about leaving you on your own. This is heavy duty. I'm a lover not a fighter.' He sank the pint. 'Anything else, just shout. Take my advice, whatever it is sort it. Rafferty's not a guy you'd want to run into on a dark night. He's an animal. King of the jungle. You're a pussy cat same as me.'

Patrick was afraid for me. I was afraid for Fiona.

I climbed the stairs to my office, expecting some knifeman to be waiting behind the door. The room was empty. I decided to confront my fears and Googled Jimmy Rafferty. Bad idea. The photograph on the right hand side of the screen wasn't recent and showed a man in his fifties staring straight at the camera beside a biography that was a litany of criminal activity but with no convictions. His sons were in there too, same eyes different faces, one with a scar. Pat Logue was correct. I wouldn't want to run into them, on a dark night or any night.

After that I was spooked enough to consider calling Andrew, laying it out and getting his opinion. DI Platt was the official option. He was the senior investigating officer; it could take his case in a new direction.

In the end I didn't telephone anybody. Instead I rolled back time to when there was no threat from a Glasgow gangster and Fiona was still the girl that got away, to the days and weeks and years before Ian noised-up the wrong people. Drugs, money, a missing husband; what was the difference? I began as I always began. I made a list, crossed it out and made another list. That gave me an outline. And a hundred questions beginning with how Ian Selkirk came to be at Loch Lomond.

***

Platt wanted to interview me again. I told him it was pointless. He ignored me, hoping I could give him something. Turned out it was the other way round. His visit brought a piece of information I didn't have. I got the impression the inspector was off duty.

I said, 'Did you have a man at the funeral?'

He seemed surprised. 'Of course not. Why would we?'

'Isn't it standard practice to observe who attends?'

'In case the killer shows? Hollywood has a sin to answer for.'

He gazed round, unimpressed by what he saw, his feelings crystal clear. 'You do some investigating yourself, Mr Cameron. With some success, I believe.'

I didn't reply.

'Aren't thinking of going it alone on this, are you? I understand, he was a friend, but I wouldn't advise it. Better leave it to the professionals. No offence.'

'All right. Have the professionals made any progress?'

'As a matter of fact we have. His car. Abandoned at Duck Bay.'

'What tells you it's his?'

He gave a smug grimace. 'His signature on the hire agreement for one. Ian Selkirk hired a Honda Civic at Glasgow airport.'

'So how did he get from Duck Bay to Luss?'

The smile faded. 'We don't know that yet. You had no contact with him, is that right?'

I anticipated his question. 'I wouldn't expect to hear from him if he was in Scotland.'

'Did he have any other friends?'

I shrugged. Fiona was staying out of this. 'I really couldn't say.'

DI Platt brushed imaginary dust from his lap and stood. 'Thank you for your time. Remember what I said, Mr Cameron. If anything occurs to you please share it with me, will you? '

At the door he paused. 'Who you know won't always be enough. I'd bear that in mind.'

Who I knew? What did that mean?

Tomorrow I'd go out to the airport, find the car hire firm and speak to them. The detective inspector had gifted me a starting point, his little chat, the superior air and the condescending praise, had irked. In the normal run I didn't indulge in petty rivalry. Ian was an exception when I thought Fiona was his girlfriend. Platt was another. An old friend had died a violent death. Stepping on the detective's toes was the least of my concerns. If he didn't like it he could lump it. What did it matter who found Ian's killer, so long as somebody did? It wasn't a pissing contest, or if it was, to borrow one of Patrick's phrases: Game on.

***

A knife had been driven through Ian Selkirk's chest and punctured his aorta. His fingers had been torn from his hand; he would've been unable to defend himself, powerless to prevent his death. Jimmy Rafferty's interest told me he had lost his life but kept his secret.

Fiona called at nine. The line was so clear she might've been in the next room.

'Charlie, it's me. Only a day and I'm missing you already.'

'You sound good. How was the flight?'

'No problems, in and out on time. Slept most of the way. What about you?'

I paused, this was the hard part. 'There's been a development.'

'Tell me!' Excitement gave her a schoolgirl voice.

'We were followed. Not one of Platt's men. Jimmy Rafferty's taken an interest in us.'

'Who's Jimmy Rafferty?'

'You don't know him.'

She hesitated. 'Who is he? Why was he watching us?'

'Not him personally.'

'But why?'

'Because Ian had something. They didn't find it.'

Silence at the other end of the phone.

'You haven't told me the truth, Fiona. You sacked him. Why did you sack him? What was he involved in?'

No reply.

'This is too serious to keep me in the dark. I need to know. We may be in danger.'

She let me wait, then said. 'Drugs. Not just smoke. Real drugs. Cocaine, heroin, stuff like that. And he was using. I couldn't have him around.'

'When did this start?'

Her answer shocked me. 'Thailand. That was one of Ian's cons. He sold me the idea of living free. I bought it too, but it was always about drugs. Do you remember how freaked he was at Bangkok airport?'

'Yes I do, you had to calm him down.'

'He saw the sniffer dogs and those signs.'

'We had only just arrived, hadn't even been out of the airport, how could he be carrying?'

'He wasn't, not then. He knew he would be though. He had the money on him to make the buy when the time was right.'

'And this was the plan from the start?' Anger grew in me. The stupid bastard had put the three of us at risk. 'Was I the only one who wasn't in on it?'

'Don't get on your high horse, Charlie, I wasn't in on it either. He told me when he panicked. I tore a strip off him and warned him to keep his dirty business away from us.'

'I do remember.'

'We weren't close after that. He took off at night to do whatever he did. You and I fell in love and he became addicted.'

Rain tapped against the window. I couldn't think of anything to say.

'That was why, when you proposed, I put you off. The thought of leaving him in a country where the penalty for what he was doing was death was too much. In many ways he was a child. Spain was my way of getting him out of Asia and away from all that.'

'Who gave him the cash he took to Thailand?'

'No idea. In Spain we worked hard, built the business. Losing the money should've told me he was still at it. He must've been out of his head even then. Did he seem okay when he came to you?'

'No, I don't suppose he did. He was in trouble, now we're in trouble.'

'Charlie, you're frightening me.'

'Good because you're staying where you are, it's safer.'

'What about us?'

'We'll be fine, but until this goes away, Scotland's out. Ian had something Rafferty wants. I'm going to help him get it.'

'How?'

'Find it and give it to him.'

'And if you can't, what then?'

'Sell real estate in Spain?' I forced a laugh. 'Don't worry, it'll be all right.'

'Can I call you?'

'On my mobile. Don't know who might be listening.'

She whispered, 'I love you, Charlie.'

I said, 'I love you too, Fiona,' and hung up.

Two minutes later a text arrived:

I LOVE U MORE.

FI x

I stared at it, sorry for myself, wishing she was with me. Brave talk for Fiona was easy, it wasn't how I felt.

Chapter 15

Morning. My eyes opened and closed. I was wiped out, hung over, not ready to chase shadows. The face in the bathroom mirror told the tale of a troubled night: dark hollows and fresh lines, bloodshot streaks and flaking skin. I stared. The old man stared back, neither of us happy with what we were seeing. Yesterday I had fallen on the information DI Platt used to remind me of my amateur status like a big cat bringing down a gazelle. Today was a different story. Game on. That was a laugh.

Three envelopes lay behind the door: an electricity bill, an offer from American Express, and a note from Cecelia McNeil thanking me for agreeing to keep looking for her husband.

Dear Mr Cameron,

I can't tell you how grateful I am to you for taking my case. Finding Stephen means more than I can say. When my hopes fade I think of you and know you'll be successful. God will guide you, I'm certain.

I am already in your debt.

Yours, Cecelia McNeil.

I admired her old fashioned sense of politeness and envied her faith. I kept the electricity bill; the others went in the bin.

A car hired at the airport left some work to do. It was Ian's steps I was following, I could expect his moves to have been bold and lazy. I imagined myself coming off a plane and took it from there. Alba Rentals jumped out at me. A pageboy blonde called Anthea smiled a dazzling smile. 'How can I help you?' she said. Her accent marked her as east coast.

'A friend of mine hired a car from you, he thinks his keys must have slipped between the seats. Was anything handed in?'

Her brow furrowed. 'I doubt it. How long ago?'

I guessed. 'Three weeks.'

'Mmmm. Name?'

'Selkirk.'

She pulled open a grey filing cabinet, flicking through agreements with the skill of a bank-teller, plucked one out and cross-checked the registration against a whiteboard on the wall. 'Blue Civic. It's been serviced, I'm afraid.'

A yellow post-it stuck to the top sheet. She read it and the smile disappeared.

'Your friend didn't return the vehicle, the police did.'

My cover story had lasted less than forty seconds. 'I know, I'm trying to find out what happened. We arranged to meet, he didn't show up. Sorry.'

Her directness caught me off balance. 'Is it serious?'

'He's dead.'

'The police wouldn't give any information. The detective in charge was very abrupt, I didn't like him.'

'Platt. I don't like him much either. Do you recall the hire?'

She gestured to the whiteboard. 'We send out dozens of cars every week so if there's damage I tend to remember. The ones that stay in my brain are the difficult customers. This friend of yours was odd.'

'How?'

Anthea leaned towards me. 'I saw him give the Hertz guy keys. Next thing he strolls over here and hires another car.'

Bold and lazy, typical Ian.

'I wondered why anyone would do that and asked Ronnie at Hertz about him. I was right, he was handing them back.'

'Did you tell the police this?'

A shadow darkened her eyes. 'No, I didn't, as I said, the detective rubbed me up the wrong way. Should I have?'

'I wouldn't worry about it. One more thing, what was the date?'

Anthea consulted the paperwork. 'February, twenty-sixth.'

'And how long was it expected to be out?'

'Seven days. Should've been back on the fifth.'

I thanked her. 'If only Hertz are as helpful.'

'Ronnie's okay. What do you want to know?'

I told her. Two minutes later she was back. 'Vauxhall Vectra hired in Dover on the twenty fourth. One way to Glasgow Airport.'

A time line was taking shape. I had come across the body by chance on the ninth of March, Ash Wednesday, when I was looking for Stephen McNeil. It had been in the city mortuary four days by then. The autopsy established it was in the water one or two days. Death occurred on the third or fourth of the month. Ian hired the Honda on the twenty sixth of February. That meant he was in or around Glasgow for four days before he was killed. And why come back to Scotland? What was here for him?

At my desk above NYB I considered what I had. Ian's car journey in the U.K. began in Dover. He drove north; was that when he started getting creative? Changing vehicles at the airport was a ruse to make it seem like he'd taken a flight out of the country. Covering his tracks. Pity he hadn't made a better job of it. Smarter to hold on to the Honda. The moment Hertz had their car back, whoever he was escaping had a fix on him.

During the next four days they caught up, filled him with drugs and put a blade in his heart. I believed Anthea's dislike of DI Platt put me a step ahead. In fact it hadn't. I had nothing of value, no information that took me nearer to discovering who murdered Ian Selkirk or why.

***

Investigation is grunt work. A morning spent calling every Glasgow hotel in Yellow Pages produced zero. Not conclusive, he may have used another name. I tried to keep in mind who I was searching for. Ian was an in-your-face kind of guy. Hiding in a cottage in the middle of nowhere wasn't his style. Duck Bay, where the car was found, was Platt's other little gem thrown carelessly away. Cameron House Hotel sat next door. I dismissed it as obvious, even for an irresponsible fool like Ian.

From Balloch to Tarbet there were guest houses; out of season visitors would be welcomed and left to themselves. The Tourist Information Centre in George Square gave me a brochure packed with spectacular photographs and lists of accommodation. Another telephone job. Two hours later, close to giving up, the next call made me forget the rest. A male voice, gruff and impatient, was replaced by a woman's.

'The police have already been.'

Adrenalin coursed through me. 'Can I have a few words with you?'

'There isn't anything to tell.'

'Please, he was a friend, it would be appreciated.'

I heard the man grumbling in the background when she agreed.

The Lomond Inn was a cottage extended to accommodate guests during summer and the Christmas and New Year holidays. Scotland invented Hogmanay. Getting drunk and teary nostalgia were mandatory. It was a marketing fantasy the world bought into, and Edinburgh capitalised on the myth. At midnight Princes Street flooded with teenagers, pissed on imported lager, rocking the old year out and the new one in. Ninety miles away the Lomond Inn played the same game with melancholy songs and a ceilidh band.

She didn't introduce herself and kept me at the door. 'He was a friend of yours you say?' She tutted. 'The loch may look benign – don't be deceived – people have lost their life in it.'

'He was with you…?'

'Just the two nights. My husband is still angry because he didn't pay his bill. Miserable old bugger. What does that matter when a young man has been drowned?'

'Do you have his luggage?'

'The police asked the same thing. There wasn't any.'

'May I see his room?'

She blanched. 'I don't think that would be appropriate. The police have examined it, and of course it's been cleaned since your friend was here.'

'I'd still like to see. I'm prepared to pay whatever's outstanding.'

That swung it. I followed her through an empty bar with the obligatory tartan carpet, down a corridor and up some steps, still in the old building. She opened the door and waited. I wanted more for my money.

'Has anybody else asked about him?'

'No, I didn't make the connection between the man in the water and your friend until the police arrived. He went out one day and didn't come back at night.'

'Did he say how long he intended to stay?'

'He wasn't sure. I think he was waiting for someone.'

'Could I have some time by myself, please?'

'All right. I'll make up the bill.'

The room was no more than functional: the bed old the fittings older. The one redeeming feature was the view, unobstructed, clear across the water. DI Platt was in the lead on this one; my hopes weren't high. What I was after might be a key, a letter or a suitcase. I poked around but my heart wasn't in it: the wardrobe, the mattress, inside the cistern; if this was the movies a sheet of paper would be taped underneath a drawer.

It wasn't the movies.

I was certain Ian's killer had already visited the Lomond Inn. Before Platt. Before me. Nobody went anywhere without some baggage. The murderer had taken it. He'd known what he was searching for and didn't find it, otherwise why would a Glasgow hard man be having us watched?

In the bar she handed me an envelope. Ian's bill. I put it in my pocket unopened. She told me the amount and I paid. It was more than I expected.

'I'm sorry about your friend,' she said. 'I liked him. The loch's a dangerous place. I never go near it myself.'

I rested my elbow in a puddle of beer.

'Oh dear, she said, 'that ought to have been wiped up. Send us the cleaning bill.'

A beer stain on my jacket didn't concern me, other things did. 'Who hires out boats at this time of the year?'

She folded my money and slipped it in her apron. 'It's a bit early yet. In summer they sit at Luss pier. I believe somebody in Balloch might. Further up the loch Alan Walker used to. He's old now. I don't know if he still does.'

Fewer than I imagined.

'Traffic on the water isn't encouraged. The residents don't want Loch Lomond turning into the Lake District. What a mess that is. I'd try Alan, four miles along the shore. His cottage is down off the road. If he's at home the chimney will be going. Be warned, he doesn't like strangers. Since his wife died he's a recluse. Sorry again about your friend. And your jacket.'

I pulled the car to the side and walked down a broad gravelled path to a brown stone cottage surrounded by a wooden fence that could use shellacking. The ruin of a garden lay on the other side, flowers, wild and blown, poked through. Once this had been someone's pride and joy. Above, grey smoke rose in a steady ribbon to the overcast sky. At the front a short jetty stretched above the dark water, paint peeling from the boat tied to it.

I knocked the door and got no reply. I tried again, and again. The curtain moved. Behind it Alan Walker was deciding whether to answer. I called his name to encourage him.

'Mr Walker! The Lomond Inn told me to speak to you. It's about the body washed up at Luss.'

The door opened, only a little. An eye, yellow where white should be, stared without blinking. 'I apologise for disturbing you, Mr Walker. Can we have a chat about your boat?'

The eye blinked. Its owner cleared his throat but didn't speak.

'Do you still hire it out? The Inn wasn't sure.'

Alan Walker stepped into the frame and he was old, about two hundred and fifty years old. His face hung above stooped shoulders, heavy and ancient, under a tangle of steel-grey hair as overgrown as his garden. He smelled of pipe smoke and wore woollen gloves with the fingers cut out. A second cardigan peeked from the worn elbows of the navy blue one on top. Walker was a man who had retired from the world and gone to seed. I reckoned he was in his eighties – his bulldog glare told me I wasn't welcome.

'Mr Walker has anyone taken your boat recently? The Lomond said you used to hire it out.'

'Bloody tourists. More trouble than they're worth. Stopped giving them the boat a long time ago.'

'So nobody recently, in the last month?'

He repeated himself. 'More trouble than they're worth. Bloody tourists.'

I edged away. Alan Walker didn't know the day of the week. When I heard the door close I went back and looked at the boat. The bottom was caved in, six inches of water filled the shell and something green and slimy clung to the sides. Vandals maybe. I suspected the old man had taken an axe to it one night. Either way Ian Selkirk hadn't been near it. I'd try Balloch and the other one but not today.

On the drive back to the city it started to rain. Again. I thought about Fiona and Spain and missed her. She wasn't due to telephone tonight. For that I was grateful. She was convinced I was handling it – it was important not to worry her.

By the time I reached Anniesland my spirits were low. The rest of the evening was a bust. I slumped in front of the television not caring what I watched, not seeing, not hearing. While I'd been having my one sided conversation with Alan Walker I'd missed a call: Cecelia McNeil. As constant as the weather. Of course I knew what she wanted; what I didn't understand was why she still had faith in me.

I was a busy fool, telling myself effort equalled progress. Except it didn't. Perhaps I'd been a bit quick to pit myself against DI Platt and Police Scotland CID with all the manpower they could muster. Andrew Geddes had told me that on any murder investigation, depending on the circumstances, anything from twenty five to a hundred people could be involved. He sneered at the cop shows where four officers tracked down a serial killer in days. 'Forty days more like, just to establish the suspects,' he'd said.

Experience taught me grinding brought results, if results were possible. But I didn't have to enjoy it. Checking and rechecking, going over and over the same old ground. Not twenty-five people. Not one hundred. Sometimes with Patrick – usually just me.

Hard. Damned hard.

Chapter 16

Sean Rafferty said, 'Cameron's found the car switch and been to the Lomond Inn. He's good.'

Jimmy said, 'Is he good enough?'

Kevin's logic never changed. 'Why don't we lift him? Sweat it out of him.'

Sean put his head in his hands. Wasn't that why they were in this shit? If they had followed the thief he would've led them to it. He said, 'I told you this guy's different. He doesn't know where the money is. He's looking same as us. Anyway, that didn't work. Or don't you remember?'

Jimmy Rafferty interrupted before Kevin could reply. 'Shut it. Both of you, shut it. Your brother was worth more than the two of you put together.'

Paul. Paul. Paul. The old man was fixated. In life the youngest brother had been a thug; in death he'd become a saint.

Sean was with him when he died. A Friday, the night a myth began.

***

The Bell public house was crowded. A flat screen television hung on the wall with the sound turned off. Nobody was interested. Friday was for serious drinkers. The Rafferty brothers stood at the bar – an unusual sight – Jimmy's boys were rarely together. They should've been able to meet once in a while, but Paul Rafferty and alcohol didn't mix. He was a touchy bastard at the best of times and, when he'd had a few, he was better avoided. From the moment Billy Lyle spoke the evening was doomed and so was he.

Lyle was a hothead. On a busy Saturday afternoon he had beaten a stranger unconscious over a disputed parking space at Tesco, gone into the store and done his shopping. He wasn't part of any gang; none would have him: more trouble than he was worth. He resented Kevin. In a moment of uncharacteristic clarity he had told the young thug there was no place for him in the family's plans; he was a loose cannon. Rich coming from Kevin. It was a slight Billy Lyle wasn't ready to forget.

He stood at the end of the bar, Sean facing him, his eyes boring into the eldest brother's back. Kevin didn't realise he was there until he shouted above the noise. 'Heard Jimmy had a stroke, how's he doin'?'

Sean answered. 'Fine'.

Lyle smiled. 'Sorry to hear that.'

The words fell like an unexploded bomb. Conversation faded. Time passed in slow motion. Sean returned the smile. Lyle was a punk, probably a psycho. He didn't rise to the bait. 'I'll tell him you were asking for him, Billy. When he's better he'll thank you himself.'

The threat would've been enough if Paul had stayed out of it. He said, 'And tell Senga I'll be round to see her.'

Senga was Billy Lyle's sister.

'Still a tenner, is it?'

Lyle, already wound tight, jumped on the bar and dived at Paul. It was madness – he was outnumbered three to one – it should've intimidated him. It didn't. Sean pulled them apart and dragged his brother outside. Kevin blocked the door and tried to calm Lyle down. He had just about succeeded when Paul added to the insult.

'She's not bad, Billy. Not as good as her mother.'

Lyle broke free of Kevin, ran outside and pulled a gun. The first shot missed; the second hit Paul Rafferty in the eye. He died in an ambulance on the way to the Royal Infirmary. Just seventeen years old.

For his mother his death was a tragedy. For his father a legend was born.

***

Kevin threw down the challenge. 'Any better ideas, Sean?'

His brother had, though not any he cared to share. The choice was straightforward: say nothing and hope he was still standing after Rocha took his revenge, or find the money and give it back. To do that, they needed Cameron or the woman to lead them to it. He made his decision. Kevin was greedy and delusional. He presumed a right to head the family and believed force could solve every problem. Wrong on both counts.

Jimmy said, 'Do we know if Cameron's still in contact with the woman?'

'Can bet he is, so what she knows he knows. Time to turn the screw.'

'Make sure he realises we're here. Toss his flat. See what that gets us.'

***

An orange tree stood in the centre of the courtyard. In the morning it caught the sun; in the afternoon, as the temperature rose, it was cool, a pleasant escape from the heat. Emil Rocha's study overlooked it. The Raffertys had sipped iced tea there. Rocha was careful, he knew all there was to know about Jimmy Rafferty and his sons before they met. Big fish in a small pool. Forgotten the moment they left. He hadn't expected to have to think about them again. The call from Glasgow had changed all that.

He picked up the telephone. 'Tell my nephew I want him,' he said. 'And send coffee and some juice.'

The Spaniard structured his organisation so he couldn't be linked with anything illegal. The police had tried and failed – Rocha was always beyond their reach. It was a point of honour with him to keep it that way.

Honour was important to the drug lord: he never broke a promise. That made him good to do business with because he always delivered what he said he would. Of course, as many discovered, that coin had two sides. If he came after you there was nowhere to hide.

Nowhere in the world.

He had a talent for reading people, so mistakes were few. But he'd trusted Selkirk and he'd proved himself unworthy of that trust. Disappointing though easily resolved. The money was unimportant; although it was a great deal – a fortune – the loss would hardly be noticed. The other matter was more serious. Betrayal came in many forms. By Emil Rocha's code, what had happened was unforgivable.

The orange tree was almost as high as the study window. He had planted it himself, years before, not for fruit, but as a reminder of how it might have been. His grandfather had been an orange farmer, his father and his uncle too. They worked hard and died poor.

Young Emil vowed to break the chain, and if that meant breaking the law, so be it. He might have become just another gangster – the Costas had more than their share – except Rocha had ambition. And vision. He went to Morocco, to Tangier and Marrakech, making connections, shaking hands with rogues who would murder for a hundred dirham, learning, putting the pieces in place. Building. That seemed a long time ago.

On his deathbed his uncle made him swear he would take care of his wife and son. He needn't have asked.

His nephew and the drinks arrived together. When Rocha looked at the handsome face he saw his father's brother as he must have been before poverty broke him.

'Sit down,' he said. 'There's something I need you to do.'

Chapter 17

I went to work on Friday. Jackie smiled and waved hello; Gary's great body was working its magic. They say there's always somebody worse off than you: this morning it was Pat Logue. He sat at a table by the window, drinking cappuccino and reading the Express, a tan suitcase at his feet.

'Bit early to see you, isn't it?'

He looked as if he hadn't slept. A livid red lump rose on his forehead and deep scratches ran down his cheek. Patrick had been in the wars.

'Gail's thrown in the towel,' he said. 'Last night was the finish. Worst rammy ever.'

'Come to the office and talk about it.'

'Nah Charlie, nothin' to talk about.'

'I can offer you a whisky if that's any help.'

He folded the newspaper 'All right. Just don't let me drown in self-pity.'

I asked Jackie to send coffee for two and went upstairs. Patrick followed me. He slumped in the chair opposite. I poured a stiff Grouse – he took it without a word. It was strange to see him so low – disturbing in a way that was hard to describe. I'd always thought of him as one of life's survivors. Now he seemed lost. No patter, no street philosophy. None of the irrepressible spirit that marked him as different. He didn't want to discuss his situation. Not yet anyway.

'That friend of mine – the one we buried on Monday – he was murdered and dumped in Loch Lomond.'

A flicker of interest. 'Rafferty?'

'Could be he had something Jimmy Rafferty wants.'

He cradled his drink. 'The Awkward Squad. Give it a body swerve.'

'It isn't that simple.'

A knock on the door – the coffee had arrived. The dark-haired waitress set it on the desk and left.

'Yeah it is. Missing persons is your thing, Charlie. How come you're involved?'

'Long story. I shouldn't have mentioned it.'

Patrick said, 'First today,' and downed the whisky in one. His features contorted and he shook his head against the fire. 'No, tell me.'

'Better you don't know.'

'Right now I couldn't give a flyin' fuck if I live or die, tell me.'

So I told him: about the car switch, the Lomond Inn; Jimmy Rafferty's shadow and DI Platt.

'What about the woman? Where does she fit in?'

I poured him another; he didn't object. His coffee sat untouched. Whisky felt right; it wasn't a coffee conversation.

'We were pals at Uni. Ian needed looking after, Fiona got the job.'

Old friends are the best friends

'Who looked after Fiona?'

The whisky was starting to work. Patrick was being cheeky.

'Fiona and Ian sold real estate in Spain. Three years ago she sacked him. Had to. She discovered he was doing drugs, and not just using, he was selling them.'

'Where is she now?'

'Back in Spain. Don't want her anywhere near here.'

He inspected the whisky, searching the golden liquid for imperfections.

'And the plan is?'

'Killing Ian didn't get them what they wanted. We were the only people at the funeral. The only link Rafferty has. He'll be expecting us to lead them to whatever Ian stole. When we don't because we can't, he'll come after us. I'm taking your advice, Patrick. Sort it out you said. That's what I intend to do.'

He gazed into the glass, unblinking: I thought he hadn't heard. He said, 'First today.' The second whisky chased the other one. He grimaced. 'Jimmy Rafferty's a psycho; he doesn't play wee games. The rules are his rules. He'll kill you, and your girlfriend, then send out for pizza.'

'What else can I do?'

Patrick's eyes were glazed, not just with alcohol; lack of sleep and unhappiness were in there too. 'I'll do a deal, Charlie. I'm potless, I have to earn and I need a place to kip.'

'Stay with me until you're straight.'

'But not for nothing.'

Not a gift, Charlie. Not something for nothing.

'I'll work with you, how's that?'

'You'll be putting yourself in harm's way.'

He turned his face so I could see the marks. 'I'm already there, or hadn't you noticed.'

I wondered if I hadn't caught him at a low ebb and dragged him into my troubles so I'd feel less alone. Two of us. Twice as baffled in half the time? Or perhaps that bit of luck every investigation begged for would come. I gave my new flatmate a key.

Downstairs in NYB Jackie was on a break, nibbling like a rabbit on Scandinavian cardboard, drinking a bottle of something with *Power* on the label. I ordered a roll and sausage – the brown sauce tipped her over the edge. She lifted her eyes accusingly but I didn't notice until she was standing over me.

'You're killing yourself with that crap. You do know that?'

'You make money selling this crap, Jackie. You sell it, people buy it. They buy it because they like it, and they like it 'cause it tastes good.'

She leaned her arms on the table. I heard a lecture approach.

'Your body's a machine, Charlie. More complex than a jumbo jet. Put junk in it, it breaks down. Maybe not today, maybe not tomorrow, but it will. Gary says it isn't our job to convert anybody. All we can do is lead by example. And I can guess what you're thinking: crazy Jackie, off on another one, well you'd be wrong. Health is the cornerstone of a happy life. Without it, what is there?'

Her sincerity unnerved me. She returned to her seat, her work done. I pushed the plate away, not hungry anymore.

When it came the phone call shook me. It was Patrick, no lethargy now. 'Charlie,' he said, 'I'm at your gaff. I think you'd better get over here. And call the police.'

***

Possessions never held much interest for me. If it could be bought it could be replaced. So I thought. When your personal space has been invaded and trashed it's a difficult outlook to hold on to. I phoned Andrew and told him what Pat had told me. At the flat Patrick was in the kitchen drinking water; coffee and sugar dusted the floor. He stared at me; his face was pale – he knew who was responsible. So did I. Jimmy Rafferty's breath was hot on my neck.

Andrew Geddes stood in the ruin of my life. Around him books had been swept from shelves, their pages torn and scattered; CDs were tossed aside like a losing hand of cards and furniture was overturned, heaped on the carpet as if Guy Fawkes had come early. The expensive sound system, my Christmas present to myself, lay smashed against the wall beside a coffee table with three legs. Zigzag cracks ran across the face of every picture in the room. In the bedrooms, drawers had been emptied and socks and pants and shirts tossed everywhere; up-ended mattresses drooped against the bare metal bed frames like drunken walrus. A curtain, ripped from its runner for no reason, hung sad and defeated above a broken Murano lamp – a gift from a woman during a long weekend in Venice I could scarcely recall. And all the lights were on. I was stunned. It was a mess, and malicious. Some bastard had taken a hammer to the flat screen TV just for fun.

Andrew saw me and picked his way through. 'Sorry, Charlie, sorry this had to happen to you. I assume you're insured.' He seemed almost cheerful. 'Anything obvious taken?'

I didn't answer. Glass crackled beneath my shoes. 'How did they get in?'

'Door's been forced. We're interviewing the neighbours. A pound to a penny nobody heard anything. I've had a word with Logue, says you gave him your keys. That correct?'

'Yes, he's staying with me for a while.'

He raised a disapproving eyebrow. I said, 'Some other time, Andrew. I like him.'

'Your business, Charlie. I'll get a list of whatever they took, later. No need to be too exact.'

He was suggesting I inflate my claim. Insurance companies were on everybody's shit list. I wouldn't, not because of some moral imperative. I didn't have the energy; the world was bent enough without me adding to it. When the police had gone Patrick came into the lounge. I was sitting on the floor. He joined me.

'Your pal says vandals. He's wrong. Welcome to the Big Boys Club. This is how they communicate. They're tellin' you they know where you live Charlie. Warnin' you.'

He pointed to the TV. 'That could've been your head.'

'The Samaritans must've cried when you packed them in, eh Patrick?'

'They were gutted. Same as you'll be if you don't fix this.'

I picked up the leg of the coffee table and put it down again. 'I'm trying.'

'Try harder.' He took my arm and pulled me to my feet. 'C'mon, the pubs are open. Your shout.'

'I can't leave the place like this.'

'This is heehaw. I'll make a call.'

He strolled round the room, whispering into his mobile, giving instructions to people I would never meet, his footsteps crisp sounds, like walking on fresh snow.

'It's done.' He clapped his hands and studied my face. 'We need to get you to the nearest barman. Pronto.'

Patrick was being a friend. I appreciated it, glad he was there. We walked, a fair hike, all the way to Ashton Lane and Bar Brel.

A guy with a ponytail polished glasses. We were the only customers apart from an old man at the end, gazing at his reflection in the mirror behind the gantry, stroking his unshaved jaw with a nicotine-stained finger. One of my father's bottles hung upside down between *Teachers* and *Smirnoff*. The clock on the wall said ten past eleven – usually too early for me. Not today.

Pat said, 'What're we after?'

His enthusiasm might've been because I was buying. I preferred to believe it was an animated act for my benefit.

'Gin. Large. Soda and ice.'

'I'll stick to the national drink.'

I gave him a twenty. He came back with the spirits and a half pint of lager. No mention of any change. It was going to be an expensive session.

'That old boy was in the merchant navy. Dunkirk, he was there. His son lives down south. Since his wife died he spends his time here, waiting to join her. Doin' all right for ninety-two. I bought him a pint.'

'How do you know all this? You were only gone a minute.'

'Doesn't take long if you're interested. Got to be interested in people. Now ponytail there, he's a waste of space. Not a word out of him. Wouldn't last ten minutes if I owned this shop.'

'You're amazing, Patrick, you really are.'

He picked up his whisky. I put a hand on his arm. 'Don't say it.'

'Say what?'

'"First today." You always say "first today."'

'No I don't. And it isn't, you gave me one.'

'I gave you two.'

'Who's countin'?'

Our positions had reversed – my head felt heavy – I wanted to sleep. Pat Logue was bright eyed. He seemed to have forgotten his troubles. 'Go to a hotel Charlie. Tomorrow all you'll need is a new telly.'

I bought a toothbrush and booked two rooms at the Malmaison off Blythswood Square. During the day accountants and lawyers peddled their wares in the former town houses surrounding it; at night it was one of the city's red light areas. The irony wasn't difficult to spot.

The mini bar was filled with the usual over-priced booze. I settled for a coke.

Bang on cue my phone rang, Cecelia McNeil's name appeared on the screen. I took the call although it was the last thing I fancied. I represented the flimsy thread of hope she clung to. With my head filled with Ian Selkirk and Jimmy Rafferty that thread was more fragile than ever she imagined. I intended to sound upbeat but I didn't get the chance.

'Stephen's alive. He's alive.'

'How do you know? Has he contacted you?'

'He used his Visa card last Tuesday.'

Mrs McNeil was still doing my job for me. Thank God somebody was.

'Where?'

'At Tesco in Shettleston. Fifty three pounds fifty seven. That means he hasn't done anything stupid, not yet.'

In lieu of something better I said, 'Good news.'

'Yes, yes, he's still in Glasgow. I went to mass this morning - I'm going every morning again - and lit a candle to St Anthony. I mean, now you can find him, can't you, Mr Cameron?'

'I'll try, Mrs McNeil. Don't give up hope whatever you do.'

'Oh, I never would, that's the sin of despair. You haven't answered my calls. I suppose I'm a terrible nuisance.'

'Of course not.' I worked to convince her.

'You said you wouldn't walk away. I worried you had.'

'Not at all.' I lied with the ease of an adulterer. 'I'll think about the Visa card and get back to you.'

'You're very kind. The important thing is Stephen's alive and close by. I'll sleep better tonight.'

The beginning of a headache throbbed in my temple. I massaged my eyes, overwhelmed with guilt. What was I going to do? My own life was in danger; so was Fiona's. Ian Selkirk's murder hung like a weight. Cecelia McNeil expected more from me and so did I. Shopping at Tesco wasn't the action of a man on the edge of suicide. Stephen McNeil had a car so the location might not be relevant. Then again, the situation was far from normal. A Glasgow gangster was after me. Wrecking the flat put the ball in my court. I was starting to sound like Patrick Logue. My energy and whatever talent I was reckoned to have were required to keep me from joining my friend in the cold waters of the loch. Mrs McNeil had a belief system to fall back on. I wondered if it wasn't too late to join; perhaps St Anthony would toss something my way.

From day one I had been off form on the McNeil investigation. With Jimmy Rafferty on my case I couldn't think clearly enough to help anybody. Thank god Fiona was in Spain.

It was my night to call, which suited me, it meant I didn't have to be at the flat. Fiona sounded tired. I asked if anything was wrong. 'No,' she said. 'Too many things to do, that's all. Making any progress on Ian?'

I kept it vague which wasn't difficult. 'They found his car?'
'Where?'
'He booked into the Lomond Inn for three nights, he only stayed two.'

'Did you tell the police about the man following us?'
'Not yet.'
'Why not, for Christ's sake?'
'I've a better chance of discovering whatever Ian stole if I keep away from the police.'

'But it's dangerous. Those people are killers.'
I told her to scare her and keep her in Spain. A mistake.
'The flat got burgled. The police think kids did it.'

Her shock travelled down the line. For half a minute neither of us spoke then Fiona said. 'This is all my fault. I dragged you into it. I'm sorry, Charlie. You have to get out of Glasgow. You have to get away.'

The anxiety in her voice brought a strange kind of pleasure. I tried to sound confident. 'I'll be careful. I've got plenty to live for.

And don't put yourself under pressure; take your time. You're not welcome in my bed 'til this is over.'

She wasn't listening. 'Leave Glasgow, Charlie. Tonight.'

'Can't do that, Fiona. Not possible.'

'Well, tell the police. Ask for protection.'

'Against what? A couple of teenagers out of their heads on glue?'

'Tell them about the guy at Daldowie and New York Blue.'

'Fiona, calm down. The police aren't the answer, not at this stage.'

'That pal of yours, the DS. Tell him.'

'I'll consider it. I promise. It will be all right. By now they must know I don't have anything.'

She kept pleading with me to run. When the conversation ended Fiona was crying. I waited for her text – it never came.

The next call added to my misery: my father with more bad news. No *hello how are you, Charlie?* Straight in.

'Mum's not well.'

I sat to attention. 'What kind of not well?'

'She's had a stroke. Just a small one. But it's shaken her.'

'When did this happen? Why wasn't I told?'

The silence at the other end of the line told me he was choosing his words. He needn't have bothered. 'You're not exactly a constant visitor, are you, Charlie?'

Not much I could say; he was right.

'So how bad is it? What does the doctor say?'

'They thought it was a severe inner-ear infection at first. Then last Saturday night she collapsed. She was in hospital for a week.'

'And I'm hearing about it now?'

That was too much for him. 'Oh please, spare me the righteous indignation. Look, I'm bringing you up to speed. After that it's over to you. Your mother's recovering from a stroke. Visit her don't visit her. Just leave out the no-one-tells-me-anything stuff.'

The line went dead. I stared at it for a long time. What he'd said hurt because it was true: my mother had suffered because of my relationship – my non-relationship – with my father. For years we hadn't got on and, though things were better now, George Archibald Cameron had the unique ability of making me feel I was a failure. No one in the world affected me like he did.

The knock at the door made me jump. It was Patrick.

I said, 'Late for a social call, isn't it?'

'Just checkin' you're okay. The flat's clean. We can go back tomorrow.'

I thanked him. He breezed past me into the room. 'My offer still holds,' he said. 'I'm with you.'

'You're a good man, Pat.'

'Try tellin' Gail.'

'When I see her I will. There's something I need you to do. Mrs McNeil's husband used his credit card in Tesco in Shettleston last Tuesday so he may well be living local. He likes a drink and he likes darts. Do a pub crawl for two or three nights. You never know.'

'Pub crawl. I'll try.'

He opened the mini-bar, took out a can of Stella and popped the top.

'Helluva price they charge for this stuff. I wouldn't give them it.'

Apparently I would.

'Cheers,' he said. 'First today.'

***

The man fixing the lock didn't notice me. Inside the flat a woman was waiting: brunette, forties, not pretty. Business-like but empathetic. 'Best we could manage,' she said. 'They made a right mess.'

I might've been looking at the aftermath of a teenage party gone wrong, though nothing like as bad as it had been. The TV, the coffee table, everything damaged or broken had been removed, and the carpet had lost its gravel crunch.

She gestured to an assortment in the corner. 'We saved what we could. Anything personal's there.'

I followed her through to a bedroom. Order had been restored, a cover was spread on the bed under matching pillows. She pulled a drawer open; socks lay in neat rows.

'You've done a great job. What do I owe you?'

'Nothing. You're a friend of Patrick's. That's good enough.'

Before she left she made me a coffee and handed me new door keys.

The lounge was still a shambles. I felt anger at the needless destruction and let it pass; holding on wouldn't change things.

A voice said, 'Make a note of what you want. Here in two days. Cash customers only.'

Patrick stood in the doorway leaning against the facing.

'Seriously. Whatever you need. Got a telly comin' later. Same as the one they tanked. Throw in a new iMac if you like.'

It was a well-intended offer I had to refuse. For me there was more at stake.

'Appreciate it, but I can't let you do that.'

'Who would know?'

'I'd know. Fiona's telling me to leave the city.'

'Not a bad idea for a day or so. Longer's just runnin' away. Can't run from your own life.'

I could have reminded him he was running away.

'I'm going to work. See you later, Patrick. And thank you for what you did here.'

Downtown NYB was enjoying a mid-morning rush. Jackie was at a table at the back interviewing two guys. One wore a black t-shirt with *Gay Power* on the front; the other had buck teeth and hung on Jackie's every word. Behind the bar a handsome man I hadn't seen before was making espresso with a practised hand. Dark eyes flashed in a suntanned face. Across the counter the waitress adored him. Jackie was at my elbow.

'New starts. Those two on the floor and Roberto.'

'Where did your other barman go?'

'He quit. This morning. His girlfriend called. Roberto was available.'

'Lucky you.'

'Tons of experience, you can see it.'

I had to admit he was impressive. A latte, an espresso and two cappuccinos appeared in quick time, along with four glasses of water.

'Serving water now, are you? Very continental.'

'They do it for a reason, Charlie. It makes sense. It dilutes the harshness of the coffee and rehydrates. We underestimate the importance of water.'

'Do we?'

I waited. She didn't disappoint.

'Gary says water's the single most essential substance for the body, apart from oxygen. Gary says sixty percent of illness can be cured by drinking more water. Incredible, or what?'

'Can I have coffee, please? Just coffee.' I drew her towards me and whispered. 'Gary doesn't need to know.'

She glared. 'I'll send it up.'

The exchange with Jackie had amused me but alone in the office my mood fell. I pulled paper from the printer; it was time to assess where I was going, or if there was anywhere to go. I cross-checked my notes and started to write. Dover/Glasgow Airport, the Lomond Inn to the autopsy report. The same unanswered questions taunted me. Where was Ian Selkirk in the forty-eight hours prior to his death?

I called Andrew. 'Has Ian Selkirk's mobile been found?'

'No. Probably at the bottom of the loch.'

'Can I have a look at his effects?'

He took his time answering me. 'No you can't, but I'll get a list of what he left over to you.'

The people tailing us must have seen me at the airport and at the loch. They would know I was in the dark, yet they still trashed the flat. They must have sussed I didn't have it, whatever it was. Maybe it was over?

Meantime Loch Lomond was the key. The car was found at Duck Bay, Ian was a few miles further on at the Lomond Inn, and his body was fished from the water at Luss.

I hadn't been to Duck Bay Marina since my student days. In my memory it was a place to pull good-looking women. On my way out Jackie was leaning on the bar chatting to Antonio Banderas, charmed out of her socks. Gary had a rival. I wondered what he'd have to say about that. I turned towards High Street. White clouds hid the sun; still, the weather was warming up.

He was standing on the corner of Glassford Street. Not the same man. Just the same type – heavy set, self-contained, unsmiling. Albion Street wasn't a shortcut, I took it anyway.

A minute later so did he. It wasn't over. Not for them. Not for me.

Chapter 18

The overnight express got me to London at an ungodly hour on Monday morning. Jimmy Rafferty's thug turning into Albion Street convinced me I'd be better off away from Glasgow. Trashing the flat hadn't satisfied them. My father's call gave me somewhere to go.

When the steward came with tea and biscuits he knocked on the door and my heart jumped in my chest. Fear had travelled with me, and Pat Logue got it right, I was running.

Outside on Euston Road the working week had begun; the distant growl of traffic carried into the station. Soon it would be nose to tail from Marylebone Road, and the growl would become a roar. The journey on the Tube reminded me why I hadn't chosen to live in the capital: sullen faces inches apart, tension and resentment on every one. For all its compensations it could never be my home.

A second train and a taxi brought me to the house and another planet, one with manicured lawns and late flowering daffodils, a place of order and calm, on the surface at least. My last visit to Buckinghamshire had been with Kate Calder; we had made love in the bedroom that had been mine when I was home for the holidays. Not long after our affair ended, Kate was finally persuaded to join North Wind. Now she was on tour in the Far East, wowing them in Tokyo or Kuala Lumpur with her incredible talent. If I'd asked her to stay with me she would have. I didn't ask and lost her. Then, out of the blue, Fiona had come back into my life.

This house had few associations for me. My parents moved here from Edinburgh. Conservatives were all but extinct north of the border thanks to the Scottish National Party. My father's political duties insisted he be nearer London. As it was he stayed in town during the week leaving my mother alone here. They were an odd twosome: him animated, full of bluster, her quiet and precise. One fierce, the other demure; the attraction of opposites I supposed.

Although my visit was unannounced my mother didn't look surprised to see me. I kissed her. She put her arm in mine and led me to the sitting-room. Underneath her Cashmere twinset she had lost weight, her cheeks were pinched and her eyes lacked her usual confidence. Her hair had been blonde but now it was white.

She said, 'The jungle drums.'

'Dad called, yes. Why didn't you let me know you'd been ill?'

'What would be the point, Charles? You'd worry, you know you would. Then come chasing down here away from something important.' She shook her head. 'You're more like him than you imagine.'

'And how is he?'

She shrugged. 'Your father doesn't change. Up to his ears. The Party's in trouble according to the opinion polls; reading them makes him angry.'

'Everything makes him angry.'

She rapped my knuckles with a word. 'Unfair. When the Japs bought Cameron's he was left in limbo. Being on the board isn't the same as running the damned thing. Selling was the correct decision but he felt responsible. The offer from the Party came at the right moment. Your father's a doer, used to being at the centre. He has so much to offer. The downside is he doesn't pace himself – it's one hundred and ten percent or nothing.'

She sighed. 'And that awful muddle Perry got into hasn't helped. You should've heard your father. I thought he would have a coronary.'

Perry was Peregrine Sommerville: lifetime conservative activist, commentator and MP for the ninth safest Tory seat in England. The muddle, a synonym in my mother's circle for anything from parking illegally to selling state secrets, made the front page of every newspaper, the most telling detail coming from the broadsheet that carried out the investigation. Perry lied under oath about his associations with a minor member of the Saudi royal family and a Jordanian businessman called Abelsalam al-Majari. Allegations that he accepted money were denied and denied again until footage shot from a hidden camera was shown to a silent courthouse. He was convicted of perjury. A zealous prosecutor could have pressed more serious charges but for reasons that never became clear, the will to pursue old Perry was lacking.

Friends in high places. My father no doubt was one of them.

Perry got fifteen months in Longmarsh Cat. D prison and served eight. During his spell at Her Majesty's pleasure he underwent a moral sea change. On the day of his release, outside the prison gates, he told how he had opened his heart to his Saviour, and repented for his much publicised sins. The Party distanced itself still further from Peregrine Sommerville, at the double.

'He found Jesus. Is that real?'

My mother said, 'I've no idea. Perry and your father have been friends for forty-five years. He was best man at our wedding. Archie was devastated. Couldn't believe Perry would be so stupid. As if the trial hadn't been bad enough, day after day of sordid details, the press fell on it like the hunt pack.' Her gaze wandered towards the window. 'It's Arabella I feel for most, and the girls. Politically, Perry's ruined of course. Not financially, that was the thing, he didn't need the money. His wife's family have plenty.'

'He just wanted it.'

Her eyebrow arched. 'Perry's done the Party a lot of damage, Charles. Your father says it's too soon to assess how serious. Lucky the last election produced a comfortable majority, otherwise it would be a very bumpy trip.'

'Did he visit him in Longmarsh?'

'No.'

'Shouldn't he have gone to see him?'

'Absolutely not. What a ludicrous suggestion.'

A forty-five year friendship down the toilet, not because your best man turns out to be corrupt, not even because he got caught, but because, when he did, he couldn't do the 'right thing' and put a sock in it.'

'What does the doctor say about you?'

'Not much. I'm sixty-five after all. Rest, Aspirin, exercise. Avoid stress.' She laughed. 'Married to your father? More to the point, how are you? You look a bit peaky. Still snooping on unsuspecting Glaswegians?'

'I don't snoop.'

'You always were a secretive little boy. I should have spotted it. Nipped it in the bud.'

'Mother.' I smiled. 'Stop trying to wind me up. You know what I do.'

She unwrapped an old chestnut. 'When am I going to be a grandmother, Charles?'

'It isn't in the plan.'

'And what happened to the girl you brought to meet us, the one with long red hair? You seemed keen on each other.'

She meant Kate.

'It didn't work out.'

'Mmmm, I liked her, she was nice.'

'Yes she was.'

'So you haven't got a girlfriend at the moment?'

I didn't answer, she would meet Fiona soon enough.

'Pru Carrington's youngest daughter's visiting them. We could drive over. You remember Caroline, don't you?'

I remembered Caroline all right.

'No, just a flying visit to check on you. Back to Scotland tonight.'

Not the truth. I was booked on a flight to Alicante at seven a.m. I missed Fiona.

My mother's disappointment touched me. 'Oh Charles, surely you can stay a bit longer?' She picked up the telephone and dialled. 'Archie, Charles is here. No, he's going tonight; he'll drop in at Smith Square on his way through town. You'll be around? Seven, that's fine. Bye.'

She put the receiver in its cradle. 'There. All arranged. Your father's expecting you. Now you can take me to lunch. Absolutely certain about Caroline Carrington? I'm sure she would love to see you.'

I couldn't tell her why, but Caroline Carrington wouldn't be pleased to see me.

Smith Square was Conservative and Unionist Party headquarters. Security let me through and gave me a Visitor badge. People hurried past carrying memos and letters and reports. It was difficult to avoid the feeling that power lived here. The office was on the first floor. His secretary gave me an approving nod. George Archibald Cameron stared out of the window with his back to me. When he turned I caught the change in him; he was smaller, his eyes were heavy, the face florid; blood pressure, fine wine or a bit of both, but the old directness was there. 'So, Charlie, how much longer do you intend to keep playing silly buggers in Glasgow?'

'And good evening to you too, father.'

He put his hands on my shoulders and eyed me up and down. 'You look well enough, say that for you.'

'I am.'

'Could do with you down here. Place is full of incompetents determined to lose us the next election. Always room for a good man.'

We both knew that ship had sailed.

'Not staying I hear. Pity. Your mother would like to see more of you.'

'Why don't you both come to Glasgow for a day or two? It's not how you remember it.'

'Want us to watch our only son spying on the unsuspecting locals?'

He didn't like Scotland; no votes up there for his lot.

'I'm inviting you to meet my friends, see what I'm doing. Who knows, you may even approve.'

'I very much doubt it.'

'Don't be so sure.'

'Please don't take this wrong, Charlie, but under achieving doesn't impress me, never has.'

'What're you talking about, under achieving?'

He walked to his desk, sat down and started rearranging papers. 'Of course,' he said, 'it's your life, just please don't ask me to understand. You've had the best education money can buy and what are you doing with it? I had hoped you'd get this investigator nonsense out of your system. Might be ready to make a real contribution.'

Every visit to my parents produced the same conversations. With my mother it was grandchildren; my father's pet poodle was me squandering my advantages in the godforsaken north.

'Mum filled me in on Perry.'

He sighed and shook his head. 'Thirty years in politics down the drain. Probably his marriage too. And for what?'

'How much damage has he done?'

'Too soon to tell. I blame myself.'

'Why? Perry Sommerville sold political influence in exchange for money and lied under oath about it. What could you have done?'

'I should have seen it coming.'

'How? How could you?'

He leaned his elbows on the desk. 'Perry and I met at university. He was the one who got me involved in politics. Until then I hadn't been interested. He had a knack of making you believe whatever he was peddling. Tremendously persuasive.'

Particularly useful in this game.

'One time at the conference in Blackpool he stood in at short notice for somebody who had taken ill. And by short I mean an hour. Perry spoke without notes for twenty five minutes. Off the top of his head. Got a standing ovation.'

Standing ovations were thirteen to the dozen at Tory get togethers. Preaching to the choir. I wasn't surprised. 'What's your point? Why blame yourself?'

He threw a sharp look at me. 'My point is it was bullshit, every word of it. I was there, yet at the end I was on my feet with everybody else.'

'So he was a con man.'

'From the beginning. The first time he stood for parliament he lost – maybe people saw what I didn't. He got in at the next attempt thanks to me. I was his election agent. I organised his campaign, for Christ's sake. Of course I'm responsible for the mess he's got us into. This latest thing isn't a lapse – he's always sailed close to the wind, then tried to charm his way out of it. Because he was a pal I ignored his recklessness. Defended him. Perry was Perry. And he was greedy. For the spotlight, for applause, money. Whatever.'

He might have been describing Ian Selkirk.

'I should have kept an eye on him. Dumped him for the good of the Party when he got caught instead of rallying support behind the scenes.'

'Being a bit hard on him, aren't you? He was the victim of a yellow journalism sting. Entrapment.'

'Not a bit. Sommerville's a fraud who may have stuffed our chances of a second term in office. A consummate actor who took everybody in; in my case for over forty years.'

'Okay, he's everything you say, but he was your friend. Surely that counts for something?'

'Was he?'

He ran a hand through his hair, still thick and dark; the pain in his eyes said I had misjudged the depth of Perry's betrayal. 'I thought I knew him, Charlie, but the truth is I didn't know him at all.'

That admission, out of the blue, came at an opportune moment for me. The unexpected frankness of his reply took me by surprise and, if nothing else, showed I didn't know as much about this man as I imagined.

The times when we shared an opinion, far less an emotion, were rare though for once I understood exactly how my father felt and why.

Chapter 19

On a country road in the small hours, two cars cut their engines and eased onto the grass verge under a bank of trees. The headlights died and five men got out: the Rafferty brothers, and three soldiers. A lot of muscle for a simple operation, but then failure was out of the question – they were running out of time.

Sean Rafferty had lived his whole life in the city; at four a.m. on a starless night this place was very different from the east end streets. He stood, allowing his eyes to adjust to darkness like he'd never known, threatening and strange, even to a hard man from Glasgow. After a minute he was able to identify the single track cutting through fields to the farmhouse and the cottage beyond; vague shapes against the sky. Some people loved this shit; the fresh air, the space, the quiet. Not him. It set him on edge. The sooner they did what they were there to do and headed back to civilisation the better.

He had come here during the day to satisfy himself the information they'd received was correct. It was, he'd seen the cropped hair behind the wheel of the hire car and followed her to a supermarket in Kilmarnock. She wandered up and down the aisles, filling her trolley; reading labels and comparing prices; occasionally having second thoughts about a can or a packet and replacing it. The t-shirt she was wearing read: YESTERDAY YOU SAID TOMORROW on the front. At the checkout she smiled at the pretty girl on the till and paid in cash, a couple of hundred pounds, a lot of food for one person. Digging in 'til her boyfriend got a result? All told the shopping trip took ninety minutes and couldn't have been more ordinary, nothing about her suggested this was a woman with a five million pound secret.

In the car park, Rafferty watched her load groceries into the boot, bending and stretching, skirt drawn tight against her arse, and remembered her legs the first time he'd seen her. He'd wanted the bitch then, and he wanted her now; for a second he even considered taking a chance and lifting her in broad daylight. Impetuous and unwise. Something Kevin might try. Sean was more cautious than his brother; too many things could go wrong. And it wasn't the plan.

An owl hooted and flew from a branch above his head. He froze, startled. Why in the name of Christ was he here? Why were any of them here? The sense of foreboding that had dogged him from the moment Jimmy agreed to Kevin's crazy idea overwhelmed him. He saw the future and bared his teeth in a joyless grin. This was a mistake, a mistake that would bring them down. They were about to unleash something they couldn't control.

Rafferty shivered and started towards the farm.

Who was he kidding? It was already out of control.

***

They walked in silence along the track ridged and rutted by farm traffic. Vincent Donnelly, a thug who worked for the family between spells in Barlinnie, stumbled and cursed out loud. Kevin Rafferty grabbed him by the lapels and threw him to the ground, Donnelly felt the blade at his throat and a warm sensation he recognised as blood. Kevin hissed. 'Another noise and you'll wish you were back in the Big House.'

If the others needed a reminder of what was at stake they had it.

The previous afternoon, Sean had studied the farm through binoculars and reported to Jimmy and his brother. He'd told them the downside and his opinion that it was too risky. It made no difference, their minds were made up, they were for going ahead. Sean made a final attempt to dissuade the old man.

'This is a move we don't make until we have to.'

Kevin exploded. 'And when will that be? Grow some balls, for fuck's sake! We need this bitch. Cameron's an amateur, out of his depth. We know more than he does.'

Sean ignored him. 'Do this, Jimmy, and there's no going back.'

Jimmy shook his head; his middle son was weak.

'A world of shit about to come down on us and you want to wait. I think Kevin's right. You need to grow a pair.'

'It won't be clean; loose ends attract attention.'

'Clean isn't on. Never was. After a while the people at the farm will notice she's gone, then we'll have police, newspapers…'

'And Emil Rocha.'

Jimmy dismissed Sean's objections. 'There's a time for caution. This isn't it. Your brother can be an arse, but he isn't afraid to act. You can learn from him.'

Sean Rafferty had heard the same criticism all his life; on the drive from the city it stayed with him. It was always the same with Jimmy and Kevin and wouldn't get any better. Their greed had put them in danger. Now the stupid bastards were hell bent on making a bad situation worse and couldn't see it.

The five figures stopped forty yards from the farmhouse. Twelve hours earlier it had been deserted now a Land Rover was parked on the flagstone courtyard with a new BMW beside it. Somebody was home. They crept closer, crouched and tense. The house showed no sign of life; nothing stirred. That wouldn't last. From under his jacket Kevin drew a gun with a suppressor already screwed in place. Jimmy had made it clear this was his show. Unease gnawed Sean's gut. Like all Kevin's plans it was doomed – any second it was going to go tits up.

They came out of the night like phantoms, racing to the rattle of their chains, growling and barking: the downside Sean Rafferty had warned against. Every farm had a dog, this farm had two. German Shepherds. Shooting them was easy. Doing it before they alerted the people in the house was impossible.

The lead dog made for Kevin Rafferty. He saw it coming at him and fired a wild shot that missed. The animal swerved and leapt on Vinney Donnelly standing behind him. Donnelly crashed to the ground, fighting to keep the open jaws from his throat.

He screamed. 'Shoot it! Shoot it!'

Kevin spun, saw his man rolling on the flagstones with the dog straddling him and fired again. Donnelly stopped struggling; he'd served his last stretch in the Bar-L. The second Alsatian crashed into Kevin and buried its teeth in his arm. He cried out in pain and lost his grip on the gun. The other dog went for the nearest soldier. Sean was first to react. He dived for the gun and shared four shots between them.

After the bedlam the sudden silence was like a blow. Kevin staggered to his feet holding his arm, blood dripping from his fingers. He stared at Donnelly's lifeless body and swore under his breath.

The disaster Sean predicted had happened. And it wasn't over.

A light went on in an upstairs window, a face appeared and disappeared. Moments later the front door opened and a man in his fifties barged out holding a shotgun. Behind him a female called 'John! What is it? Be careful!'

The farmer saw the German Shepherds dead on the flagstones and levelled the weapon at the intruders. 'Who the fuck are you? What do...'

His question went unfinished, Kevin grabbed the gun from his brother and this time hit what he was aiming for. The farmer collapsed and fell backwards into the hall. Kevin ran into the house and up the stairs, when he returned Sean caught the wild look in his eyes.

Kevin said, 'Those loose ends you were worried about, forget them.'

Two hundred yards down the track, the cottage was as silent as the farm had been before the dogs came round the corner and ended any hope of taking the woman quietly. In daylight it had the look of a property on its way to dereliction; the original whitewash had yellowed, plaster cracks scarred the outside walls and rust stains from broken guttering ran brown to the ground. Internally it hadn't been updated in fifty years. It would be damp and cramped and hard to heat in winter. Fiona Ramsay hadn't rented it for its quaint appearance or sparkling amenities – it had more important qualities; the track petered out and became field, so there was no traffic apart from the farmer, his wife and a few labourers coming and going. No neighbours. Perfect.

Kevin signalled his men to cover the front. He moved slowly round the side testing every step with Sean behind him, half expecting the place to be empty. The woman must have heard the commotion and escaped across open land into the night. Searching would be a waste of time. Kevin dreaded having to tell Jimmy they'd lost her.

At the back door his luck changed: the old lock gave without a fight; one tap of a screwdriver covered with a cloth to deaden the sound was enough. No sweat. He stepped into the kitchen, ran his hand along the inside wall for the switch, found it and turned it on. A naked bulb threw bleak light over a sink full of unwashed dishes and a rubbish bin overflowing empty wine bottles onto the floor. The cloying smell of reheated Chinese take-away caught in his throat. He tutted disapproval like a health inspector who had discovered a restaurant's dirty secret. Killing the farmer and his wife energised Kevin Rafferty. Now, standing in the kitchen, a feeling of power surged through him.

She was here.

Sean had seen his brother's arrogance too often and knew he was watching a psychopath. Kevin seemed not to have noticed the plan to lift the woman quietly had fallen apart. Three people dead, killed by the same gun, meant triple murder. Front page news Emil Rocha would hear about before the end of the day. The consequences were inevitable. Between them Kevin and Jimmy had signed his death warrant.

Kevin said, 'This won't take long.'

He found the bedroom at the first try, not difficult, there was only one. The figure under the clothes was asleep. Kevin put the gun in his pocket – he wouldn't need it.

For a minute he stood in the middle of the room listening to her breathe, relishing his success. Sean had been against it; his father, the deluded old bastard still believing he was in charge, had taken some persuading. But he had been right. And now, thanks to him, they had her.

He sat on the edge of the bed, studying the woman, knowing even before he drew the bedclothes away that she was naked. His finger ran the length of her thigh; skin like velvet. She shivered under his touch and began to come awake. Rafferty covered her mouth with his hand and in the half-light saw her eyes flash open. The terror in them made him smile. Fiona Ramsay struggled against him. All in vain. Soon she stopped and lay trembling.

Kevin lowered his head letting his lips brush her ear and whispered.

'Sorry to disturb you. You look as innocent as an angel lying there. But you're not, are you Fiona?'

Chapter 20

A river of people poured from Victoria Station flooding already over-crowded London; the tourist season was beginning. Eastern European, oriental and black faces. A tanned young man with blonde hair and a backpack brushed against me. He said, 'Sorry, mate', his accent a flat drawl. I wondered what the Aussie in the boat off Koh Tao a couple of lifetimes ago was doing now. The underground was less busy. We passed Ravenscourt and Boston Manor; by then only those headed for Heathrow remained.

I punched Patrick Logue's number in speed dial. He didn't let me speak. 'Call you back,' he said and hung up. Five minutes later he did. 'Sorry about that, Charlie. Any idea how many pubs there are out here?' He answered for me. 'Dozens. I'm in the Cottage Bar in Dennistoun. Thought I saw your man, why I cut you off. False alarm. Been in ten pubs since last night – so far no sign. 'Course he might come in at a different time. Can't be everywhere.'

'Stay with it, Patrick. We need a break.'

'If Rafferty's goons are hangin' around they're makin' a better job of keepin' out of sight. Nobody suspicious at the flat or NYB and I was there all day. Mother all right is she?'

'Fine. I'll be gone a few more days. Let's hope Stephen McNeil decides to show.'

Speaking to Pat Logue reminded me I had a call to make. My mother sounded tired. For once the energy to quiz me wasn't there. I told her to take it slowly, knowing she would do exactly as she pleased.

At nine I tried Fiona's number from the airport: her mobile was switched off. I tried again. Same thing. And again. By midnight I was seriously worried. This wasn't our arrangement. Something was wrong. It was going to be a long night. The idea of surprising her was in the bin. My imagination gave me dark thoughts to feed on. I devoured them. In the lobby of the Hilton I logged on to the Internet and Googled the address of RealSpain. Images of sandy beaches and golden sunsets jumped out at me. And business was slow: under 'Properties For Sale' scores of flats and villas were marked down; a sign of the times. Nevertheless the site boasted a remarkable tally of hits. My interest was the address and telephone number.

In the morning I was tired and irritable. A group of teenage boys in front of me in the check-in queue started as they meant to go on, drinking cans of lager and talking loudly, well impressed with themselves. One of them, trying to run before he could walk, called to a passing dark-haired stewardess in her thirties. 'All right darlin'? Fancy a bit, do you?'

She ignored him. I wished I could.

On the ground I hired a car and drove south, following the instructions from the RealSpain web pages through mile after mile of white boxes piled on each other. Living the dream? I didn't think so.

RealSpain supplied the background. Porto Estuto had been a quiet fishing village three decades previously. Weren't they always? What they didn't tell was how tourism and the nineties building boom erased every authentic fragment and replaced it with pizza joints, a fish and chip shop and a handful of English pubs. I clocked the *Prince of Wales Feathers*, *The Green Man* and the *Albert Bar* within yards of each other, crazy golf, bingo, karaoke, and more estate agents than I could count; it was about as Spanish as the Great Wall of China.

RealSpain was off the main drag. Not a great location though Fiona had said it did well. I pressed my face against the glass. Two desks occupied most of the space and a small couch sat in the corner. The windows were dressed with colour prints of villas and long-term rentals, priced in euros. It was unremarkable and it was closed.

A swarthy guy came out of the jewellers next door. He lit a cigarette and looked me up and down. I made an odd sight: polo neck sweater and jacket, overdressed for the climbing temperature.

'Excuse me, what time do they open?'

His reply was an indifferent shrug. If I wasn't in the market for over-priced bracelets and gaudy rings I was no use to him. I kept with it. 'My girlfriend works here. I want to surprise her.'

He threw the cigarette on the cobbled street and put his foot on it. 'Haven't seen her in a while.' His English was perfect. 'Nobody's been lately.'

'Since when?'

He gave another shrug. 'Weeks.'

That didn't make sense. 'Any idea where she lives?'

'No. Try the Lord Stanley down by the harbour – all the English go there.'

The harbour was easy to find. Any lingering trace of the fishing village had been obliterated. Every spare foot of space was a restaurant offering a menu turistico, or a club with a name like 007 and Diamonds, ready to supply music and watered-down sangria. At night this place would be a neon car crash.

I parked and walked, blinking in the sun so different from Glasgow. The Lord Stanley was all I expected it to be: a hole in the wall selling John Courage and Stella Artois. Even this early in the day a few diehards sat at the bar reading the Daily Mail, treating hangovers with a hair of the dog and examining me through their pain.

The barman grinned. 'What'll it be?'

'Coffee, please. Espresso.'

The boozers sussed we had nothing in common and went back to reading the latest attack on the England football team.

'Just arrived?'

'Actually I'm trying to find someone.'

'Yeah? Who?'

'A woman, runs RealSpain real estate. Know her?'

'Fiona, of course. Comes in regularly. Haven't seen her lately. Keeps herself to herself.'

'But you know her?'

'Oh yeah, knew her pal better. Ian was a card. Hasn't been around either. Might have moved on – the property market's as flat as a witch's tit.'

'Any idea where she lives?'

His expression changed. Too many questions.

'Who's asking?'

'I'm a friend of hers, thought I'd surprise her but the office isn't open.'

He wasn't convinced. 'A friend? From where?'

'Scotland. Thinking of buying a villa. Fiona said she'd help me. Can't spend another summer in that god-awful climate. Nothing but rain.'

The coffee was bitter with a metal aftertaste. I pretended not to notice. The barman needed time to accept me; criticising wasn't the way forward. 'Property market's dead,' he said again. 'You might land a bargain.'

'That's what Fiona told me.'

He laughed. 'She's okay. He was a spaceman, challenging people to drinking contests, passing out on the floor. She wasn't amused. Reckoned he was an alki.'

'Ian always was a crazy hombre, even at Uni. Nobody could stand the pace he set. Fiona kept us out of jail more than once.'

That little piece of fakery convinced him I was okay. 'Her place is a mile out of town on the north coast road. Big gates. Impressive, you can't miss it.'

The villa was more than impressive and he was right, I couldn't miss it – on a hill above the long ribbon of road to Alicante and eventually to Valencia. A high wall ran all the way round. Behind it tall palms swayed in the breeze beside a kidney-shaped pool, while the blue Mediterranean stretched to the horizon. In the mature garden, acacia and jacaranda, lilac and bougainvillea offered colour and shade. A lot to trade for grey skies and Glasgow. I hoped I was worth it. The gate wasn't locked. Ominously, neither was the front door. I walked in on a familiar scene: the house had been wrecked. Mine had been bad enough, this was worse.

I hated Ian Selkirk for what he'd done to us. Patrick called them the Big Boys Club, and I had been a fool. Scotland or Spain, it made no difference to them. Of course there was a chance she got out before they arrived. Her built-in wardrobe still held clothes. I couldn't say if any were missing. I scanned what was left of a beautiful home. Pat Logue's friends weren't around to fix it this time. There was no blood but, like my flat, the damage went beyond a search – the same malicious hands had been at work. Behind the villa I found more bad news. A red Vauxhall estate. Fiona's car. She hadn't escaped.

I told myself fairy stories to keep from going insane. After my place was done she had moved. The villa was empty when Rafferty's thugs arrived. She was on her way to Scotland and we'd missed each other. I heard my logic and didn't buy it.

It was one hundred metres to the nearest house. The neighbours might have seen or heard something. But there were no neighbours – the windows were shuttered – it was too early in the year. I drove back to Porto Estuto with my heart hammering in my chest and stopped at the first bar I came to. My hands were shaking; a large gin steadied them. I sat at a corner table and tried to think. If Fiona had fled where would she go? Glasgow wasn't safe, so where? Maybe to a friend, except the only friend mentioned was Ian Selkirk and I knew where he was. She could be anywhere in the country, or close by, a victim of kidnapping. Her abductors might be torturing her, filling her with drugs like they had Ian.

She could be dead.

The sunshine failed to warm me. I was cold and sweating, my hands and arms were numb, pins and needles lanced them.

Lifting the glass to my lips was almost impossible. Black thoughts ran wild in me. I was having an anxiety attack.

It passed, clarity returned, enough to allow me to consider the options. The obvious one was the police, yet involving them had negative implications. Fiona had disappeared, her villa was wrecked and the business closed. Then I show up asking questions. The barman and the boozy Daily Mail readers would have no problem remembering me. I might even be detained. That couldn't happen, not while Fiona was at Rafferty's mercy.

A name came, the contractor Ian and Fiona worked with: Sebastian. "More like a partner" was how she described the relationship. They depended on his business. The arrangement barely survived Ian's first fuck-up – there wouldn't be a second chance. I'd seen the villa. It took money to own a place like that. Fiona was afraid she was going to lose everything she'd worked for. Understandable self-interest made her weep in Glasgow.

Sebastian could be the key, might even be involved. Might even be in danger.

I trawled estate agents, ignoring the ones who specialised in re-sales – my man was a builder. There were fifteen agents in Porto Estuto, nine full service outfits. It took two hours to get round them and none had heard of a developer called Sebastian. The last was the most helpful. A German woman telephoned the architect they used. No luck. He had never come across a construction company run by anyone with that name. With nothing better to do I tried RealSpain again. It was still closed. The properties in the window didn't carry any information other than the spec. Just as I was about to go I noticed Fiona's villa, asking price one point four million euros; she was delivering on her promise to sell-up and join me. Life without her was unimaginable.

I drove the coast road again to her place as afternoon made way for evening. They might be watching, waiting for me. The magnificence of the property had distracted me on my first visit, now it seemed less attractive. I searched for some indication of where Fiona might have gone, assuming she left ahead of whoever

Rafferty sent. The action of a man out of ideas. Once a house has been invaded and vandalised it was never the same. I thought of my flat – I'd probably sell it. The villa was already on the market, Fiona wouldn't come back here. It occurred to me I was surmising she'd got away, that they didn't have her, an emotional trick to keep pain at bay. I lifted a small Moroccan urn lying unbroken on its side and imagined her haggling over it in the souk on a trip with someone else. There was so much I didn't know about her, so much I wanted to know. I prayed it wasn't too late.

An alcove set-up as an office had been trashed beyond belief. Everything was in pieces: the pc, the printer, the desk hacked with something heavy and sharp; the contents of a black filing cabinet torn like confetti. A rattan waste paper basket spilled its contents with the rest. I picked it up, stupidly hoping Fiona had printed off a receipt or some clue to where she was going. I didn't find it. Stuck in the bottom, ripped to shreds was an image I recognised. I gathered the bits and smoothed them out. The picture, shot from across the road on a sunny day, flattered just as it was supposed to.

I was staring at a photograph of the Lomond Inn.

Chapter 21

She'd seen their faces. They hadn't bothered to hide them. They didn't care. As soon as they got what they needed, they'd kill her. Ian had stolen from dangerous people. Not these people and not their money, but they wanted it and assumed he'd told her where it was hidden. While they believed that, she had a chance.

Fiona opened her eyes to nothing. No sight, no sound. She was on the floor, in the dark, with her back against an uneven wall. Something scurrying nearby startled her. Mice she could handle, rats were…better not to think about rats.

What seemed like hours later, heavy footsteps brought her awake; paralysed with fear her body had closed down and she had fallen asleep. A door opened and two men pulled her upright. She blabbered. 'Please. Where are you taking me? This is a mistake.'

Iron fingers gripped her arm; a rough voice said, 'Shut it.'

At the top of a narrow flight of stairs, she stumbled and felt it sting where the skin had broken. The thugs dragged her into a lift that travelled from the basement to the fifth floor; the smell of stale cigarette smoke and piss was overpowering. The doors slid open. An elderly couple waiting to go down held on to each other and stood aside as Fiona was manhandled across the landing.

She pleaded with them. 'Help me. Please. These men are going to kill me.'

Their eyes stayed on the ground; whatever was happening was no business of theirs. This was the high flats, a place the police considered a no go area, dope dealers and junkies, shooting up yards from their home. The old people witnessed violence every day and knew better than to get involved. They wouldn't be calling for help. Nobody would. Not if they valued their legs.

Those who know don't speak.

The room was not unlike her mother's lounge; patterned wallpaper, a solid coffee table and a floral three piece suite. Kidnapped and held against her will, the very ordinariness of it shocked her.

A man leaned on a stick. He looked frail and unwell. Two younger men flanked him, one with a scar marring an otherwise handsome face. The old man spoke. 'So at last, this is her, Kevin.'

'This is her, Jimmy'

Jimmy Rafferty pointed a trembling finger at Fiona. 'Don't go with hurting women. 'Course if I have to, if there's nothing else for it, then…' The shrug absolved him from responsibility. 'You've brought this on yourself. We can do it three ways, the easy way, the hard way,' he paused for effect, 'or Kevin's way. Your choice.'

Fiona Ramsay had been told about the east end gangster family, Jimmy and his psycho sons. Paul, the one who died, was supposed to have been mental, a maniac even by Glasgow standards. Christ! Of them all, Sean was the only Rafferty who was even half sane.

She'd seen him before.

Sean took control. He said, 'Tell us what Selkirk did with the money and I'll ask them to go easy on you.'

Words poured from Fiona. 'Ian was out of control, doing drugs, lots of drugs. Some days he was so wasted he couldn't talk. People complained, he'd become a liability, I fired him. After that…'

Kevin turned to his father. 'This is bullshit. She's giving us her life story. Let me have a crack at her. Have I ever let you down?'

Jimmy snorted contempt. 'Only every day since you were born, Kevin.'

Sean spoke to Fiona. 'You getting that? D'you realise what my brother's asking, do you understand? Where did your coke head pal hide the cash?'

Fiona didn't answer.

Kevin said, 'Make a decision, Jimmy. You're the boss.'

Jimmy said, 'What do you think, Sean? Should Kevin have his fun?'

***

They tied her hands behind her back and blindfolded her with a piece of cloth. Behind it fear became panic. Why blindfold her now?

The same hands hauled her to her feet and marched her away, minutes later she heard a door slide shut and felt the floor move beneath her. She was in the lift again. Then there were steps, another door, and the wind ruffling her hair, cooling the sweat on her face.

'Where are we? What are you going to do to me?'

Sean Rafferty whispered in her ear; his breath was warm. 'In Spain Selkirk was your oppo and, judging by the turnout at his funeral, you were the only friend he had in the world. You two go way back. Where does Cameron fit in?'

Fiona didn't hesitate. 'Charlie discovered Ian's body at the mortuary and called me. I hadn't heard from him in years.'

'What's the plan, get the cash and you two run off into the sunset together?'

'No! No! He'll give it to you, then you can leave us alone.'

'Think my head buttons up the back, Fiona? About Cameron maybe, as for the rest, I don't believe you.'

Rain started to fall, a few drops that became a steady drizzle. Rafferty held out his upturned palm and sighed. 'We're all going to get wet. Don't fancy getting wet. What did Selkirk do with it?'

Fiona's head sank to her chest; she sobbed quietly. Kevin shot a glance at Jimmy and spoke to the heavies. 'Untie her. Lift her up.'

Fulton and Tumelty did as they were told, gripping her on either side so tightly she couldn't breathe. Soon she'd know why. Kevin Rafferty said, 'Take a look. And think before you answer. Where is it?'

Fiona loosened the cloth. Terror shot through her, she buckled and almost blacked out. She was on a wall no broader than her foot, on the roof of a block of high rise flats. Under a dark sky, Glasgow sprawled as far as the horizon; low lying clouds close enough to touch, lines of miniature cars crawled in both directions on the motorway, and beyond, Celtic Park, rising silver against the landscape.

'Some view isn't it? Even better where you are. Sorry about the weather. On a clear day you can see the coast.'

The wind tugged her skirt, her hair matted her head, she didn't notice. Her legs wouldn't support her. All that prevented her from falling were Rafferty's men.

Kevin said, 'Twenty eight stories, a long way down.'

'Please. Please…' The words were lost. Fiona swayed over the edge.

Sean stood in front of his father, he said, 'Jimmy, listen to me. The instructions were clear: the woman has to be returned unharmed, that's the most important thing. Fuck the money, the money doesn't matter, we don't need it. Rocha doesn't care about it. Or the thief. If we kill her he'll come after us. And we won't be on the winning end. Give her to me. I'll get whatever she knows out of her. But either way she goes back. We can still make this all right.'

It pleased Jimmy Rafferty to see his sons competing against each other. He had no intention of cutting the rivalry short. Sean wasn't like his brothers; secretive and deep as the ocean. At last he was showing some gumption. Thank Christ for that.

'Calm down, Sean, you'll get your turn.'

Kevin said, 'People who jump are dead before they hit the bottom. Heart attack, so they say. Think that's true?'

Fiona howled into the wind.

'Where is it?'

'I don't know! I don't know!'

'Twenty eight floors. Seven seconds from here to the bottom. Two hundred and six bones in the human body, every one of them broken.'

'Please. Please. Oh please. Ian didn't tell me.'

He prodded the small of her back and felt her shudder. 'Last chance, Fiona.'

Fiona Ramsay bawled and collapsed against the men supporting her. Kevin lost patience, he turned to his father. 'The bitch is at it, Jimmy.'

Jimmy had seen enough. He said, 'Get her off before she falls off.'

They lifted Fiona down. She knelt, shaking, crying hysterically. The old man stood over her, unmoved. 'You're a tough lady, give you that much. Just remember, what comes next you've brought on yourself.'

She looked up at him, emotionally spent, rainwater and tears rolling down her face. 'Bastards. How can I tell you what I don't know?'

Rafferty signalled his eldest son to come forward. 'Make her talk, Kevin. Any way you like. To hell with Rocha. I'm done fucking about.'

Chapter 22

Tracing missing people took patience and instinct. Ruling out the possibles, hospitals, haunts, jails and the like was the necessary slog; often it was enough. When it wasn't I tried to get in touch with their motivations and followed my gut. Then there were other times when I couldn't get there on my own and frustration or desperation drove me where I didn't want to go. This was one of those.

Off the main square the Spanish flag moved in the breeze, yellow and red, vivid against the bleached white walls. In front, a row of parked cars with POLICIA on their sides sat idle. No one had the energy to break the law during the day. At the desk I told a uniform I wanted to speak with whoever was in charge. He asked me to take a seat. Two hours later I told another officer the same thing. Since Fiona failed to answer her phone fear had been building inside. Now it screamed. A calendar on the wall told me it was the thirtieth of March, three weeks since Cecelia McNeil came to see me and sent me down this road. Eventually I was shown to an interview room where a policeman sat at a table; his eyes said there was nothing left in the world to surprise him. I gave him a version of the truth: I was visiting my girlfriend, she worked for RealSpain, but instead of a happy reunion the office was closed and her villa was ransacked. He heard me out without interrupting, got up and left, leaving me to sit through the longest three hours of my life.

When he returned a man in plain clothes was with him. He didn't speak, even to introduce himself. I got it. He was a detective. They were taking me seriously. The questions came slowly, most of them about me and why I was in the country. I wanted to drag the cop over the desk and beat some urgency into him. Didn't he realise what I was saying? Fiona had been abducted; she might even be dead. If I was involved why would I stick around to report it?

The detective caught my irritation. 'Mr Cameron, I'm Inspector Santimaria. I understand your anxiety. I've just come from your girlfriend's villa. It's as you say. My men are going over it. So far we've found nothing to suggest a struggle. It may be a straight forward case of burglary. However, the fact that RealSpain isn't open may be significant. The neighbours tell us it's been closed for weeks. Your woman might have already gone, which would bring us back to robbery.'

'Not possible. I spoke to her a couple of days ago. She didn't mention going anywhere.'

'In that case we have something more serious to consider. Any idea who might wish her harm?'

'Absolutely none. In her work she met different people, strangers, any one of them could have her.'

He toyed with a ragged nail. 'You're suggesting she's been taken against her will. What makes you think that?'

I admired his skill, the casual tone in his voice as he teased my opinions from me and made me test them. 'What else is there to think? Her home's been trashed, the business is closed and Fiona's disappeared.'

Nearer the truth than I wanted.

'Then the question is why. Why would anyone do it? Why destroy her beautiful home unless they were looking for something?'

He sensed I wasn't telling all of it. 'I wonder, what could they have been looking for, Mr Cameron?'

'I wish I knew.'

He made some notes. 'You're not planning to leave, are you? Not a good idea, not at the moment. Try the Dolphin Hotel. I'll contact you when I need to.'

The Dolphin Hotel wasn't a hotel at all; it was a bed and breakfast not far from the Lord Stanley. My room was functional, a cramped bathroom, tiny bedroom and an even tinier kitchenette with one ancient electric ring. I lay on the bed and studied the plaster cracks on the ceiling. Sometime later I fell asleep and woke in the dark, hungry, with two missed calls on my phone; Patrick and Jackie. The will to return them wasn't there.

It seemed my thinking changed with every new development. Given what I'd discovered at the villa, they, whoever they were, could have Fiona; a prospect too terrible to consider. The alternatives were few, straws to cling to, and I did; she was still in Spain, hiding, or she had made it back to Scotland. The latter appealed most because at least she'd be free, and she'd need transport. I got hold of Pat Logue and asked him to check.

He said, 'How're you doin', Charlie?'

I lied. 'I'm fine. Don't worry about me. Fiona hired a car at the airport the last time. Might have done the same again.'

'I'm on it.'

I ended the call, threw some water on my face and went out. The illusion of action made me feel marginally better, although illusion was what it was.

The town was livelier at night; tourists roamed the harbour drawing easy promises from the touts about the food in their restaurants. Neon added to the holiday atmosphere. In different circumstances I wouldn't have minded. Arm in arm with Fiona, far from Glasgow and gangsters, I might have enjoyed its down-market charm. As it was I hated it almost as much as the inedible pizza I had for dinner.

The crowd at the Lord Stanley were watching Tottenham play Huddersfield in the cup on the big screen in the corner. Conversation was limited to whispered asides apart from one spectator, standing rather than sitting, offering wide ranging opinions on every aspect of the game, and shouting 'Dirty northern bastards!' whenever Huddersfield had the ball. Where I was from, both teams were dirty southern bastards. I didn't correct him – he wouldn't have appreciated the geography lesson. Instead I sat at a table on the crumbling shelf of cement that passed for a pavement, ordered a beer and listened.

Every voice was English, holidaymakers and a few ex-pat residents. When Spurs scored, a cheer went up. I left them to it and walked the cobbled lanes until the noise faded and I came out in a street with RealSpain facing me, dark and abandoned behind the window. The reason I was in Porto Estuto struck me so hard I almost fell.

Damn Ian Selkirk. Damn him to hell. I had found Fiona and lost her again. Images of what Rafferty might be doing haunted me, and I blamed myself for not keeping her with me.

There was no sleep that night. Or the next. I wandered in bad dream country, tossing and turning, and on the second morning drove to the villa and sat in the car, watching, willing her to appear. Or failing that, somebody, anybody to lead me to her. In the old town I hung around the Lord Stanley, staring into my drink, filtering the chatter and despising the people around me because they were safe and Fiona wasn't.

'Still here?' It was the barman. 'The police were asking. I told them about you. No sign of her yet?' He wiped the table with a filthy cloth. 'Probably gone off with some bloke – no offence – she's a good looking woman. Had to beat them away with a stick in this place. Maybe why she stopped coming in.'

'Who were her friends?'

'Apart from the guy she worked with I never saw her with anybody.'

'There must've been somebody.'

'Not that I noticed. It was always just her and him, nobody else got a sniff.' He laughed. 'Thought about trying myself more than once. Don't worry. She'll turn up with some rich Arab in tow.'

The nightmare wasn't happening to him – he could afford to be confident. Patrick called to say the newspapers had hold of it. "Scots Woman Missing on the Costa Blanca" headlines in the Daily Record with a muggy picture that could've been anyone. There was little to report though that didn't stop them spinning the few facts into a story. Fiona's disappearance would be discussed over JC and tequila by beer-bellied lechers in every bar on the coast. Pat said, 'And nada on the car, at the airport or anywhere else.'

But he hadn't spotted any of Rafferty's crew and took that as a positive. I didn't. Instinct told me the answer to everything was back in Glasgow. That was where Ian Selkirk had gone with whatever was so important to Rafferty and, assuming she was free, Fiona would make her way there too. Our future together depended on ending this thing. There could be no life until it was over, and we both knew it.

After two days hanging around Porto Estuto Inspector Santimaria informed me the police had made no progress and I was free to go. At the airport I tried every desk for a cancellation. Thompson's had a seat on a flight to Newcastle leaving at noon the next day. I called Jackie and Patrick and told them I was on my way home. But not before I'd had a look inside the RealSpain office. In the early hours of the morning the street was deserted; there was no one to hear the glass door panel shatter or witness the only crime I'd committed on foreign soil. To my surprise the place wasn't alarmed. Inside I turned on a light and hurriedly thumbed my way through a couple of unlocked filing cabinets looking for God alone knew what. All I found were folders, set out in alphabetical order, filled with contracts and correspondence. Suddenly I felt sad. Fiona had put her energy into building this business from scratch. Now, thanks to Ian, it would fold. He was dead but, as so often in the past, somebody else had been left with the job of clearing-up the mess he had created.

Pat Logue was there when the plane touched down, older than when I last saw him. Depressed and hung-over, the down-side of drinking his way round the city on my behalf.

'So what happened? Any word?'

'Tell you later,' I said. 'How're things with you and Gail?'

'Don't ask. McNeil was a waste of time.'

I'd hardly given Cecelia McNeil's husband a thought. Patrick had been left to pick up the slack and his efforts in the east end of the city had come up dry. No Stephen McNeil. I'd be getting a call from his wife or one of her notes thanking me and making me feel bad.

He said, 'Your pal was askin' after you.'

'Which one?'

'Rat eyes.' He meant Platt. 'Told him I hadn't seen you.'

We drove north. Neither of us felt like talking. The weather fitted the mood. Twenty miles from the Carlisle by-pass Patrick noticed the dark green Vectra cruising behind us, no attempt at disguise. There were two men in it.

'You didn't tell anybody I was back, did you?'

His reply was defensive. 'Like who?'

'Like anybody.'

The car trailed us to Glasgow and when we left the motorway at the Royal Infirmary it kept going, but the message had been delivered.

At the flat so had the television.

Chapter 23

Fiona Ramsay's mistake hadn't been stealing – that came later. Her error was listening to Ian Selkirk's dangerous fantasy, a dream that had become a nightmare, and allowing his obsession into her head. In the end greed triumphed over logic. This was the price of failure. Ian had always been a reckless fool. Now he was dead and the man in front of her was his killer. Charlie hadn't told her the details – it wasn't necessary – she could guess and knew what to expect. They would torture her until she gave them what they were after. Except she couldn't; she had no idea where the money was.

Kevin Rafferty let her see the knife and savoured her fear; they'd wasted enough time.

'Which part of your face don't you like? Your nose maybe? Personally, I think it's fine but no problem, I'll cut it off for you. Or you can tell us about the money and keep the nose.'

Her eyes fixed on the weapon, her voice trembled. 'Ian had it.'

Rafferty grabbed her hair and pulled her head back. 'Don't fuck me about, bitch.'

He held the blade to her throat, ice against her skin. His fingers brushed her lips, her neck, and moved to her nipples. She closed her eyes and shouted. 'I don't know! I don't know! Please, I don't know!'

Sean Rafferty walked past his father and put his hand on his brother's wrist. Kevin glared at him. 'Let me try.' He looked to Jimmy for permission. Jimmy nodded.

The woman was familiar to Sean; he had seen her lying by the side of Emil Rocha's swimming pool, her body slicked with oil. Behind the sunglasses her eyes would have held no fear that day.

Not like now. He bent close and said, 'You have to tell us, Fiona, it's your only chance. What did he do with it?'

She sobbed like a little girl. 'I can't tell you what I don't know.'

Sean Rafferty was gentle. 'What was the plan?'

'To meet at the Lomond Inn.'

'And he had the money?'

'Yes. He called me when he was driving north, said it was done.'

'Did you speak to him about it after that?'

'Once more. He was high. He said it was with someone safe.'

'Who?'

She didn't answer.

'Where did you intend to go?'

'Somewhere. Anywhere. New Zealand.'

He shook his head. 'Selkirk was your partner. You understood him, if he told anyone it would be you.'

'Why would I still be here? I'd have disappeared. He didn't tell me.'

Sean wiped tears from her cheeks. When he spoke his voice was reassuring, almost tender. He sighed. 'Then I can't help you.'

She panicked. 'No! No! He'd seen Charlie.'

Sean said, 'When?'

'Before he went to Loch Lomond.'

'How do you know?'

'Ian told me.'

'Told you he'd seen Cameron but not a word about where the money was? No, you're making it up.'

'It's true. They were friends. Ian was afraid something would go wrong. Charlie knows where it is. I can get it. He's in love with me and thinks I'm in love with him.'

'Still don't believe you. If Cameron knew where it was hidden you'd have it by now. You've got three choices, Rocha, my brother, or me. The truth, last chance.'

Fiona burst into tears again. 'How many times. I know Rocha. I've seen what he does. I wouldn't be here if I knew what Ian did with the money. I don't. I don't know.'

Jimmy turned away, Sean tried one more time. 'Jimmy, Jimmy…'

His father kept going. Sean had lost. Jimmy spoke to Kevin, 'And get the mobile this time.'

Kevin let the criticism pass and waited until they'd gone. He hunkered beside the woman. 'So,' he said, 'Selkirk told Cameron, that's your story and you're sticking to it?'

She nodded, desperate to be believed. 'Yes, yes. Ian told Charlie not me.'

Rafferty stroked the ugly line on his face with the knife. 'In that case we don't need you, do we?'

Fiona vomited on the floor. It was no dream.

***

The woman had started something all right. Jimmy Rafferty was witnessing a power struggle. The surprise was Sean, the quiet man. Not so quiet now. Kevin would have his work cut out keeping him in line. If they joined forces they would be a formidable team. Except that was unlikely. As children they kept their distance from one another; as adults it was hard even for Jimmy to believe they were brothers: Kevin, vicious, impetuous, an easy man to fear, essential in their business, and Sean. What about Sean? The boy was a stranger to his father; always hanging back, listening not speaking. Until recently. This thing with Rocha had brought him out of his shell.

Kevin said, 'Cameron's back. Got him covered night and day, we should pull him. See the look on his face when he discovers it was his girlfriend who put him in the frame.'

Sean said, 'She was lying to save herself.'

'Maybe.'

'Does he act like he's sitting on five million? Either he's in the dark or he's the coolest guy on the planet.'

'So let's give him some encouragement, find out how cool he really is. Forget softly softly.'

'Sean Rafferty lost it. Is that what we've been doing? Fuck's sake, Selkirk and the woman are out of it. We have nothing. Nothing!

Charlie Cameron's all that's left. We're in deep shit, or haven't you noticed? Any day Rocha will get fed-up waiting for us to do what we were supposed to and come here himself. He'll discover what happened to the thief, put two and two together, and we'll be face down in the river with our throats cut. We should never have taken him on.'

'But if she was telling the truth…'

'No Kevin. Once we go down that road there's no turning back, we've proved it twice already. Cameron's all that's between us and Emil Rocha. We lift him and we're fucked. No, we use the woman.'

Kevin barked at him. 'How?'

Sean brought Fiona Ramsay's mobile from his pocket. 'Who says the dead can't speak?'

Chapter 24

The Big Issue guy ignored me again.

He thought he had problems – he should try mine.

NYB was empty except for a couple of young women at the bar basking in Roberto's smile. Jackie had gone home. I went to the office to check the ansaphone and mail. Nothing. That couldn't be right. If Rafferty had Fiona why were they still interested in me? And if she had got away why hadn't she called? There should've been contact by now.

Until recently Cleveden Drive in the west end had been a good place to live. I stood in the lounge trying to see it the way it was before somebody took an axe to it. Patrick read my mind and repeated his offer. 'Just tell me what to get. Cash buys anythin'. And by the way, you're not landed with me. I'll find somewhere else to doss.'

I sat down. 'No, don't. Stay as long as you like.'

'Thanks, Charlie. Options aren't too impressive right now. Wonderin' if I need to get myself a lawyer.'

'It won't come to that.'

'You reckon?'

He didn't believe me. Neither did I.

'Gail keeps movin' the goalposts. Just about had it with her. Says I have to give up the drink. Apparently I'm a bad role model for the boys. What's she talkin' about? I like a drink, never denied it. But it doesn't affect our marriage.'

'Doesn't it?'

'No. Money's always there. Nearly always. If I stay in she complains I'm makin' the place look untidy. I'll tell you, Charlie, I'm this close to blowin' the whistle on the whole thing.' He was building up steam. 'And when I'm offski, I'm offski for good.'

'Give her time. Gail loves you.'

'Tell her that. A month ago everythin' was fine. All of a sudden it's not workin'. Women. I don't understand them.'

'Join the club, Patrick.'

'You and Fiona okay?'

The story poured out of me.

'Somebody got there before me, her villa was wrecked.'

'Rafferty?'

'Can't be sure. Had to involve the police.'

'What did you tell them?'

'As little as I could get away with.'

'If Rafferty has Fiona, why were they waitin' for us at Newcastle?'

'I've been trying to work that out. I can't.'

'Because they don't have her. She's out of sight. You're all they've got.'

I hoped he was right.

'One more thing. The TV. It has to go back, Patrick. I can't accept stolen goods.'

'Think it's stolen?'

'Okay, goods of unknown origin.'

The knock at the door made us jump. Patrick answered it. He said, 'Somebody for you, Charlie' and left. The detective smiled his grim smile.

'Mr Cameron. Charlie. Is it all right to call you Charlie? You're a hard man to track down.' He swept the room with his eyes. 'Looks like you've upset somebody, did they take much?'

I didn't reply.

'May I sit down?' He made a deal of getting comfortable. 'Pity,' he said. 'Must've been nice. You've been on holiday, I hear. Got into a spot of bother too.' He tutted. 'My, my, you do live an interesting life.'

'Is there something I can do for you, Inspector?'

'Well I really don't know. The Spanish authorities contacted us about a missing woman. Fiona Ramsay, another old chum I believe.'

'Fiona and I know each other. I went over to see her. Friends do that kind of thing.'

'Do they?'

He was enjoying himself, wagging a finger like he was amused.

'You're a dark horse, Charlie. Your pal, Ian, led a colourful existence. Before it was cut short. Ever heard the name Emil Rocha? No? Quite a character. He's French, or Catalan, or a bit of both, depending on who you listen to. Spain's been after him for two decades. A friend of a friend of yours. Small world, isn't it? We're sure Selkirk worked for him. Over the last three years he was in and out of this country every eight or nine weeks.'

'Could be visiting someone?'

'Then they were short visits. In one day, out the next or the day after.'

'So?'

'An odd way to behave, don't you think?'

'I really couldn't comment. Ian was as much a stranger to me as you are, Inspector. I keep telling you it was long ago. You keep expecting god knows what from me. For the last time, yes, I knew the guy, once. And no, I haven't seen him.'

My irritation bounced off him. 'You see, when you were talking to the police in Porto Estuto you left out a couple of details. Loch Lomond for one.'

'What had that to do with anything? I was there to see Fiona.'

'Of course, but when this place got turned-over, then the villa in Spain...I've seen the pictures, a terrible mess...I asked myself where was the connection. It wasn't difficult.'

'I don't know what you're on about.'

'Really, it's always a mistake to think you're smarter than everyone else, Charlie. I advised you not to try your amateur powers on with me. Now my advice is different. Don't get clever because I know.'

I called his bluff. 'What? What do you know, Inspector?'

'Selkirk and Ramsay and you. Thick as thieves. He's dead, she's missing and you're right in front of me.'

'You've lost me.'

'Good decision not to go into politics, by the way. Not nearly sharp enough, I'm afraid.' He leaned towards me. 'The sale of illegal narcotics in Spain is split between five people. Emil Rocha runs the south east, from Valencia to Cadiz. Selkirk was one of his bag men. Something went wrong, he ends up dead. Not so unusual, it's a dangerous trade to be in, but why run to Scotland, he hasn't stayed here in years? And his old friends, suddenly they're not safe in their own homes. Innocent people...except they're not innocent.'

He got to his feet. 'This isn't about getting some old lady's cat out of a tree or whatever it is you normally do, Charlie. Emil Rocha's a player. I think your friend stole from Rocha and I think you're involved. You and Fiona Ramsay. Rocha thinks so too. Next time it won't be your fancy flat. If he has the woman you can forget about seeing her again. When he's finished with her you wouldn't want to.'

He saved his final chilling comments until he was at the door. 'A Spanish police informant says the word on the streets puts it at five million pounds, give or take. Selkirk's dead, Ramsay too probably, that just leaves you.'

'I'm not a part of anything. Neither is Fiona.'

His pupils were flinty and dark. I got Patrick's rat eyes thing. 'Tell it to Emil Rocha, let's hope he believes you. I don't.'

***

I wasn't in the mood to work, all I could think about was Fiona. I passed through NYB with my head down, hoping nobody stopped me to talk.

Mrs McNeil was the last person I wanted to see. Since I'd found Ian Selkirk's dead body at the city mortuary on Ash Wednesday, her calls and letters, the whole case, had been an annoyance to me. Maybe I shouldn't have taken it on. Easy to think that now.

The door opened and there she stood, not gentle and trusting; angry. She hadn't come to thank me; her face was set hard, the lips drawn in a line, resentment alive in her eyes. 'You're here,' she said. 'Good. I wondered how you spend the day.'

'Mrs McNeil, come in.'

'You were just about to call me, is that what you were going to say?'

'Come in. Please. I understand how you feel.'

'No you don't. To you I'm a sad woman whose husband walked out on her after her son committed suicide. You pity me. Not enough to stick to your word, mind, just enough to convince yourself you haven't done anything too bad. You promised. You promised me.'

The slender fingers I'd admired clenched at her side.

'Please sit down. You're right.'

She preferred to stand, deaf to excuses. 'I put my faith in you. I was foolish. Finding Stephen is all that's left. There's nothing else to live for.'

'Stephen doesn't want to be found, Mrs McNeil.'

'What about the credit card? If you'd tried harder I might know where he is.'

'My guess is he won't use the card again. As long as the money lasts he won't need to. He may've had a breakdown. None of the things he's done suggest he's a danger to himself.'

She wasn't convinced. 'You're so plausible, aren't you? Talking as if you know, as if you care. My Christopher's dead, Stephen's out there and you haven't tried to find him. You said you'd give it your best shot, remember?'

Charlie Cameron, honest injun.

'We have tried, Mrs McNeil. I went to Newlands yard, the El Cid, even the mortuary; a friend on the Force put a trace on the car, and my colleague spent three nights trawling the pubs around Tesco in Shettleston. Nothing doing.'

'And is that your best? I mean, aren't there other things you could try? It is what you do after all. I expected more.'

I didn't tell her so did I.

'I promised I wouldn't give up and I won't. We need your husband to show himself, otherwise we're in the dark.'

She mellowed, a little. 'Tell me the truth Mr Cameron. Do you think you can find Stephen? Don't lie to me, it's too important.'

'I can't answer that, I'm sorry, if we get something to work with, of course, if not...'

'I haven't been sleeping well, my nerves, I expect you're doing all you can, it's just that...it's hard to keep believing. Stephen used to say I was neurotic. Maybe he was right. Phoning you every five minutes, sending notes.'

'I like the notes.'

Cecelia McNeil backed towards the door, now the fire was spent she was the timid, good-living lady I'd met on Ash Wednesday. 'I was very rude just now, forgive me. Please keep looking, Mr Cameron.'

'I will, I promise I will, and when I have anything I'll be in touch.'

No sooner had she gone than my mobile sang its bright little tune. I had a message. I read it and my heart stopped.

Chapter 25

Glasgow was Sunday morning quiet. In a few hours that would change. The Sabbath wasn't a day of rest any more. I drove carefully. If the police breathalysed me my license was a goner. I'd let Patrick talk me into the pub crawl, now I was paying the price.

The message from Fiona had rocked my world.

SAFE FOR NOW

DONT KNOW FOR HOW LONG

WHERE IS IT

FI x

Every time I closed my eyes the text was waiting for me. I called her number, the mobile was turned off. But she was okay, though not knowing where she was meant I couldn't protect her. I studied the words again and again, willing them to tell me more.

I texted.

WHERE ARE U

I WANT TO PROTECT U

A minute later she replied.

BETTER U DONT KNOW JUST GET THEM WHAT THEY WANT

A feeling of powerlessness took hold; my head went down.

Pat Logue didn't stay at the flat on Friday night. It was Saturday evening before I shared the news with him. He was pragmatic. 'At least she's safe Charlie, that's somethin'.'

'But why won't she tell me where she is?'

'If you don't know Rafferty can't get it out of you. And hold your horses, Fiona got away, it's a start. She's contacted you once,

161

she'll be in touch again, meantime we keep lookin'. But not tonight, tonight we're out for a few jars. You and me.'

I started to object. Patrick would have none of it. 'Stand on your uncle Pat, you need to chill. Havin' a heart attack won't make it better. We're goin'.'

He was right. By myself I'd sit around and worry, and a night with Patrick Logue wouldn't be dull, that was for sure. 'Won't be much fun with me. You'd do better on your own.'

'Not happenin', Charlie. Not a skinful, just a few. Nothin' over the top.'

In his world over the top was a relative term. His advice was a warning of what was to come. 'We need somethin' in our bellies before we go anywhere. I'll dive out for fish and chips, you get the plates. And drink milk, puts a linin' on your stomach.'

'I don't like milk.'

'Doesn't matter what you like, drink it.'

He switched off his mobile and insisted I do the same. 'No interruptions,' he said. 'Tonight we're free as birds.'

We began in Cottier's in the West End. Patrick ordered and gave me the history.

'Daniel Cottier worked on this church. A conservation trust is tryin' to save the building. They've turned the interior into a theatre. There's a restaurant upstairs.'

He was enjoying himself. It hadn't occurred to him I might already know all this. He passed a lager to me and eyed the glass. 'Get that down your neck.'

I sipped it; it was good. Pat gulped down a third of his without trying. 'First today.'

'So why Cottier's?'

'I like the place. The crowd's a bit young but I appreciate their energy.'

One of the barmaids – a brunette, small waist and big brown eyes – smiled and shouted 'Hiya, Pat!' and I realised his restoration-patron chat was bullshit.

'You're a well known gun here, Patrick.'

He turned away. 'Moira's all right. Her brother was in my class at school.'

People left. We slipped into the booth they'd been in. Pat said, 'Listen Charlie, I can only guess how you're feelin'. If it was me I'd be off my nut. Treat this wee jaunt as a battery recharge. Your problems will wait. Guaranteed.' He stopped speaking. 'There's our man at the bottom of the bar. Sticks out like a sore thumb.'

I took a look and found myself in a staring contest with a thickset skinhead in a black donkey jacket.

'I don't get this, Patrick. Why doesn't Rafferty order his thugs to pull me in and beat what they want out of me. They tortured Ian, why not me?'

'If Jimmy Rafferty wanted it that's how it would be. So he doesn't. They're usin' you.'

'Using me for what?'

'To find Fiona.'

'Then why trash the flat?'

'Makin' sure. Always pays to be sure.'

'But I've no idea where Fiona is.'

'She knows where you are, that's enough. Yesterday you thought Rafferty had lifted her in Spain; thanks to her text you're certain she's safe. For now. Got to be reassured with that. The game's still going and we're still on the park. Finish your pint, it's Saturday night. Places to go.'

We made our way to Lauder's on the corner of Sauchiehall Street. It wasn't busy. Patrick sat at a table. 'Your shout,' he said.

When I brought the drinks he wasn't happy. 'They've ruined this pub. Look at it.' He shook his head. 'No heart, no soul. Space Invaders and a kiddies menu. Shame. C'mon, can't stay here, too sad.'

And I learned something about him – it wasn't just about the alcohol. I followed him out, down West Nile, across Buchanan Street into Exchange Square and a surprising choice. The Rogano.

'Now this,' he said, 'is a place.'

I agreed, the Rogano was a favourite of mine. He pointed at the ceiling. 'Art Deco.'

'I know.'

'Rennie Macintosh influence.'

'I know, Patrick.'

The Oyster Bar was crowded. Pat got served right away, just like always. He handed me a small glass of claret-coloured liquid. 'What's this?'

'Dubonnet. Always drink Dubonnet in here.'

'Why? Nobody drinks Dubonnet.'

'I do.'

'You're a strange man, anybody ever tell you that?'

'Gail tells me all the time. I prefer to think of myself as singular.'

'And you're a snob, I'd never have guessed.'

'Don't understand that word, never have.'

'Means you're a pretentious twat.'

'Shut up and drink your Dubonnet.'

The Rogano crowd were a mixed bag; thirty-somethings plus a sprinkling of middle class middle-aged men and women; business types out on the weekend, and some fine looking females hanging on the arms of geeky guys. The guys had to have money. I brushed shoulders with a group of laughing women, their glasses filled with Champagne. I kept my drink out of sight. Sipping Dubonnet wouldn't do much for my image. One of them smiled at me. I smiled back, then Fiona and the awful mess rushed in and wiped the smile away.

Patrick was at my shoulder. 'The thinkin' man's fanny. Another reason to like it here.'

'This is a mistake. I shouldn't be doing this.'

He pulled me aside. I'd never seen him so serious. His face was inches from mine, close enough to smell the sweet scent of the aperitif on his breath. 'Listen Charlie, really listen. What we're doin' tonight, there's a point. You need it.'

The woman who'd been interested in me was watching. 'You're good at what you do. Very good. Except not this time, this time it's too personal. Ian Selkirk was a pal and you're in love with Fiona. That puts you at a disadvantage unless you sort your head out. So far you haven't had a decent idea. Not one. Same with McNeil. Anybody could've done what you've done. Anybody.'

'Cecelia McNeil says I've let her down.'

'You have. And you're lettin' Fiona down too. You'll get nowhere 'til you start treatin' it like any other case. While you're worrin' about Fiona you're no use to her. You can't think straight. Since you discovered Ian's body you've tried to dump the McNeils. Anythin' positive has come from the wife. We've been goin' through the motions. Sure she's disappointed. So am I. I told you I'd help and I will. But you're the Man, Charlie. Tomorrow we sit down and figure it out. Right now we're doin' this – crawlin' our way round Glasgow. Not to get drunk. Not to get lucky. To get free. Fiona needs you on the ball, Cecelia McNeil too. Know what I'm talkin'?'

I knew what he was saying. My mojo wasn't working because my responses were emotional not analytical. By forcing me to face the uncomfortable truth about my efforts Patrick was doing me a favour.

The lady with the Champagne had moved on. 'I hear you, Pat. And thanks.'

'All right,' he said, 'all right, Charlie. In the mornin' we'll start fresh on both cases. Now,' he punched my shoulder the way mates do, 'your shout.'

'Another Dubonnet?'

He considered. 'Make it a Guinness, get a chronic hangover from that French shite.'

Tonight Patrick was the leader. I followed. To the re-opened Clutha by the river, where a police helicopter had fallen from the sky one Friday night and destroyed the place – another disaster from out of the blue – to Heraghty's bar on the south side, and a couple more bars only half remembered, until we fell into Babbity Bowser's in Merchant City. The red-haired barmaid didn't recognise him; about the only one who hadn't. We hung around until she did. Three more drinks I could've done without. I was drunk. As far as I could tell he was unaffected.

Two whiskies appeared. 'Supportin' your old dad, Charlie. Like he needs the money.'

'Japanese company own it now, and I've had it. No more.'

'Oh well, happy birthday to me then. First today.'

He drank both of them.

Saturday had grown old and so had I. Getting wasted wasn't the fun it had been when I was nineteen, laughing at Ian Selkirk's craziness and lusting after Fiona. We waited on the pavement for a taxi. Patrick put his hand on my shoulder.

'Time we were home, Charlie, you're a wee bit over-refreshed.'

I almost didn't see the car parked across High Street, a sinister reminder of another Glasgow, a Glasgow I'd be better off without.

Chapter 26

NYB was empty. Jackie gave me a bright 'Good morning.' I tried to fake the same but my headache wouldn't allow it. 'Just coffee, please.'

'No breakfast?'

'Coffee's fine.'

I lifted the Herald and pretended to read. Words jumped from the page. The world was still a crazy place, nothing about it interested me. In the sports section the editor drooled over the prospect of the Old Firm meeting in the Scottish Cup on Easter Sunday, three weeks down the line. The day before, Celtic had lost at Inverness and Rangers got a last gasp winner against whoever they were playing. I couldn't have cared less.

Andrew Geddes arrived. 'You look rough. On the bevy were we?'

'Should've been a detective, Andrew.'

He grinned. 'That bad, eh? Thought a man of your experience would know better.'

'Sod off, Geddes. Let me die in peace.'

He dropped a sheet of paper on the table. 'Your pal didn't leave much. Wasn't intending to stay very long.'

'Anything significant?'

His scowl said he wouldn't be answering any questions. He walked away and sat down by himself. The coffee tasted awful. I downed the water that came with it and asked for another; Jackie's continental innovation. I made a note to thank her then changed my mind. Once that door opened Christ knew where it might finish.

Andrew folded the Mail On Sunday, leaned back in his seat and called to me.

'Any further forward on the other stuff?' He meant Ian Selkirk. 'Haven't seen Platt around. How you getting on with him?'

'Like brothers. What do you think?'

'Yeah, he's not an easy guy to like. Supposed to be good though, cracked some big cases down south.'

'So why's he here? Don't see it as a career move, somehow.'

'Wife died. New start, far as I know.'

'He doesn't like me, he thinks I'm involved.'

'Well, are you?'

'You're a pal, Andrew, now sod off back to your paper.'

He laughed and gave it a rest. It was okay to noise-up someone with a hangover;

self-inflicted made it alright. It took an hour before I could even consider eating, and toast at that. Andrew Geddes dipping a bagel in his coffee didn't help – my stomach turned.

Patrick Logue sailed in at a couple of minutes to twelve, the picture of health. He waved and came over.

'Great night, wasn't it?'

He pointed at the toast. 'Need more than that to keep body and soul together. We've got work to do; have to be fit. Breakfast's the most...'

'Patrick, not now.'

'Oh. Sorry, not feelin' too hot? Good job we gave the Dubonnet a body swerve.'

'Can we not talk about alcohol? Better still, can we not talk?'

'You see,' he said, 'Gail wouldn't put up with that. You'd be gettin' told.'

'About what?'

'That tetchy thing you do, that man-on-the-edge crap.'

I couldn't deal with him. 'Look, I'll meet you in the office at one. Beat it. Andrew Geddes's over there, go and torment him.'

I got a glass of orange juice and took it upstairs. The office was cool. In the dark with my eyes closed, wishing I felt better, the thoughts booze had blocked out for a few hours returned. I pushed them aside and looked at the list. DS Geddes was right: beyond a change of clothes and some toiletries Ian hadn't left anything.

Pat Logue came in holding two pints. I said, 'Not for me, Patrick. Couldn't face it.'

'Not for you, you can get your own. For me. Saves runnin' up and down.'

'Thought you didn't drink on Sunday. Your golden rule.'

'Important to stay flexible, Charlie. Did you see him?'

'Who?'

'The Big Issue guy. Poor bastard looks nearly as bad as you.'

I fought down nausea and took a breath. 'Whenever you're done, we'll get started.'

'Fire away, Charlie.'

'The McNeil case. What's driving Stephen McNeil? His wife feared her husband was a danger to himself because he ran out on her the day before their son's funeral and took his guns. But he withdrew a substantial amount from the bank. Fifteen thousand pounds. A man thinking about ending it doesn't need money.'

Patrick sipped his drink.

I said, 'And Tesco. Shows he's taking care of himself.'

'Yeah, when the shock of the suicide passed shouldn't he remember he left his wife to cope on her own?'

'Unless he doesn't want to go home.'

'Runnin' from the marriage?'

'He packed in his job, stopped meeting his mates, and he's okay on the cash front.'

It was beginning to make sense. I said,' Stephen McNeil bailed on his whole life. He's not coming back.'

'Mrs McNeil's a good woman.'

'What if her husband got tired of living with a good woman? What if there's somebody else and he's starting again? Might be driving for another company.'

'I'll start checkin' first thing in the mornin'. Go back to the El Cid. If there is a woman, somebody might've noticed them together.'

We sat in silence until Pat said, 'Are we any closer, Charlie?'

I was coming round. 'Yes we are, but we're not seeing something. Probably right in front of us.'

'You always say that.'

'Because it always is. It's about the boy. It's about Christopher.'

'We know that. The guy's riddled with guilt and grief.'

'So Cecelia McNeil says.'

Patrick wasn't convinced. 'But we saw how close the father and son were. Fishin'. Football. Wish my relationship with our two was that good.'

'We saw pictures and heard a story. Everything we believe we believe because Mrs McNeil told us.'

'Why lie?'

'You asked why a seventeen year old boy would kill himself, remember? We've never answered that.'

'Aye. Gail wants to kill Liam and Patrick, they've no notion of toppin' themselves. At that age you believe you'll live forever.'

'Christopher McNeil didn't. He locked the garage, turned on the ignition and went to sleep. Because he had a row with his father?'

'Kid must've been unbalanced.'

'Not something his mother would be keen to talk about. I'll try her again.' I stood. 'Time out,' I said. 'I need to eat.'

We went downstairs. Patrick headed for another beer, I wolfed my way through two rolls and sausage and two espresso. Back in the office Pat Logue picked up the newspaper.

'Nothin' but bad news. Can't depend on anythin'. Celtic lost to Inverness Cally. What's the world comin' to?'

'Celtic.'

The word jumped from my mouth.

'What?'

'Stephen McNeil's a Celtic supporter, he'll be at Parkhead.'

The paper rustled. Patrick scanned the pages. 'They're at home against Motherwell next Saturday. If we can find him. It's a big place.'

I called Rhona and told her to ask Andrew to join us. Pat Logue rose out of his chair.

'Better I'm not here, Charlie. Your chum doesn't fancy me.'

'Sit down, we're working together on this.'

'The people I do business with wouldn't like me associatin' with the other side; my credibility will be shredded.'

'Cool it, Andrew can help us. He isn't interested in you, not today anyway.'

Andrew Geddes knocked and came in, nodded to me, ignored Patrick and took a seat.

'What's up, Charlie?'

'Question for you, Andrew. If I wanted to know where a season ticket holder sat, could you get that information?

'Which ground?'

'Celtic Park.'

'The Gyro-dome? Of course. Who're you looking for now?'

'Stephen McNeil.'

He made a face. 'Still him. Has he broken the law yet?'

'I'm almost certain he hasn't.'

'Then that's all I can do without at least suspicion of a criminal act. As it is I wouldn't like to explain why I was requesting access to confidential information. Believe it or not, because you asked isn't a good enough reason.'

I gave him the address. 'How's the hangover?'

He shot a glance in Patrick's direction that had blame written all over it.

'Not like you to go overboard.'

'I'll live.'

'Never again, right?'

I rubbed my head. 'Absolutely. How soon will you know about McNeil?'

'Beginning of the week, Tuesday at the latest. Good enough? That it?'

'Has Ian's mobile turned up?'

'No.'

'And there's a Spaniard called Emil Rocha.'

'Never heard of him.'

'DI Platt dropped the name, says Ian worked for him as some kind of courier. Probably the guy he robbed.'

'I'll see what turns up.'

When he'd gone Pat Logue spoke. 'He's after me. Pretends he's not bothered but he is, sure of it.'

'Then don't do anything to attract his attention.'

'Too late, Charlie.'

'By Tuesday we'll know Stephen McNeil's seat. Have to be close so we can follow him when the game ends. I'll stay outside; you'll be in the ground. We'll need a ticket in the same section. You manage that?'

'Against Motherwell. Shouldn't be a problem.'

'Good. Now, the Ian Selkirk case. Ian got killed because he took something that didn't belong to him. Could be drugs. Money's the favourite. Platt talked about five million. Since then, my flat's been trashed. Fiona's villa got the same treatment. She's hiding and won't tell me where. And every time I turn round one of Rafferty's thugs is with me. They haven't made a serious move because they're depending on me to lead them to whatever Ian stole.'

'You're all they have.'

'Then they have nothing, Patrick.'

'They don't know that.'

'Even Platt believes I'm involved.'

'You are, just not the way he thinks.'

The hangover made a come-back, my head ached and it wasn't the booze. The thought of Fiona, alone and frightened, scared for me as well as herself, was too much.

'I could go to Rafferty, tell him he's wasting his time. Unless we get a break it might come to that.'

'Not a good idea, Charlie. Gangsters don't do reason. They want what they want, and they get it or somebody gets hurt. Wind-up in Loch Lomond same as your mate. How would that help Fiona? Forget the direct approach.'

Of course he was right. 'So it's back to the beginning,' I said. 'When Ian went AWOL before, he couldn't resist cruising gay bars. Chances are he did the same this time. Loch Lomond isn't far from Glasgow. He might've hooked-up with somebody.'

Patrick shook his head. 'Count me out. I'll concentrate on McNeil.'

'Homophobic? Who'd have guessed?'

'Nothin' against gays. Live and let live I always say. I'll fit in more easily at the darts.'

'All right I'll take the bars.'

He winked. 'Go easy on the drink. You know what you're like when you get the taste.'

'Don't push it, Patrick.'

He grinned. 'Tetchy, tetchy. Not good. Turns people off. Did Ian hang around with anybody apart from you and Fiona?'

'No. It was the three of us. Our little club.'

'What a pain in the arse you must've been. Family?'

'An aunt he used to joke about, in Lesmahagow, I think. Could be dead by now.'

I dredged my memory. 'Aunt Jean. Ian stayed with her in the school holidays.'

'Over twenty years ago. Good luck, Charlie. Any more contact from Fiona?'

'No. I sent two texts, no reply.'

Mention of Fiona brought me down. My mood was already low; the previous night's excess didn't help. Our big powwow had produced some ideas. We'd made progress, just not enough for me, but it wasn't too late to make it right. That meant putting aside distractions like love and old friendships and starting again.

'Ian double-crossed Emil Rocha. How come a Glasgow heavy like Rafferty's in the picture?'

Patrick said, 'Could be Rafferty's contracted.'

'Hired help?'

'Makes sense, a bunch of dagoes runnin' about the town won't get far.'

I lifted the sheet of paper Andrew Geddes had given me. 'We've seen the list of personal effects. No key. That rules out safety deposit boxes and lock-ups. He could've used the old auntie; she might not even be aware of it.'

'I'll say this for you, Charlie,' Patrick stretched, 'you're an optimistic guy. Parkhead's an opportunity, unless McNeil's dropped it the way he has everythin' else, the rest is wishful thinkin'. Gay bars, ancient aunties. Tell the truth, it's not much, is it?'

'It's what we've got. On Tuesday night you hit the darts. During the day find out if he's driving for somebody else. I'll do the pubs since you're so prudish, and look for Jean Selkirk.'

'That it?'

'Till we know where McNeil sits.'

'Celtic are a bad lot this season. Wouldn't be surprised if he's given up on them.'

'Let's hope not.'

'And I could use some cash.'

'How much will a ticket be?'

'No idea. Won't matter, only need money when I'm dealin' with strangers. Anybody else knows I'm good for it. Put in a word with Geddes, will you? I like NYB, it suits me, don't want to drink somewhere else.'

'Won't help, Andrew's a policeman.'

'Supposed to be on the same side, aren't we?'

'Not sure he sees it like that.'

'Speak to him anyway. Got enough on my plate.'

I doubted anything I said would alter Andrew's opinion. Downstairs Patrick's nemesis had gone. He took his place at the bar content to let Sunday afternoon roll on by. In the corner Jackie shared a table with a guy, both of them wearing track suit bottoms and sweat shirts. She waved me over. With her hair tied back she looked younger, fresher. Jackie Mallon was happy. She said, 'Charlie, this is Gary.'

His bald head reminded me of an over-sized baby. He probably carried ID to prove he was old enough to be served. Gary held out a confident hand. 'Hi. Jackie's told me about you.'

She jumped in before he could say any more. 'We've been to the gym. Get those endorphins going.'

Gary said. 'Best drug on the market.' He ran his eyes over me. 'Work out much yourself, Charlie? Any day you want a partner to pump some iron with let me know.'

'Thanks, Gary, doubt you'll be hearing from me. Whenever I feel like exercising I lie down in a darkened room until the notion passes.'

I left them feeling smug and good about themselves.

Chapter 27

At ten minutes to two on Monday my mobile played its annoying jingle, a fanfare to the worst night of my life.

TELL ME YOUVE FOUND IT.

IM SCARED CHARLIE

A stake through my heart.

I read and reread; it didn't get any better. My reply was frantic, my fingers stumbled over the keypad.

STILL LOOKING COME BACK 2 HEADS BETTER THAN ONE

Nothing.

Next door Patrick snored. I wanted to wake him and share my pain. Instead I made coffee and sat alone in the kitchen with the lights out. How long I stayed like that I had no idea. Pat found me slumped across the table, neither awake nor asleep, in a place I'd never been. He brewed more coffee and began the rebuilding process. When I showed him the message his reply was gentle, wise beyond anything I expected. He touched my arm, waiting for my attention. 'Charlie' he said. 'Nothin's changed. Nothin' at all.'

And I knew he was right.

Later he pointed me towards the shower. The hot water restored my body though my mind stayed numb, as if a circuit had fused somewhere inside. But that loss had value; my heartbeat was steady and I was calm, ready to face whatever was out there. When I came back scrambled eggs and bacon were waiting. 'Breakfast.' he said, 'My speciality.'

He pattered for my benefit. There was no need; the long night had passed.

'You do this at your house?'

'Yep, Gail isn't a mornin' person. Ever since the boys were wee I've been in charge of gettin' the show on the road.'

I was impressed. I said, 'You're a good guy, Patrick.'

He crunched toast. 'Nah, nah I'm not. I make decent scrambled eggs, I'll settle for that.'

We travelled into the city together. I reckoned he was keeping an eye on me. NYB was quiet. The two guys Jackie had hired were lounging against the end of the bar. Their conversation wasn't about clearing tables. I overheard Roberto championing Fair Trade with a female – preaching to the converted – the lady hung on every word. I asked one of the waiters to bring coffee to the office. He was a strange looking boy with lazy eyes, prominent teeth and a neck that was too long for his body; probably a student paying his way through university before going on to become a doctor or some such and earn real money. Unfortunately that's how he saw it too; he seemed to resent being interrupted. Not good. If a well-known face couldn't get service what chance did anybody else have?

Patrick said. 'He the best she can get?'

The other guy brought our coffee. A smile played around his mouth, a joke he wasn't willing to share. I wanted to give him a slap; he had that kind of face. He was gay and flaunted his sexuality in a mini performance.

'So,' Patrick clapped his hands, 'let's get to it.' He drew a chair over to the desk and reached for Yellow Pages. 'What's the approach? They're not going to give out information on employees just like that.'

'Ask to speak to Stephen McNeil. They'll tell you if he doesn't work there. Apologise and move on to the next one.'

He grinned. 'Ever lookin' for a new gig, Charlie, there are people who could use a devious bastard like you.'

I pushed a pen and paper towards him 'We want haulage companies in the Greater Glasgow area.'

'Snookered if he's gone south.'

'Let's hope not. Cecelia McNeil's been disappointed enough.'

The list was longer than I'd imagined. Patrick worked in silence, now and then whistling snatches of a tune unfamiliar to both of us. When I couldn't take any more I left him to it.

'Where you goin'?'

'Lesmahagow.'

'Ah, the Gow. Mamba country. Miles and miles of bugger all. Take it easy, Charlie.'

Jackie called me over to the baby grand. She said, 'Missed the drama last night. Danny stormed out. Won't be back until the piano's fixed.'

'What's wrong with it?'

'He says it's out of tune.'

'Sounds fine to me.'

'Yeah, but with respect, Charlie, you're not a musician. Danny is, and he says it's way off.'

'Does Glasgow have piano tuners? Where did you find him?'

'Yellow Pages. When he's finished I'll call the maestro, tell him his integrity isn't threatened and it's safe to come back.'

A man leaned inside the body, tinkering, doing whatever piano tuners do. He played a chord, then another, fingers drifting across the keys and turned to me. His features were delicate, the skin white and smooth as porcelain. I recognised him. It was George Lang, Christopher McNeil's music teacher.

'We've met before. Almost. At the McNeil house.'

His aesthetic features changed. His reply was stiff. 'Really?'

'I'm working for Christopher's mother. Have you got a few minutes? Can we talk about Christopher?'

He looked at his watch, suddenly he was a man with a schedule to keep. 'I haven't…'

'Two minutes?'

His shoulders sagged, resigned. 'I'm not keen to discuss Christopher. Not with you, not with anybody.'

'How long were you his piano teacher?'

'A couple of years.'

'How did you get on?'

'Good. Chris had talent, discipline too. He loved to practise.'

'So why did he need you?'

Lang's skin was more bloodless than I remembered, as pale as bone. 'You'd have to appreciate where he was coming from. Christopher couldn't cope with the pressure at home. It affected him, affected his music.'

'How?'

'It confused him. The father wanted him to be a sportsman, the mother a musician. He couldn't concentrate. People think talent arrives in a box, all you have to do is take it out and put it on. They're wrong. It demands attention. And it'll make you unhappy if it doesn't get it.'

'Sounds like a curse.'

'In a sense. Gifts come at a price.'

'Are you saying Christopher was unbalanced?'

George Lang's voice was an anguished whisper. 'I told you I won't talk about Christopher and I won't.'

I'd lost him and I knew it. He brushed past me. I ignored how upset he was and called after him. 'Did you ever meet his father?'

He said something I didn't hear and hurried away.

***

The Big Issue seller waited in his usual place. I fingered coins in my pocket and steadied myself for today's recitation. He saw me coming. I pressed money into his hand. He gazed at it as if it was unexpected. I was three steps past him when he spoke.

"'Gie fools their silks and knaves their wine. A man's a man for a' that.'"

His voice held controlled contempt. I understood the couplet, just not how it applied to me, and I made a decision: I'd resist his emotional blackmail. In future, as far as I was concerned, the guy was on to blank. I wasn't having some geezer hurl Robert Burns at me. Enough was enough.

Glasgow has an advantage over many cities: minutes after you leave you're in the country. I drove past the cathedral on to the M74 and followed the signs for Carlisle. In-coming traffic was backed-up into the distance, a couple of miles of vehicles moving at snail-pace.

April, and still the sky was muddy, heavy with rain, temperatures in single figures. Porto Estuto it wasn't. At Strathclyde Park a few people in boats braved the cold – a strange sight on a Monday morning. On a whim I took the Clyde Valley scenic route. Places with quaint names, Rosebank, Hazelbank and Tillietudlum, came and went. Lesmahagow was neither scenic nor quaint; it was typical of villages in South Lanarkshire, an odd mix of houses clustered on the rise above the single main street, some more than a hundred years old. Jean Selkirk might be in one of them, on the phone telling a cousin in Australia about the unexpected arrival of her nephew, Ian – what a lovely boy he was – and how he'd asked her to keep a package for him.

It took an hour to find her, or at least find her name, etched in granite in the little graveyard by the river. The drive back to Glasgow seemed long.

At NYB I avoided the Big Issue guy but not Pat Logue. He was at the bar. I frowned when I saw him. He slid off the stool, drew me aside and whispered. 'No luck, nobody's heard of Stephen McNeil. Could be usin' another name, of course.'

'Why? He hasn't done anything wrong. We can't find him because he's kept it simple. His mistake was using the card at Tesco, and it wasn't a mistake, he doesn't know his wife hired us. As far as he's concerned nobody's looking for him.'

'Fifteen thou won't last forever. On that subject, Charlie, sub me, will you?'

I let my irritation show. 'Patrick, keep going and you'll have drunk all your due.'

'Surely not? I mean I'm full-time. My other interests have been set aside to concentrate on your stuff. A couple of dips won't make much of a hole, will they?'

'What other interests?' I gave him two twenties and a ten.

His mobile rang. He checked the screen and switched it off. 'Gail.' he said. 'Been tryin' to get me all weekend. I'm diggin' in my heels. Saturday night decided it, I'd be all right by myself. Better than all right.'

'Always wise to keep a dialogue going.'

'No point. Not with her.'

I told him he knew his own business best but I didn't believe it.

'We need to discuss expenses for hangin' around dodgy pubs and sufferin' shite beer. I've got standards Charlie, thought you knew that. And I'm still owed from the east end.'

'Bring me receipts. No receipts, you're buying your own. Understood?'

Receipts for a couple of pints. What a cheap bastard I could be.

'You're as bad as Gail. Ian's auntie was a bust and you're takin' it out on me, am I right?'

He sloped off, pretending to be hurt. And he was right. The trip to Lesmahagow had been a waste. Seeing Pat Logue at the bar set me off. It wasn't his fault, it was me.

Andrew Geddes called over. 'A word, Charlie. Platt's making noises. Your name keeps cropping up. He'll be along to see you. My advice would be to tell him anything you know. The case hasn't caught fire and his ego's screaming blue murder. No news on your break-in, by the way. Spoke to Celtic Park this morning – they'll have the information tomorrow. Best I can do in the circumstances.'

He spelled out the circumstances he meant.

'No crime. No suspicion of a crime. Just doing a pal a good turn. You'll understand why I don't push harder.' He was joking. But only a little.

'I appreciate it. Tomorrow's fine, and thanks.'

'Platt. Watch it with him. He's after a result. Make sure you don't oblige him.'

'How would I do that?'

'Oh, I don't know, withholding evidence, maybe? He has a reputation for not letting go when it comes to bringing a charge. Just be careful.'

'Right now he's the least of my troubles. What about Emil Rocha?'

'Spanish police haven't got back yet. How does he figure?'

'How does any of it figure, Andrew? I wish I knew.'

I dropped my voice so no one else could hear. 'Listen, about Pat Logue. He's doing some work for me so go easy, will you?'

He sighed. 'He isn't Public Enemy Number One, Charlie, but he's always got an angle on the go. Only a matter of time before he falls on his face. It's my job to be there when he does. The Logues of the world do plenty of damage on the quiet. Your pal's a thief and his sons are right behind him. Liam got caught lifting a leather coat out of Paul Smith's on Saturday. Can't say he lacks ambition. Security camera caught him and the staff are witnesses.'

'Patrick doesn't know.'

'He will soon. The boy's too young for the Big House but the Children's Panel will be delighted to make his acquaintance.'

'First offence?'

'Don't be daft. First time he's been nicked, that's all.

'Patrick's wife's been calling him. They're at war. He stopped answering his phone.'

'Better tell him. The boy's mother collected him. In a right state she was. Wondered where the Wild Rover had got to.'

'He was with me. He's been avoiding her.'

'Shame she didn't do the same with him. She's nice enough.'

Andrew had a habit of sounding pleased when trouble arrived. He'd been the same when the flat was burgled. Perhaps he couldn't help it. He wandered off to spread cheer in other lives. I wasn't unhappy to see him go. I went upstairs and waited a few minutes then buzzed down to Jackie. 'Ask Pat Logue to meet me in the office.'

'He's talking football with Roberto. Boring.'

'Tell him it's important.'

Patrick sauntered in, pint in hand as usual. 'That Roberto's an interestin' guy. Big Inter fan. Hates A.C. I mean, he really hates them. He was sayin'…'

'You need to call Gail, Liam's in trouble with the police. She's been trying to reach you for two days.' The grin disappeared. 'Use this phone if you like, just make sure you get her.'

'Who told you? What kind of trouble?'

'Andrew Geddes. Shoplifting. Gail was at the police station. She was upset.'

I gave him space. The irony of Saturday night didn't escape me, while we drank our way round Glasgow, Gail Logue was in a police station crying for her son. That was at the heart of her sudden objections to her husband.

Alex Gilby stopped me at the bottom of the stairs. 'Jackie's losing it, Charlie. Best to keep a low profile'

'How so?'

He shook his head. 'You'll find out.'

And I did. A minute later when she introduced me to somebody. 'This is Mr Strang, Charlie. Mr Strang has offered to help.'

'Help with what?'

Mr Strang peered down his long nose, a character from a Dickens novel with the charm of an undertaker. 'I'm here to resolve the unresolved, Mr Cameron.'

'Really?'

Jackie got between us. 'Mr Strang is an accredited consultant with the Feng Shui Society; he's doing a bagua.'

'Is he indeed?' I hadn't a clue what a bagua was. 'Let me know how it goes.'

Patrick passed me on his way out. He didn't say goodbye. Very different from the guy who talked football with the barman. I guessed he'd been on the receiving end of hard words. I didn't envy him. Likely this wasn't the first time one of his sons had crossed the line and been caught, but it came at a critical moment; divorce was in the wind.

Andrew Geddes was at my shoulder. 'Got the word, has he? He'll get used to it. It's only the beginning.'

His pleasure got under my skin. 'He's a man worried about his son, Andrew, cut him a break. Patrick's wide, that's all, he's not a child molester or a serial killer.'

Geddes was unimpressed. 'Never had you down as a bleeding heart, Charlie. Wide? What does that cover? I wouldn't give him house-room.'

I went to the office. Another word would be one too many; we'd fall out. Andrew had his view, he was entitled. Later in the afternoon Jackie was behind the bar.

I said, 'How did the bagua go?'

'Not good. Not good at all, Charlie.'

'How so?'

'It's the club.'

'What's wrong with it?'

'It's facing the wrong way.'

Alex was going to love hearing that.

Chapter 28

The Cumberland Arms on the corner of Argyle Street and Wellington Street claimed to be the oldest gay pub in the city. I'd take their word for it. When Ian Selkirk did a runner the first time, I tracked him here and missed him by minutes. It was as good a place as any to begin. I had a plan, two places a night; any more was headless chicken stuff, running around trying to get lucky, never sure if I was too early or too late. As a strategy it was limited but until I had better it would have to do.

The Cumberland wasn't busy, though not bad for a Monday. It was no different from any pub anywhere; guys drinking and shooting the breeze, talking politics, laughing too loud.

I sat at the bar. As a strange face I expected the regulars to check me out and keep their distance. Someone called 'Two heavy, Norrie!' and gave me the start I needed. Norrie was a tall thin guy, black t-shirt, jeans, designer stubble and an earring. I asked for lager.

'Haven't seen you in here before.'

It didn't sound like a question but it was.

'Friend of mine recommended you.'

'Oh aye, who would that be?'

I drank the top off the beer and took my time. 'Ian. Comes in whenever he's in Glasgow. Lives in Spain these days. Told me to say hello to Norrie for him.'

'Doesn't ring a bell.'

'Really? He will be disappointed.'

'When was he in last?'

'Not sure, a month, five weeks, something like that.'

'And I know this guy?'

I laughed. 'No sweat. I won't say a word.'

He moved away to serve another customer. He'd be back, I'd bet money on it.

Everyone on the planet is the same – so long as we're in the story we're riveted. Norman was no exception. He edged down the bar 'til he got to me.

'Describe this friend. What does he do in Spain?'

'Real estate. Very successful, so he says.'

He shook his head. 'I'm losing it, too many drugs.'

'Always cracking jokes, tons of personality. Ian Selkirk. Been coming here off and on.'

Norman signalled to a guy in a leather jacket and tight jeans. 'Derrick, you see me with anybody you didn't recognise recently? A pal of his,' he waved his thumb at me, 'reckons he knows me. Don't remember a thing about him.'

'What was his name?'

'Ian. Mean anything?'

'A Tommy, yeah. A couple of Davids, sure. Easier if you weren't such a tart, Norrie, even you can't keep up with it. What chance do I have?'

I put in my tuppence worth. 'He was only in Scotland a few days. Stayed out at Loch Lomond.'

Norman scratched his ear. 'You've got me at it now. Won't be able to sleep for thinking about it. Hate that.'

Derrick said, 'Try it sober next time. It's nearly as good.'

I watched the barman do my work for me, talking to this one and that, enjoying the notion he couldn't recall some sexual episode with a partner from abroad. He found out what I would've found out in a quarter of the time. Nothing. Ian Selkirk hadn't been near the Cumberland Arms.

I headed towards Central Station. Under the bridge a beggar with sad eyes and a haggard face held out his hand. In broken English he told me he was starving. I gave him a big photograph of the queen. Further along three youths shouted an invitation to violence. Gratuitous agro. A mountain of uncollected rubbish lay by the side of the road near bins that hadn't been emptied in weeks. This part of town was dirty and dangerous.

The Polo Lounge was a different animal from the Cumberland; a club for people born to party. I tried the same stunt with the fresh-faced young man who served me. His name tag helped: Colin. Maybe Colin was more secure than Norrie because he wasn't interested. I hung around without connecting with anyone. When I'd had a bellyful of sympathetic looks for being a sad old bastard I drank up and left.

It was still early. Going home wasn't an option. I couldn't face it, so I walked. My mood hadn't lifted from the afternoon; if anything I felt worse. For a month the mystery of Ian Selkirk's murder had refused to reveal itself. I still wasn't sure exactly what he'd done, for Christ's sake. Fiona was in hiding, depending on me to resolve the nightmare we were living. Images I was powerless to resist bombarded my tired brain. At one point I thought I heard footsteps: Rafferty's goons come for me at last? I stopped. The footsteps stopped too. My mind was running wild, I'd spooked myself, it was an echo. On another day I might have laughed. Not tonight.

I'd quit the Polo Lounge around eleven fifteen. Now it was twelve thirty. I must have walked in circles because I was in High Street. The car was miles away.

Glasgow was dark and deserted. At the bottom of the hill the Tron clock chimed the half hour. There was no one to hear it but me.

***

Cecelia McNeil's body language was stiff with the same kind of hostility I had seen the day the piano teacher showed up uninvited. No tea this time. Maybe she'd thought about our conversation in NYB, recalled my efforts and was angry again. I was after what I hadn't had so far: the truth.

There was an edge to her voice. 'Why do you want to talk to me, Mr Cameron. Is there a development?'

'Of a kind, Mrs McNeil. I bumped into George Lang. Told him I was working for you. When I asked about Christopher he couldn't get away quick enough. Almost ran. Any idea why he'd react like that?'

'George is a very private man.' Her reply had a hollow ring. 'I'm not surprised he wouldn't discuss my son. As far as he's concerned you're a stranger.'

'Tell me about Christopher.'

'There's nothing to tell. He doesn't come into this.'

'But he does. He took his life after a fight with his father. I've asked you before what the argument was about. Must've been pretty serious.'

She wouldn't look at me. 'I really don't remember. It seems like a hundred years ago.'

'How did it start? Did Christopher say something? Or was it Stephen?'

She sighed and trembled. 'I've no memory of how it began. One minute things were all right – the next... Christopher stormed upstairs. Stephen got into the car and drove away.'

'What did you do?'

She made a bleak attempt at a laugh. 'Me? I was caught in the middle as usual. It was always the same.'

'What's George Lang done to make you dislike him so much?'

She pulled herself together. 'You're wrong. George is okay.'

'Didn't look like it the time he was here.'

'I don't mean to be rude, but I'd prefer if you would go, Mr Cameron. These questions are very upsetting, and I've been upset enough.'

'I'm not trying to upset you, Mrs McNeil, believe me. I'm asking what the row was about. Difficult to credit you can't remember.'

'Well I can't. Please leave.'

I stood on the steps, still short of an answer to my question, but accepting I wasn't going to get it. The sobbing coming from the other side of the door made me wish I had listened to my father; since I found Ian Selkirk's body at the mortuary this wasn't a job I fancied anymore.

I dropped in at the flat first. No sign of Patrick. It was possible he and Gail had put their differences behind them and become a family again. Andrew Geddes was due to come through with the information about Celtic Park sometime today and Pat Logue was a genius at getting things, but it took time. At NYB Jackie Mallon's face told me all wasn't well.

'What's wrong?'

She nodded. 'Over there.' Patrick sat at the bar, his head on the counter, a half full pint in front of him, as drunk as I'd ever seen.

'How did he get in that state?'

'He seemed fine when he came in. You know Pat, usually he can down enough to sink a battleship and still look okay. One minute he was fine, the next blotto. Didn't have the heart to toss him out.'

'I'll take him to my place; he's crashing there anyway.'

She helped me manhandle him to the car. 'When Andrew Geddes appears tell him I won't be long.'

'Sure you don't want me to come with you, he weighs a ton?'

'I'll be fine.'

Patrick snored all the way to Cleveden Drive. It took twenty minutes to get him inside. I dumped him on the couch and collapsed into the armchair opposite. When I recovered I dragged a quilt off a bed and threw it over him. Back at NYB Jackie hurried over. 'Okay, Charlie?'

'Yeah. He's sleeping it off. Any sign of Andrew?'

'Hasn't been in yet.'

'I'll be in the office. Send him up.'

Pat Logue was supposed to be going to the El Cid. I had intended spending the evening trawling more gay bars. Change of plan. I couldn't be two places at once and the darts teams only played on Tuesdays. Finding McNeil on his favourite double wasn't such a long shot. The chat with Patrick had exposed a flawed assumption.

Stephen McNeil wasn't hiding.

I wondered if Stephen blamed Cecelia for Christopher's death.

Andrew picked that moment to put his head round the door. 'Got what you need,' he said and sat down. 'Jock Stein Stand. The Celtic end. 123. G19 and 20. Good enough?'

'Better than that. I owe you one, Andrew.'

'Make it dinner for two. Sandra loved it here.'

'Book it. On me.'

He stood. 'Seen Logue?'

I lied. 'Not today. What's he done?'

'Nothing I can prove. They've just discovered a container robbery on the docks. Happened weeks ago. Electrical goods. Stereos, MP players, televisions. Top of the range. All gone.'

'Doubt he had anything to do with it, Andrew. Different division.'

'Your pal feeds off the bigger rogues. Got to get his supply from somewhere. Kick his granny if the price was right.'

Harsh.

'He's a dodgy bastard, surprised you have anything to do with him.'

If he only knew.

'I'm expecting a fax from the Spanish law about Emil Rocha. Get you a copy when it arrives.'

'Appreciate it. Sort your reservation. I'll put Jackie in the picture.'

I went back to the flat to make certain Patrick was okay. I needn't have bothered; he hadn't moved an inch. The empty space where the flat screen TV had been reminded me of Andrew's words:

a dodgy bastard, surprised you have anything to do with him

When I left, the dodgy bastard was still unconscious.

The El Cid was busy. A petite woman, hard-faced, too much make up and big tits, gave me a breezy hello.

I said, 'They're all here tonight. What's the occasion?'

'Semi-final. Grudge match. The Vault put us out last year.'

Both teams had their supporters, probably guys who were quite good, just not good enough. A man in corduroy trousers and a check shirt readied himself to throw. His eyes were cold, like a gunslinger in a cowboy movie and his belly rolled over his belt. He took his time, measuring the distance, and let fly straight into the double. Somebody shouted 'Played!' The marker wiped the blackboard clean. His mates whooped. He took their appreciation in his stride.

The standard was high – a game was over in minutes – it took thousands of hours of practice to get that good. The players added, subtracted and multiplied in their heads, weighing the options each new score presented, rarely pausing to consider the next throw. I couldn't keep up. The surly foreman from Newlands was in the thick of it, representing the pub. He was the only one I recognised.

The Vault won game after game. I ordered another pint and spoke to the barmaid.

'You're getting hammered. Is this your strongest team?'

'No. We've lost one of our best players. The guy standing in isn't as good.'

'Run off with another woman, has he?'

She gave me a funny look. 'Don't let Carol hear you say that.'

'Is Carol the wife or the girlfriend?'

'Girlfriend. She's devastated. Serves her right for trusting a man.'

Bullseye. There was a woman or at least there had been. A roar went up from the other end of the bar; the El Cid had pulled one back. The marker cleared the board, ready to begin again. Stephen McNeil had done the same, abandoned everything, even his bit on the side.

'Come on,' I said. 'We're not all bad.'

'Yeah? Have I just been unlucky then?'

'Must be, it's tainted your judgement. Would this Carol go for somebody like me? What d'you think?'

She leaned across, her breasts rested on the counter, the smile turned off as easily as a light switch. Flowery perfume mixed with cigarettes and gin.

'Listen,' she said, 'you seem like a nice guy but you're a stranger. That accent tells me you're not from round here. And for a stranger you ask too many questions, that's what I think. Now shut it and watch the fucking darts.'

Patrick was awake when I got back, nursing a can of beer, staring at the wall. There were red marks on his cheek. He didn't say anything. Neither did I. I made myself coffee and sat down next to him. I didn't offer him any.

He said, 'Did you bring me here?'

'Yeah, this afternoon. You passed out in NYB.'

'Last I remember I was in Glasgow Green with a bottle of Bell's. Definitely not recommended.'

'Thought you were with Gail?'

'I was. She threw me out. Literally.'

'She'll be worried sick about Liam.'

'No, Liam'll be fine. He's too young for jail. She's scared this is the start. Can see herself a couple of years down the line takin' the bus to Barlinnie every week.'

'Could be the best thing that's happened to him. Just the fright he needs.'

'Don't think so, Charlie. He's not bothered. Caught him on the phone boastin' to his pals. Gail heard him too. That was when she attacked me. Went mental.' He fingered the scratches. 'She blames me for everythin'. No way back this time. Gone too far.'

'Let the dust settle. Everything looks better in daylight.'

He touched the red welts. 'This won't.'

Pat Logue had to work out his life by himself. I said, 'Gail's in a bad place. She's terrified of losing her son and her marriage is falling apart. Could be time for a rethink, Patrick.'

He didn't respond. At the door I stopped. I had my own fear going on. 'You still up for this Rafferty business? I have to be sure.'

'I promised to help. That promise stands. Whatever happens to Gail and me I'm there. Depend on it.'

I hoped he was as good as his word. His wife wasn't the only one who needed him to deliver.

Chapter 29

On Wednesday I parked outside NYB and fed coins into a meter. The weather was better today, fresh and clear. Not sunny, not yet. The guy selling the Big Issue was smack dab between me and my destination. I stuck a hand in my pocket looking for money; I'd given the last of it to Glasgow City Council Road Traffic Department. He seemed to sense what was coming and kept his head down, shifting his weight from one foot to another in a rocking motion; preparing himself. The greatcoat he wore was too big for him – the same one I remembered from before Christmas when a hard frost lay on the pavement and mounds of dirty-white snow piled against the kerb. He'd been a sorry sight that day; shivering, almost dancing to stay warm, fire red cheeks pumping his breath out in clouds to condense and fade in the icy air. I'd had a word with Jackie, but there was no need, soup and rolls were on their way. I added a twenty pound note. We could all feel better.

That was forgotten, he'd taken against me. His face was animated; he waved an accusatory hand and shouted. '"For a' that an' a' that, it's coming yet for a' that. That man to man the world o'er, shall brithers be for a' that!"'

Passers-by gave both of us a second glance, wondering as I did, what was going on. I quickened my step taking me past him. Jackie and Alex were standing outside NYB. At the door. The red door.

I said, 'Why do you suddenly have a red door, Jackie?'

'For luck, Charlie. A red door attracts good fortune.'

Alex said, 'Don't you think we should be discussing this kind of thing, Jackie?'

'We are.'

'I mean before.'

Only fight the battles you can win.

I interrupted. 'The Big Issue guy, what's the story?'

'How do you mean?'

'He's got a thing about me. Keeps quoting Burns. Can't think what I've done to upset him.'

'Maybe he sees you as an establishment figure. The enemy.'

'Don't be ridiculous.'

'Drugs then.'

'Him or me?'

I said hello to a couple of regulars; it was still a bit early for Andrew or Patrick. At a table against the wall two pug-ugly men stared at me, coffees untouched in front of them. The one on the left was familiar; the skinhead I'd seen in Cottier's the night of the pub crawl. We had moved to a new level; the game of hide and seek was over. Anger burned my neck. These goons had dogged me since the crematorium – before that for all I knew. Fiona and I were no part of whatever Ian had done. It was time to say that and be heard. Resentment gave me courage. I started towards them. Halfway across the doors flew open. The Big Issue seller was shouting at me again. 'The car! The car's on fire!'

Seconds went by while I tried to make sense of what he was saying.

The car? Whose car?

Then I ran.

***

People gathered on the pavements; it wasn't every day you saw somebody's car going up in smoke. One of the windows was broken; flames rose to the sky from inside. There was nothing to do except watch.

On the street, traffic stopped; progress was impossible. The police cordoned the street off in both directions and the fire brigade appeared. Thick jets of water brought the inferno under control in a matter of minutes but the car was a blackened shell. I had stumbled into a bad dream. An officer took my statement and interviewed the principal witness, the Big Issue guy. The whole of NYB stood amazed at the drama on their doorstep. Jackie squeezed through the crowd and tried to console me. 'It's only a motor, Charlie. It's only stuff.' She took pictures on her phone. 'Insurance,' she said.

Rafferty's thugs were at my elbow. One of them spoke without looking at me.

'A message from Jimmy. You've got one more week.'

I moved towards him but Jackie got between us. He stepped back and laughed.

'Next time your car goes up you'll be in it.'

***

One week, ten weeks, it made no difference. I still hadn't a clue. I wanted to beg Rafferty's heavies not to hurt Fiona, to let us get on with our lives; the words stuck in my throat. Jackie took my hand and led me to NYB.

Andrew Geddes's advice was to tell Platt what I knew, it never felt right. Now holding back didn't seem such a good idea. I didn't like the policeman or trust him, but at least he was on our side.

Thirty minutes later he was in my office, smiling his rat smile, reinforcing my original decision. 'That your jalopy out there, Charlie? Dear oh dear, what a mess. And no sign of the girlfriend, I hear.' He was baiting me. 'Where can she have got to?'

I came close to hitting him. He sat down, crossed his legs and straightened the crease in his trousers. 'Five million pounds is an awful lot of money. Not easy to write off to experience, especially when every dago in Iberia's paying attention to see what you do. Emil Rocha isn't liable to forget about it. Can't say I blame him, I mean, he's the king of the castle, everybody's afraid of him, until someone makes him look a fool. Won't do. Won't do at all. Never trust a junkie, that's the lesson. Did you know your pal was an addict?'

Since Ash Wednesday Ian Selkirk had dominated my life. My flat had been ransacked, people followed me, and Fiona was in hiding, terrified. Now my car was lying in the street, a smouldering husk, while Detective Inspector Platt smirked offensive questions at me. I was tired of it.

The policeman was having too much fun at my expense to notice how close to the edge I was. 'A little bird tells me Jimmy Rafferty has taken an interest in you.'

He did his tutting thing.

'Hardly the sort of company a well brought up chap like you should be keeping.'

He was enjoying himself, drawing a languid finger across a table top and inspecting it for dust. When he got up to straighten a picture I realised it was an act; he still had nada.

I bit back. 'How's the investigation coming along, Inspector? Any nearer to understanding the first thing about it?'

Platt dropped the phony casual. 'You amaze me, Charlie. Your world is falling apart yet you can still make jokes. Admirable. Fucking stupid but admirable. I know Rafferty's watching you because so am I. Two of his men were here this very morning. I'd guess about the time your banger caught fire. I asked myself why Jimmy Rafferty would be bothering with you. The answer is he's working for Rocha. Rocha wants his money and he's hired the local strength to find it for him.'

He laughed. 'It's a foolish man who'd go up against that pair.'

'How much did you say?'

'Five mil. Give or take.'

I couldn't listen to any more. 'What is it with you, Platt? You don't really think I had a part in this. So why are you on my back? I thought it was because you didn't approve of a civilian poking around your case but it isn't. You disliked me from the beginning. You're making my life difficult instead of doing your job. The only one trying to get to the bottom of this is me.'

'Difficult? I haven't even started.' He stroked his chin with the insufferable half-smile on his face. 'You want to know why? Okay,

I'll tell you. I worked on a case in London involving a chum of your father's, Peregrine Sommerville. Know him, do you? Old school. Up to his armpits in all kinds of corruption. Aren't they all? Ten years would've been about right; instead he got a paltry couple of months in a country club. The evidence was there. Spent sixteen months pulling it together. But I made a mistake, didn't I? Forgot who I was dealing with. Sommerville had clout. Got off with a slap. Guess who was behind it Charlie.'

The sins of the father.

'And here I am, in the arse end of nowhere, my career down the river, quietly putting in my days, until the Almighty has a rethink and throws me a bone. And not any old bone. Archibald Cameron's son and heir, out of his depth and as bent as a nine bob note. Not a surprise, considering. Must be in the genes. Except this time the law will prevail.'

His rat eyes sparkled. 'Nice idea, isn't it? The law prevailing.'

'You're looking in the wrong direction, Platt. Resentment is blinding you. Whatever happened between you and my father has no place here.'

His face twisted, the words flew at me. 'He was guilty as hell. He got away with it because of who he was. Him and his cronies make me sick. My wife was ill, I was too busy building the case against Perry Sommerville to be with her. The night she died I was fifty miles away arresting that Tory bastard. Then he got off. Bitter? Absolutely! They paid some quack to say I was unfit for duty. Tried to push me out. After twenty eight years. I wasn't having that. Glasgow was the compromise.'

'I had nothing to do with it.'

'Ah, but you do Charlie. You're his boy. One of the gang. The chosen few. And no, you don't seem like it, not at the moment. I'll give you that. Today it's playing detective in the frozen north. Tomorrow, when you get tired of it, and you will, you'll be welcomed back into the fold. The prodigal returns.'

'You don't believe I had any part in what Ian Selkirk did. This is about revenge. Where does justice figure in that?'

He dismissed the question. 'Very plausible. Sommerville was the same. You're better than he was. I almost believe you. Almost, Charlie.'

'You've decided I'm guilty without a shred of proof.'

'On the contrary, I invited you to work with me. First thing I said. You haven't behaved like an innocent man. That business in Spain, for example, must admit that was odd. I mean, why would someone with nothing to hide lie to the police?'

'I didn't want to put Fiona in danger.'

'By telling the authorities? My my, don't have much faith in the system, do you?'

He turned a chair round to face me and straddled it the way cops in the movies did.

'There were three of you in on it; the details are unimportant. I couldn't give a flying fuck about them. Selkirk wouldn't tell where he'd stashed the cash so they killed him. Willing to bet the female's gone the same way. Shame, especially if as you say, she didn't know. That leaves you. Rafferty's after Rocha's money. My plan is simple. Stay back 'til you break cover and lead them to it. At that point I'll step in and have the lot of you.'

His black eyes filled with malice.

'And your father can't help this time. Drug money. Murder. Sweet. Maybe you put the knife in your old pal. Never thought of that.'

He stood. 'I'm a patient man, Charlie. However long it takes I'll be there.'

You've got one more week

It just got better and better.

Chapter 30

Around two in the afternoon a contractor took away what was left of my car. Quite a sight hanging twelve feet above a Glasgow street.

Jackie was wonderful. She called the insurers and dealt with them on my behalf. That let me get on with the business of staring at the wall. The only witness was the Big Issue guy and suddenly he wasn't around.

Platt's admission about Perry Sommerville and my father muddied the already dirty water. He had crossed the wrong people and they destroyed him. In his haste to implicate Archibald Cameron's son he had gifted information I didn't have, the hire car abandoned at Duck Bay, and what exactly it was Ian had stolen. Five million pounds. A man with no axe to grind would've been more cautious; the inspector's enmity made him careless.

It was the sixth of April, exactly four weeks since Cecelia McNeil's first visit, twenty eight days from when I discovered Ian Selkirk's body at the city morgue.

Jackie arranged for a replacement vehicle to be delivered later in the afternoon. Nice one, Jackie. On her way out she stopped at the door and fingered the coat hanging behind it.

'Not the time, I know,' she said, 'but this has seen better days. You hardly ever wear it.'

'It's Armani.'

'Doesn't matter. If you don't wear something it clogs up the energy. This is clogging-up the energy.'

DS Geddes came by. He had already heard about the arson.

'Somebody doesn't like you, Charlie. The fax came through from the Spanish police.'

He put his hand in his pocket. 'Emil Rocha's a big fish, not the kind of hombre you want to fall out with.'

There were two sheets; in the right hand corner of the top one was a grainy image. I studied the photograph. The poor quality didn't disguise how handsome he was. Moody and dark. He might've been a movie star. The eyes told a different story – they stared from the page, cruel and unforgiving. And this was who Ian Selkirk had chosen to rob. Mad bastard. The drugs must have separated him from reality. No one in their right mind would mess with this guy.

No one in their right mind; a description of Ian, perhaps? Fiona said he was uncontrollable and if she couldn't handle him, who could?'

Andrew said, 'Making any progress with Platt?'

'You might say, Andrew.'

'Word is he won't be with us too long. His boss thought he was getting a high-flyer. He's pretty disappointed. Platt's put in for a transfer.'

I was sorry to hear it. Andrew wasn't aware of the background. DI Platt was a victim; he deserved a better shake. Though I still couldn't bring myself to like him I had sympathy for the way things had turned out. Later I had a surprise visitor. Patrick. He came through NYB straight to the office. The change was miraculous – not quite his usual self, but close.

'You should've told me you were after a new motor. I would've taken the other one off your hands. Got you a fair price too.'

'It slipped my mind, Pat. Maybe next time. Didn't expect to see you.'

'I called Gail. She apologised. I'm meetin' her in the Hilton to talk about Liam.'

'Good.'

'Meantime I was earnin' my corn. The barmaid at the El Cid? Her name's Janet. She's divorced. "Between husbands" was how she put it. Been workin' in the pub for eight years. Eric, her boyfriend, works there too. Knows everybody and everybody knows her, that type. Thinkin' about packin' it in and movin' abroad. The Greek islands are the favourite. I asked about Stephen McNeil. Hasn't a good word to say about him. Reckon they might've had a thing at one time. She's a nippy sweetie to start with. When I mentioned McNeil she really let go.'

'I'll never understand how you do it, Patrick. A woman you've never met tells you her life story. What's the secret?'

'No secret. I'm a people person. See, you're all business, Charlie. No interest in small talk. I'm the opposite. Never came across anybody who didn't have a story. Trick is to get them to tell it to you.'

'By doing what?'

'Listenin'.'

I was certain there was more to it than that.

'Janet,' the way he said it made it sound as if they were pals, 'is up in arms about poor Carol.'

'The girlfriend.'

'Ex-girlfriend. McNeil's been messin' around for years. Carol's just the latest. Nobody was judgin' until he packed her in. One night he told her he was goin' away, that it was all over.'

'Did he say where?'

'Didn't say anythin'. Carol is Janet's mate so Stephen McNeil's the biggest bastard that ever walked the planet.'

'Are these women aware he already has a wife?'

'So what? McNeil dumped Carol, that's the only thing that matters.'

He fished out a crumpled scrap of paper and handed it to me. 'Carol Thom. There's the address. Hasn't got a job. Or a man. Spends most afternoons down the bingo. Most nights in the El Cid.'

'Patrick, how could I have doubted you?'

'I'll leave it with you.'

'And I almost forgot. Stephen McNeil's seats are in the Celtic end. 123. G19 and 20.'

He played it low key. 'See what I can do.'

***

I stayed later than usual at NYB. When I left, the replacement car still hadn't arrived. I walked – it wasn't far. Nothing is in a city the size of Glasgow; something I liked about living here. Patrick had lifted my spirits. I envied his ability to shuck off his worries, even if he was faking it.

I was headed for Bennets and another night trying to connect with someone who might've spent time with Ian Selkirk shortly before he died. Wednesday was karaoke night. I'd make this quick – Karaoke at the best of times was crap.

He was at the bar. I didn't recognise him at first; the old fashioned three piece suit was gone; tan chinos and a check shirt took its place. His pale face was creased in a grin. The two men he was with were younger than him by a good ten years. In their company he seemed younger too. This was the third occasion our paths had crossed. The first time he'd struck me as diffident, unsure of himself, easily intimidated by the older woman. At NYB he'd been more confident, still shy, but willing to be drawn into conversation – until I reminded him of our mutual acquaintance and asked the wrong question.

Amazing how obvious everything appears as soon as you can see it, like the winning lottery numbers the day after the draw.

5 15 24 25 41 49

Of course!

This was the same. He was having fun. I wouldn't interrupt him. No need – he'd told me more than enough just by being there. I hung around for another fruitless hour until the few conversations I had managed to start petered out. I glanced up and down the street looking for some sign of Rafferty or Platt or both. Nada, as Patrick Logue would say.

Maybe they were having a night off.

A taxi stopped for me in Queen Street. I used the journey to reflect on how stupid I had been. George Lang was in Bennets. I was willing to bet he'd taught young Christopher more than the piano.

Cecelia McNeil's dead son had been gay.

***

On Wednesday night I made notes on both cases and put the information into some kind of form. Christopher McNeil's sexuality would hardly be news to his mother. Of course she might've been in denial, hoping against hope for the grandchildren she would never have. Not what she wanted, no doubt, but no surprise.

So far I'd been able to lay the black thoughts about Fiona aside, telling myself she must be somewhere with poor reception. At ten o'clock I went to bed. Around three I fell into a shallow sleep and woke tired and depressed. Fast becoming the norm.

I made coffee and did something I'd only ever seen in movies: pulled the curtain back and scanned Cleveden Drive, expecting two strangers to be parked in an unfamiliar car. Spooking myself. I lived with the constant expectation of another terse message from Fiona, or worse, none at all.

Mid-morning I left. Any longer and I would've gone insane. Jackie Mallon sat at a table near the bar watching Roberto give a virtuoso macchiato-making performance for the benefit of three women at the start of a girls' day out.

As I passed she said, 'Message from the hire car people, they'll be here later. They apologise for the delay.'

'Has the Big Issue guy been around? He shot off as soon as the police took his statement. Wouldn't have minded a word, seeing as it was my car that got it.'

'Haven't seen him.' Her voice was flat and her eyes were red; she might've been crying. She went behind the counter and returned with two cappuccinos and two pieces of cheesecake. One of the coffees was for me, the rest was for her. Her shoulders sagged,

'I better tell you, Charlie, it's over between Gary and me.'

I guessed I'd heard the last of Gary's wisdom.

'Sorry, Jackie, you liked him a lot.'

'Yeah. But I couldn't handle his jealousy. A guy only had to glance at me and he'd go off the deep end. Accused me of having an affair with Roberto, can you believe it?'

Silence was the safest option.

'I mean Roberto's great,' she spooned cheesecake into her mouth, 'but I'm his boss, he's an employee for god's sake.' Another spoonful followed. 'How's Fiona?'

'Still in Spain.'

She made a start on the second portion. 'Relationships are tough, believe me I know. Hope you have better luck. You'll need it.'

I didn't want to talk about Fiona.

'Any strangers been in? Any odd characters?'

She gave me a look. 'Loads, that's why the takings are so good. Don't let yesterday get to you. Fortunately we have Andrew here to protect us.'

Andrew had just come in the door. I said, 'You ever work, Geddes? You spend more time drinking cappuccino than anyone I've ever known.'

He nodded to Jackie and defended himself. 'Not true, Charlie. Just thought I'd tell you, Platt's in trouble.'

'Really?'

'Yeah. The incident on the street yesterday brought things to a head. His boss wants something he can take upstairs. So far our friend Nigel hasn't unearthed a single line of enquiry with any meat on it. Been ordered to turn it round or else.'

'Bit soon to condemn him; it's only been four weeks.'

'He hasn't made any kind of progress. I mean none. Is he up to it? That's the question the brass are asking.'

'So what'll happen?'

'Another officer will be assigned the case. Hope to Christ it isn't me. If it is, you're the first person I'll be interviewing. No offence, but what went on in Porto Estuto smells and now deliberate fire raising on the city's streets. Platt's convinced you're in it up to your ears. It's not difficult to see where he's coming from. Selkirk and Fiona Ramsay were mates of yours once upon a time.'

That annoyed me. 'Once upon a long time, Andrew. Thanks for the vote of confidence. Don't worry, DS Geddes, I won't expect special treatment.'

'Hold on, Charlie, they were friends.'

the best friends

'Now one's dead and the other's missing.'

Andrew and I were friends too; he seemed to have forgotten. I gripped the edge of the table. Jackie put a hand on my arm, afraid I was about to lose it. First and foremost Andrew Geddes was a policeman, that's what he was telling me.

'Putting you in the picture, that's all.'

'Appreciate it.'

When he left Jackie admonished me. 'You bit his face off. In his position what would you do?'

She had a point. My reaction wasn't about Andrew. Or Platt. On the outside I appeared to be doing okay. Not the truth. My head was out to get me. A ball of anxiety lay in the pit of my stomach from morning 'til night. I couldn't sleep. When was the last time I ate? Since Spain all I'd thought about was Fiona. The search for Cecelia McNeil's runaway husband was a distraction. Thank god Patrick was making a come-back.

Speak of the devil.

I made a show of looking at my watch. Pat grinned. 'Is this the new Pat Logue? That's what the fans are askin'. Quick out of the traps. No more lettin' the day slip away.'

He was pleased with himself. I wondered why.

'Got us a ticket. Ten rows behind your man, McNeil.'

'Well done, Patrick. How much?'

'Call it a donation to the cause.'

'Thanks. I want to have a look at the lie of the land before Saturday.'

'Good idea, Charlie. Easy to lose him in the crowd. When?'

'This afternoon?'

'I'll call Gail and tell her where I'll be.'

This was unusual. Patrick did his own thing. He never asked if it was all right. He ordered a pint, orange juice and lemonade, sipped it and didn't add "first today".

I said, 'Three o'clock okay?'

He was already dialling the number. I moved away, trying not to hear and failing. His voice carried. "Honey" and "love" figured a lot in the conversation. The new Patrick indeed. Gail was calling the shots probably for the first time in their marriage. It was her turn. She had her husband where she wanted him and by the sound of it he wasn't unhappy about it.

'Fine,' he said. 'I'm all yours. Gail needs an idea where I am, what with the Liam carry-on at the weekend. Can see her point.'

'Getting better, is it? You and Gail?'

He looked away. 'That wee tyke shook her up. She's startin' to see me in a new light.'

'Oh yeah?'

'Yeah, but it's a slow process. Know what I'm talkin'?'

Bullshit was what he was talking.

'We'll leave at half past two and drive out there. Tonight I'll try Carol. Like you to come along. That be okay?'

He squinted at me. 'Okay? Why wouldn't it be okay? We're a team on this, aren't we?'

'But Gail?'

His reaction made me smile. 'Gail's got nothin' to do with it. This is business. I'll call her, sure, just so she knows. I'm on a case, for Christ's sake.'

Things had altered in the Logue household. In future New York Blue would be seeing a lot less of its best customer.

The replacement car was delivered at noon. I had wheels again. I signed something without bothering to read it, drove to High Street and parked. Still no sign of the Big Issue guy. A quiver of concern passed through me. As far as I understood, he was the only one who had seen the arson attack; wilful fire raising, DS Andrew Geddes's description. The people who murdered Ian wouldn't tolerate witnesses.

I invited Patrick to have lunch. He cleared his plate in record time and said, 'Ever been to Celtic, Charlie?'

'Never. Football doesn't do it for me.'

He made that sound car mechanics make when they lift the bonnet, a this-is-worse-than-I-thought noise. 'The accent is one thing, you might be from the islands, I suppose, but not into football? Serious. Some guys go for rugby. Even golf's a pass – but most of us worship the beautiful game.'

'Not me, Patrick.'

'Then do yourself a favour, don't tell anybody. And you hardly touch whisky, even your own.' He might have been describing a felony. 'Strange kind of Scotsman you are.'

'I didn't have the best of starts.'

'Still blamin' your old dad? Take responsibility, Charlie. Gail's favourite word right now. Plank yourself in front of the telly on Saturday and Sunday and watch twenty-two millionaires run after a ball. Better still, start goin'. I'll come with you if you like. Explain the finer points. Soon pick it up.

'Thanks but no thanks.'

We walked to Cochrane Street. The Big Issue seller wasn't there. He might've switched to another location. I didn't think so.

In the east end of the city, down-market met derelict and the nearer we got to the ground the worse it became. We were in a war zone, or so it seemed; blocks of flats, dull grey and dilapidated, every other window boarded; sectarian graffiti, shaded in green, scrawled on the walls of public houses no sane person would enter. We stopped at traffic lights. On one corner two young boys wearing hoods did a drug deal in broad daylight, on the other an old man in a heavy coat scavenged a bin, searching for god knew what. Rough stuff.

I watched rubbish drift across scraps of scrub land that hadn't a snowball's chance of being developed into anything except another pub or a betting shop. The few people we passed walked with their heads down. I couldn't see their eyes; there would be no hope in them.

It was a helluva place to live but according to Pat Logue the beautiful game was alive and well in the middle of it. Loch Lomond might have been another galaxy instead of twenty-odd miles. But bad things happened there too.

From a distance Parkhead rose like the coliseum in ancient Rome, just about the only cared-for property on London Road. A Mecca for some, the enemy's lair for others. We turned left into the car park, deserted apart from a dozen vehicles near the main door. Patrick pointed to the red brick façade with *Celtic Football Club* in large green lettering.

'Paradise,' he said, his face lit like a child's. 'Been comin' here since I was a kid. Got in for nothin' umpteen times.'

'How did you do that?'

'It was pay at the turnstile. We'd ask an adult to lift us over. Somebody always did. Saw loads of games that way. Wouldn't work now. Tickets only. When they're on a run it's a full house. 'Course it didn't look like this. We were headed for bankruptcy. Fergus McCann stepped in and saved us. He built the new Paradise. Impressive, isn't it?'

It was. But where I saw a modern sports stadium Pat Logue saw glory. He walked across the empty concourse, explaining how it would be. 'Twenty minutes before the end of the match they open the gates.' He stopped. 'Stephen McNeil will come out this one. I'll be behind him.'

I tried to picture the scene. 'How difficult will it be to keep him in sight?'

'Depends. The hard part is stayin' with him when the whistle blows.'

'Can we do it?'

'We'll need help.'

'Assume there are four of us. You, me, Liam and young Patrick.'

'Depends,' he said again. 'We don't know which direction he'll take.'

'Or if he has a car.'

'That could be a problem. If he drove away we'd be none the wiser about where he was staying. We'd have found him and lost him in the same afternoon.'

It had sounded like a good idea but tailing Stephen McNeil wasn't going to be easy.

I said, 'Let's figure it out back at the ranch.'

In the office we worked on a plan. I sketched a map of the ground and thought about the best way to use our resources. 'Do your boys have mobiles?'

'Phones are no good – won't be able to hear over the crowd noise.'

'Forget talking, we'll text.'

'Nice one, Charlie. And everybody can have a picture of McNeil on the phone. Might be possible for me to photograph him and send it to the rest of you.'

'Just message what he's wearing, we'll go from there.'

Pat Logue stroked his chin. 'You really don't get this, do you, Charlie? Message what he'll be wearing, I can tell you that right now. He'll be wearing a green and white football shirt or a scarf, same as forty thousand other fans.'

'All right, you'll have him in sight for the best part of two hours. After that he'll be easy to lose. Stay with him as long as you can. Liam will be waiting in front of the main stand; young Patrick can be further along London Road towards the city if he goes that way.'

'What about you, where will you be?'

'I'll try to pick him up when he comes out. With luck we'll both be on him.'

'And?'

'The further he gets from the stadium the better our chances. He used the credit card at Tesco's in Shettleston Road. I'm hoping he's pitched his tent near there.'

'Walkin' distance. More trouble than it's worth to use a car.'

'Still a possibility. We've got the reg. The boys can wander around the streets looking for it. Forty-five minutes each way, plus the interval. They can cover a lot of territory in that time. And if they find it all the other stuff isn't necessary. I'll get parked early, ready in case we get lucky.'

Patrick arranged to meet me later at NYB. I put my feet on the desk and closed my eyes. It was tempting to let Carol Thom go – she wasn't in the loop. Another trip to the El Cid didn't appeal.

Talking it through with Pat Logue made it seem so simple; he would spot Stephen McNeil and follow him to the car the boys had already located. I'd be waiting. McNeil would drive to his house and we'd know where he lived. What to do after that was up to Cecelia McNeil. My job would be done.

I must have dozed off because I woke sweating with my heart hammering in my chest. Finding what Ian had stolen and getting Fiona back safe was my job. Nothing else mattered.

And I had six days to make it happen.

Job done, who was I kidding?

Chapter 31

My third visit to the El Cid failed to improve my opinion. The pub was one of those land-that-time-forgot boozers. In the lounge it was 1972. We arrived after ten. Carol Thom was a bingoid. Patrick assured me she wouldn't be there any earlier.

We got our first piece of luck as soon as we went in: the barmaid who thought I asked too many questions wasn't working. A smiling younger woman took her place. In the car we'd agreed Patrick would do the talking. This was Pat Logue country. Besides, as the blonde barmaid had pointed out, my accent was against me. My brief was to watch and learn. I ordered our drinks, leaned on the bar and did just that.

Music filtered through tiny speakers high on the wall. Two or three regulars stood at the bar, alone and apart. I wondered why they preferred it in here. A boy and girl held hands; her head lay against his shoulder. Young love. By the door a middle-aged couple ignored each other and stared into space. They'd made an effort – he had on a shirt and tie and she was wearing make-up. Big night out.

The bingo girls were easy to spot: five of them, in a booth at the far end, talking and giggling. Patrick turned on his patter like a market trader.

'Any joy, ladies? Who should I be pally with?'

A brunette whispered something that made the rest cackle, deep and dirty.

'Anybody scoop the rollover?'

The women snorted their disillusionment. 'Fat chance,' one of them said. 'Hardly got a tickle.'

More sniggers.

Patrick squeezed in beside them. 'Rubbish when it goes like that. Last time I played I was dead unlucky. The Pyramid. Almost knocked it off.'

A hard faced redhead in her fifties helped him out. 'Close were you?'

'Really close. The woman sittin' in front of me won it.'

They laughed and he was in.

Some instinct told me to take a look outside. The street was deserted except for a man standing in shadow; one of Rafferty's thugs, an officer there on DI Platt instructions, or just a punter waiting for the number 17 to Castlemilk? Six days to go, and I was spending energy on a womaniser who'd done a runner.

Pat Logue had the bingo women eating out of his hand. At a guess, Carol Thom was in the centre of the group, protected by the sisterhood; blond highlights streaked her hair, her bust strained against the too-tight blouse and every finger had a ring. Twenty years in the past she wouldn't have had to try so hard.

Pat said, 'So, no luck tonight. What will the men say?'

The redhead answered for them. 'Who cares? Gave up caring what mine thinks long since.'

'Communication breakdown. Not good. When that goes what's left?'

The brunette had a suggestion. 'Three kids and the family allowance.'

Patrick smiled at the joke. 'You're too cynical. Where would you be without us? You need us, we're your rocks.'

They hooted.

'Nah, come on. We have our uses.'

'Aye, but the rest's a waste of space. Rather have a plate of home-made soup.'

'Ladies, ladies, you've been taken for granted, I can tell. Don't let your bad experience prejudice you. A few bad apples. Know what I'm talkin'?'

'Shite, that's what you're talking. This girl's an example.' The redhead pointed to Carol Thom. 'Bastard didn't even say goodbye.'

Patrick spoke to Carol. 'Maybe he's havin' a breakdown?'

Carol Thom choked on her drink. 'If anybody's having a breakdown it's me.'

Pat shook his head. 'Guy's an idiot then. No idea where he went?'

'Don't know, don't want to know. Cared more about his football team than me. I'm well rid of him.' It was bluster, a performance for the others. Redhead took charge again. 'The easiest way to get over a man is get another one. Who's your friend?'

Patrick pulled out of the booth, hooked a thumb in my direction and feigned surprise. 'Him? He's my parole officer.'

In the car he said. 'The girlfriend's as much in the dark as the wife. Cross her off the list.'

'I agree. You did well, Patrick.'

'Thanks, Charlie. Leave them laughin'. Always leave them laughin'.'

The next day was Friday. Five days until Jimmy Rafferty's deadline ran out. Deadline. How was that for irony? I had to face it, I was out of ideas. Not quite accurate, I hadn't had any to speak of. In the middle of the night I called Fiona's number; it rang and rang. No one answered. If I asked, Andrew would run a trace except that meant telling him the truth. Too complicated.

Pat Logue had already left the flat when I finally dragged myself out of bed. He had graduated from a shady character to a man of mystery. I guessed Gail was leading him by the nose and he was loving it.

Though it had been two weeks, signs of the burglary were still visible. I hadn't moved on replacing the damaged furniture. Mrs McCall wasn't happy, as she cleaned she muttered disapproval, not all of it directed at the intruders.

I threw a jacket in the car – the one I'd dipped in beer at the Lomond Inn, overdue for dry cleaning but in the circumstances hardly a priority – and headed for the office.

Jackie Mallon was in better spirits, the disappointment of Gary was fading. Even from a distance I could tell she'd turned the corner. As I arrived, a customer who had been coming to

New York Blue as long as I had was leaving. I held the door open for him and made some comment about the weather. That's when I saw the small marble figure under the window. A frog with three legs. I picked it up; it was heavier than it looked. Jackie came towards me faking a smile. 'You've found him then?'

I weighed it in my hand. 'Have I? What is it?'

'The Toad God.'

'Oh, right. Of course. And why is he here?'

'The Toad God's the bringer of prosperity, Charlie.' She could see I needed more. 'It's about energy. Ancient forces. Gary was a physical guy…'

'You said.'

'…but he was blocking the flow. I'll explain it when you've got the time.'

'I'm not sure…he's an ugly little fucker.'

'Who? Gary?'

I laughed. 'No, your new friend.'

'Touch him when you're passing. Get him on your side.'

I handed her the totem and walked away. She pointed to the jacket over my shoulder.

'That for cleaning? Shall I put it in for you?'

This unexpected generosity made me suspicious, especially coming from her.

'Thanks, I'll do it myself.'

Then she asked her real question: 'Do you think I should change the seats in the restaurant so nobody's facing the door? Bad Feng Shui.'

'What does Alex think?'

'He says to leave them. I'm not sure, we're losing power.'

The world was going mad. I didn't know whether to laugh or cry.

In the office I emptied the jacket pockets and found the bill I'd paid for Ian. I tossed it in the in-tray and opened the mail – one crisp white envelope – the kind I'd come to know so well. Cecelia McNeil. She was unaware of our plan for Celtic Park. I hadn't told her. And wouldn't, unless her husband was there. I was struck again by the precision of the handwriting and the economy of the words, in spite of how she must be feeling. Mrs McNeil was stronger than I had realised.

Dear Mr Cameron,

My sister in Dumfries wants me to stay with her. There is nothing for me here so I have decided to go. The house is on the market, too many memories. Please send me your invoice and thank you for your efforts on my behalf. I know you tried.

Cecelia McNeil.

No mention of God; he'd had his chance. Perhaps it wasn't too late to change the outcome, for Mrs McNeil at least. If Stephen McNeil was at the game and we discovered where he was living, we might produce a different ending. Then I'd get a note thanking God and me for saving her marriage.

Patrick arrived in the afternoon, all smiles. He was wearing his Jesus sandals, a good omen. He knocked and came in. 'Gail's okayed the boys for tomorrow. She wasn't keen, I talked her round. Told her it was a payin' event, help them appreciate the value of money. All that stuff. Promised to bring them home as soon as we tracked McNeil. She's happy.'

'Then we're set. We'll meet here at one o'clock and get in position early. Do the boys know?'

'Not yet, don't want them talkin' to their mother. They'll be alright. Anythin' on the Ian front?'

The look on my face answered for me. 'Rafferty's given me a deadline.'

'How long?'

'Five days and counting. Surely he can't believe I'm holding out on him? If he thought I had the information he'd have kneecapped me to get it and thrown my body in the Clyde.'

'Nah, you're a detective; he thinks you can lead him to the money and Fiona.'

I lost it.

'The money! The money! We're not absolutely sure if it even was money Ian took. And I've no idea where Fiona is. Why doesn't somebody listen? I haven't a fucking clue, Patrick.'

I was showing more of myself than he could cope with. 'Take it easy Charlie. Freakin' won't help. By the way, what's that wee statue doin' on the floor?'

'Toad God.'

It might've been the most obvious thing he'd ever heard, he didn't bat an eyelid.

'The Toad God. Right. Jackie's idea?'

'Yip.'

'And switchin' the chairs, what's that about?'

'Not taking no for an answer.'

'Not a word women recognise.'

When he'd gone I ran my eye over the list of Ian Selkirk's possessions again. I saw nothing – there was nothing to see. Downstairs in the diner chaos ruled, as Roberto and Jackie struggled to make the seating plan work. I had bigger problems. On my way out I checked no one was watching and rubbed the Toad God's fat little head.

Because you just never know.

Chapter 32

Mrs McCall cleaned the flat on Saturday mornings. It didn't suit; still, that was the deal. She came in twice a week; Wednesday was the other day. I must have tried fifty times but she refused to alter "the arrangement" as she called it. If there was someone with me we stayed in bed 'til she'd gone. I'd learned that sex with the Hoover going in the next room is a disappointing experience. Mrs Mac made no concessions. No matter how late it had been when I got home the night before the vacuum began its awful sound at nine sharp.

But that was BP. Before Patrick. Pat Logue's talent worked on everybody, with the exception of his wife and DS Geddes.

I found them sitting on the sofa drinking tea and talking. 'Charlie, Lorna's askin' when you're thinkin' of puttin' the house straight.'

Mrs McCall had been my cleaner for five years. I didn't know her name was Lorna until today. It had taken Pat Logue five minutes to find out. He said 'New television arrives on Monday.'

I looked at him. In days I wouldn't need a TV or anything else. They went back to their conversation. I became invisible. "Lorna" was bitching about her daughter-in-law. And all the time the Hoover stayed silent.

At NYB the Toad God hadn't moved an inch but the seats in the restaurant were back in place. I scanned and cropped the photograph Cecelia McNeil had given me of Christopher and his father on the water, printed four copies, took a picture on my phone and forwarded it to Pat Logue. By now I assumed the tea-drinking competition was finished, Patrick was collecting his sons, and Mrs McCall was doing the work I was paying her to do.

Today was a big day: the last chance to locate Stephen McNeil.

Without the McNeil case to distract me I might've gone insane worrying about Fiona. I hadn't seen her in almost three weeks and hadn't told her about the warning. My final warning. If Rafferty made good on his threat all I could hope was that Patrick would keep Fiona safe.

Liam Logue was fourteen, shy, and already as tall as his father. His brother was smaller and over-weight. Patrick introduced them. 'Charlie, meet Batman and Robin.'

The boys shuffled and stared at their shoes.

'Sit down guys. Anything to drink?'

I passed the shot of Stephen McNeil and let them study it.

'This is who we're after. It isn't recent.'

I laid out the plan, gave them the colour, make and car registration and told them what to do.

'At the end of the game you have to be in position to pick him up. If you come across the car we'll use plan B. It'll be down to you not to lose him in the crowd. Any questions?'

Young Patrick spoke. 'How much're we on? Da says a tenner.'

I flashed a hard look at their father. Andrew said Pat Logue would kick his granny if the price was right. Not so far from the truth. 'We'll make it twenty, how's that?'

'Twenty-five,' Liam said. His genes were doing the talking.

'Twenty, that's your lot. Don't push your luck. Wait for us outside.'

Patrick pretended to be embarrassed but secretly he was pleased. In their universe if you didn't ask you didn't get. 'What do you make of them?' he said. 'Couple of yahoos, aren't they? Got their mother's heart roasted.'

'And that's your job, right Patrick?'

'Not anymore, Charlie, not anymore. Name's in the book. The appeal procedure's exhausted. One more offence and I'm sine died.'

'Then behave.'

'Easier said.'

'Seen the Big Issue guy on your travels?'

'Have not. Must be keepin' a low profile. I notice the wee man's still hoggin' the door though.'

He meant the Toad God.

'He stayin' then?'

Even if I understood, which I didn't, I couldn't be bothered to explain.

'Something Jackie's interested in.'

'A lucky charm.'

'That's the one.'

His mood altered. 'Look, this Rafferty thing, I could get some muscle. Have to pay them mind but I could get them if it's any help.'

He'd made the offer before.

'Thank you, Patrick, you're a good guy. It has to end, whatever way it ends, otherwise Fiona and I won't ever be free of it.'

'This is Jimmy Rafferty. On a contract. He'll do you in, Charlie.'

'I'm not being brave, either these people realise I have no part in it and leave us alone or they kill me. But it has to end. And it will.'

'In five days.'

'Four days. Five days was yesterday.'

'Christ,' he said. 'Jesus Christ Almighty.'

***

Nobody spoke in the car. Patrick tuned the radio to a football phone-in, fans asking the experts their opinion, letting off steam and giving their own view. Football wasn't my game. I didn't have a game; sport had never interested me. I knew enough to realise Celtic against Motherwell wasn't the match of the season. Nevertheless, in London Road the police were already refusing entry to the main car park. Patrick and his sons got out, I drove through the lights and took the second turning. I didn't notice the boys until I was locking the car; eight or nine years old, kicking a ball around, on the lookout for a mark.

'Hey, Mister,' the bigger one said, 'watch your car for you?'

He flicked the football out of his hands and caught it, his expression on the right side of friendly. Just. His pal had the look of a cherub, cheeks smeared with dirt and big brown eyes that stared up at me.

'Watch it? Why?'

'In case something happens. It's a nice car.'

They teach them young in Glasgow.

'How much?'

The smaller kid piped up. 'Fiver.'

'Two pounds, a quid each.'

'Three. Three quid and it's a deal.'

I wanted to slap his angel face.

'Okay.' I started to walk away.

'Where's the money?'

I turned, still walking. 'When I get back. Do a good job, I'll make it four.'

'We might have to go.'

'Then you'll miss out, won't you?'

Saturday afternoon extortion was the easiest cash they would ever come by. Ten years down the line, when their menace had been sharpened on somebody's unpaid debt, their mothers might be sitting on the bus next to Gail Logue, on the way to Barlinnie. For now, they had a decision to make. I was changing the rules.

I gave a thumbs-up. 'Do a good job, lads.'

On another day I would've given in and paid them to leave my car alone.

This wasn't my car.

Patrick and his sons were in a queue at a burger van. 'Want anythin', Charlie? This guy does great onions.'

The sky was overcast. It could rain anytime. We gathered in a circle for a final run-through the plan. 'Okay.' Patrick clapped his hands. 'Got the car reg? Got the photo? Know what our man looks like?'

They nodded and kept on eating.

'Put my number in your phones and call me if you come across the car.'

A beeping sound pulsed inside young Patrick's jerkin. He brought out his mobile.

'Should've charged it,' he said. 'Forgot.'

I glared at Patrick senior not pleased.

'Sure your boys are up to it? This is our last chance on this thing.'

'They're fine, Charlie. Honest. I spoke to both of them this mornin'.'

I didn't share his confidence. My watch said twenty past two. Forty minutes 'til kick-off. Liam and Patrick Logue were quiet. Whenever they spoke it was to their father. I was invisible again. A group of Motherwell fans passed close to where we were standing, chanting defiance, claret and amber scarves in the air, eyes blazing with intensity. The home fans ignored them; they had nothing to prove against the Motherwells of the world.

Pat Logue saw the boys off and shook my hand, a very un-Patrick thing to do.

'Here's hopin', Charlie,' he said and walked away.

At five minutes to three the place was mobbed. At five past it was deserted. The crowd cheered each name when the team was announced over the PA. Standing in the car park was like being beside a huge bee hive, the constant buzz broken by the Ohs and Ahs of thousands; an occasional roar, massive applause, and a return to the drone.

Liam and his brother would be roaming the streets looking for Stephen McNeil's car. We were due a break. I fingered the mobile in my hand. Nothing from Pat Logue. Did that mean he couldn't see McNeil, or did it mean he wasn't there? The temperature was fourteen or fifteen degrees yet my palms sweated. Suddenly getting a result was the most important thing – it had become a symbol.

Every couple of minutes I looked at the phone. At half-time Patrick called. Background noise made it difficult to hear but the part that mattered got through.

'No McNeil. I'll speak to the people around where he sits, see what they can tell me.'

I was more disappointed than I had a right to be. Thirty minutes later Pat Logue came towards me. 'Had to wait until they opened the gates. Never realised you can't just leave. He's not there, Charlie. Spoke to a guy who knew who I meant: said he hadn't seen him in weeks.'

'Well that's that.'

'Don't beat yourself up. Can't find him if he isn't here. We gave it our best shot.'

'Did we, Patrick?'

He shrugged. 'I'll call the boys, tell them to pack it in. About time you told the police about Rafferty. Joke's over. Keepin' it to yourself was fine when there was a chance of sortin' out the mess your pal dropped you and Fiona in. Now it's down to the wire. You need protection. You need help, Charlie.'

'What can I tell them? Some thug threatened me?'

'Start with the truth. Give them the whole story. Ian and Fiona, why Rafferty thinks you're in on it, the heavies following you. The flat. The car. The messages from Fiona. And the reason you didn't include them.'

'She's the reason.'

'I know. That's not enough anymore. You can't win because killing you means nothing to them. It's what they do, for Christ's sake.'

'I'll take it under advisement, Patrick. Will you be at the flat later?'

'Not sure. Got to get these two back to their mother, otherwise it'll be my fault.'

'What'll be your fault?'

'Everything. See you when I see you. Good luck.'

I rolled the car into the traffic, past stalls selling trainers with Nike on the side for a tenner and shops that only opened at the weekend. The flat was tidy. Mrs McCall – Lorna – had done some work after all. I emptied my pockets and lay down on the bed. I must have slept because when I opened my eyes it was dark. Something had woken me – Pat Logue, maybe. Or perhaps Rafferty's patience had run out?

It was neither. I had a message.

THINK THEYRE ON TO ME

WHAT HAVE U FOUND OUT

FI x

I went crazy. This whole mess was Ian Selkirk's doing. If he was standing in front of me I'd kill the stupid bastard myself. I replied.

STILL NOTHING

CALL THE POLICE AND GET AWAY NOW

Cx

Chapter 33

However much I resented beating the bushes for Cecelia McNeil's husband, the interviews, the phone calls and the neat little missives had kept me sane. Now that distraction was exhausted a river of failure and fear washed me away.

Three days left. Rafferty had won.

I hadn't heard Patrick come home – perhaps he was with one of his barmaid admirers. His business. I had the impression he was pulling back. Wishing me good luck; what was that all about?

Jackie didn't pull her punches when I arrived. 'You look the way I feel,' she said. 'Had breakfast?'

'Not hungry.'

She took my arm and sat me down. 'Scrambled eggs and toast. Tea not coffee. Got to take care of yourself; nobody else will.'

She brought the food herself. 'This is the most important meal of the day, did you know that?'

'Yeah, I'd heard.'

'So eat.'

I pushed the scramble around the plate, buttered a slice of bread and didn't touch it. The tea tasted weak and watery. I left most of it too. A poor attempt; she wasn't pleased with my efforts. 'Charlie, dear oh dear. When Fiona comes back I'll get blamed for letting you starve. Eat the toast at least.'

Lost in my own troubles it took a while to notice Jackie wasn't doing so well. I tried to be funny. 'How's the Toad God performing? Any miracles yet?'

'He's off to a bad start, Roberto's gone AWOL. Supposed to be on this morning. No show. He's not answering his phone. Surprised at him. Thought he was happy here. I'm understaffed as it is.' Her frustration went deeper than a barman. 'He has to know he's left us in the shit.'

'Maybe he's ill?'

She laughed. 'He look unwell to you? Guy's as fit as they come. Saw him in a gym once, when I was with Gary, pumping iron. Real weight. He isn't sick, he's quit.'

More often than not Andrew Geddes and I had lunch on Sunday. Today he took a seat at the bar and kept to himself. He nodded, opened a paper and buried himself in it. Strange. Everybody had their problems this morning. Jackie tried a cheerio smile that didn't get there. DS Geddes kept reading. Maybe the city fathers were putting something in the water.

I walked and walked. St Vincent Place, St Vincent Street, up the hill and over the motorway. Twenty-five minutes it took. I resisted looking back. If Rafferty's thugs were coming for me, let them come. Kelvingrove was the last place I expected to find myself. It seemed light years since I'd listened to the tour guide with Fiona Ramsay holding on to my arm. The dinosaur was there, so was the Dali painting, she was missing.

The flat was empty. I fell asleep in a chair and allowed a precious day to slip away.

My mother called around eight. We had a long chat about nothing very much. Most of her conversation was centred round my father. However I judged him, and knowing DI Platt's experience how could I do otherwise, he was her life. Archie was fine – more than could be said for Perry. According to her, beaten down by loneliness and rejection, Peregrine Sommerville had taken to drink.

'So finding Jesus was just an act?'

Eleanor Cameron had learned early it was unwise to admit to a definite opinion, even in conversation with her son. She said, 'I couldn't possibly comment. Arabella tells me he's been drinking heavily for a long time. Perhaps that accounts for the behaviour that put him wrong in the first place?'

'Is he getting help?'

I heard her sigh. 'Too late, I'm afraid. Liver's gone. Weeks rather than months.'

'Does father intend to see him?'

'He hasn't mentioned it. He's very sad about the whole thing. Poor Archie.'

I ended the conversation with my usual promises to call.

The resolve I'd enjoyed in the afternoon deserted me, I edged the curtain aside and peered into the night. A figure stood across from my building. I sensed rather than saw a familiarity, then the feeling passed. Platt's man or Rafferty's, I no longer cared.

Monday morning: two days to go.

An unnatural calm settled in me. My expectations of myself were based on the premise that I knew Ian Selkirk. That wasn't so. I'd known him, or thought I did, in the past. The long dead past, when we were young, crazy and naive, giving the world the finger, completely confident in the possibilities of tomorrow. But the body on the mortuary slab belonged to a stranger. What his motivations had been, what moved or inspired him, was beyond my knowledge. It had been foolish to assume some special insight into someone I hadn't seen in a dozen years. People change. I had. Ian Selkirk too. Only Fiona stayed the same.

The sun was shining, the first decent day in a month. Outside the Italian Centre the Big Issue seller was back in position. As he was the only witness to the car burning I had been anxious to speak to him. Today that wasn't important. For once he let me pass without the Burns rant: defeat carries; even those less fortunate can smell it. I gave him a coin and took the magazine.

Jackie was behind the bar pouring lattes and cappuccinos. I said, 'Roberto didn't show up then?'

She made a face. 'Serves me right for depending on a man.'

The barmaid at the El Cid would agree.

Patrick Logue was reading the Daily Record with his feet on the desk and turned when he heard me come in. 'Mornin', Charlie. Thought I'd stick around today. Run over the facts one last time.'

I sat across from him. The feet went where they belonged, on the floor.

'What facts? There aren't any facts. I've learned in five weeks about darts, football, and the gay scene in Glasgow. Unfortunately none of it's any damned use.'

He folded the newspaper and stuck it in his pocket.

'So we start again. What we don't do is lose hope.'

I shook my head. 'Sorry, Patrick, it's too late. I just want the nightmare to be over.'

He started to speak – I waved his words away. 'You don't understand. If I hadn't discovered Ian at the mortuary none of this would've happened. But I did and contacting Fiona drew her into something she had no part of. We were the only two at Daldowie. That's why Rafferty believes we're in on the theft. While there was a chance I might lead them to what they wanted they were content to follow me. Ian was a fool, out of his league from the beginning. The Raffertys and Rochas of the world don't give up. Ever.'

'Neither does Charlie Cameron.'

'You're not listening. The deal was to give them what they wanted and get these monsters out of our lives. Well, I haven't.'

'Still think you should tell Platt.'

'Platt's as obsessed as Jimmy Rafferty with me. Another one who credits me with knowing more than I do.'

'So what's the plan?'

I put my head in my hands. 'Christ, Patrick, how many times? There is no plan.'

'And the next couple of days? Will you just wait for them, or will you make it harder than that? See, I need to tell Gail where I'll be.'

'What're you talking about.'

He drummed his fingers on the table. 'Like glue, Charlie, I'm stickin' to you like glue.'

'No no. This is my trouble. You need to consider your family.'

'I am,' he said. 'Mrs Logue wants a positive role model for her sons. How about a man who stands by a friend? Is that positive or what?' He grinned. 'Accept it, I'm here and I'm stayin' here.'

Pat Logue was incorrigible, but it was working. I managed a fair attempt at the fry-up he ordered for both of us. He was the only person who knew how serious it had become.

Patrick lifted a glass of orange juice and saluted. 'First today. Time is it?'

'After eleven. Why?'

'Let's get out of the city for an hour or two.'

It made sense. Andrew Geddes was at a table by the door, a yard from the Toad God, enjoying his soggy bagel, killing time before his shift started. His eyes were heavy. I wasn't the only one who had difficulty sleeping. He offered me a weak smile and said hello to Pat.

I said, 'Andrew's warming to you, might escape his clutches yet.'

'I'm an acquired taste, so Gail says. I'll catch you up, want to talk to this bloke.'

He stepped away from me and chatted to the Big Issue seller. The poetry lover smiled. Gail's husband had a talent for leaving people better off than he found them. He hurried after me. 'Interestin' guy,' he said, 'was an English teacher. Got hooked on heroin. Been clean for years, just can't find his way back.'

'You think everybody's interesting.'

'Everybody is, Charlie.'

He rubbed his hands together. 'So where do we fancy? The coast? Largs? Knickerblocker Glory in Nardini's? Or the Trossachs? Beautiful countryside.'

'You decide. I'll point the car in the right direction.'

He considered where he wanted me to take us and said, 'Head for Balloch, not too far.'

He'd forgotten. I checked the mirror to see if we had company and drove towards Great Western Road.

'I made a poor show of checking for a boat. I only tried one.' I told him about old Alan Walker. 'It's a loose end. We'll follow it up. Properly. Like I should have done when I had the chance.'

The route was all too familiar. In Luss, Patrick made his way down Pier Road, out along the jetty to the water. He was quiet now, the boyish enthusiasm and the non-stop patter were left in Glasgow. He gazed across the loch, his hair ruffled by the breeze, a look in his eyes I hadn't seen.

I said, 'You brought us here on purpose, didn't you?'

The sun dipped behind a cloud, turning the loch black. 'Where was his body?'

I pointed to the narrow strip of beach and the rough fingers of wood poking from the loch. 'Cold,' he said. 'Dead cold.' He faced me. No jokes now. 'And that's what they did to your friend, Charlie. To your old friend, Ian.'

Old friends are the best friends

'Doesn't that make you angry? Don't you want to tear their fuckin' heads off? Ian Selkirk wasn't my pal. If he had been I'd never have given up on the bastards who did for him. Never.'

My face flushed. He said, 'There's a sayin', you'll have heard it. Don't get mad, get even. Well that's crap. Get mad. Get even. And get the cunts who murdered your mate. Now that's a philosophy I can go.'

He walked away. I watched him standing on the sand, skimming stones.

Of course he was right. I had been on the back foot from the very beginning, wishing Ian's death would go away so Fiona and I could live happy ever after.

There was one more day before Rafferty made his move. Twenty-four hours. If I was going down it wouldn't be without a fight.

Chapter 34

Tuesday, the last day: the time Jimmy Rafferty had given me was almost up.

And I was glad.

They were still watching the house: one of them had skulked the night away in Cleveden Drive. It didn't bother me now. Tomorrow things would change. Maybe they'd kill me, but it would be over. I was in surprisingly good spirits for a condemned man, I even caught myself humming a tune I'd heard somewhere.

Normally I avoided going into banks unless it was necessary. No one had authority to make a decision – that took a phone call, and a difficult conversation with someone in Rajasthan or Gujarat, reading from a script. This morning my request was simple: I wanted to withdraw more than the hole-in-the-wall limit. It wasn't a problem the smiling cashier told me. Good to know, considering it was my money. Out on the street two thugs fell in behind and made no attempt to disguise their presence. One of them spoke into a mobile. My visit had caused some excitement. Maybe they expected me to run down Sauchiehall Street with five million pounds.

When I got to NYB Pat Logue saw me and slid off his bar stool. I stopped him.

'Upstairs is as far as I'm going. Only one way in and out. No need to become Siamese twins. Read your paper and drink your juice, I'll be all right.'

He sat down. 'Like glue, Charlie. Know what I'm talkin'?'

Patrick's heart was in the right place but then I already knew that. His words on Luss pier had hit their mark. I had a reputation: finding missing people was what I did, had been doing for years. My instincts, normally needle-sharp, had been dulled by memories, resentments, guilt in Ian's case, and love for Fiona Ramsay. Cecelia McNeil never had a chance. My mind was always on Loch Lomond, or Thailand or Spain. Charlie Cameron, honest injun. My guarantee to give it my best was cheap talk. Christopher's mother had come well down the list.

I gave my order to Jackie. 'Coffee and two rolls and sausage, with mustard please. Send it up.'

'Feeling better?'

I didn't reply. Yesterday I was beaten. Not today. I stuck most of the cash from the bank in an envelope, scribbled a name on the front and put it in my pocket. The coat hanging behind the door caught my eye – I really should get rid of it. Getting mad. Getting even, and all the rest of it was set aside and I gave the food my undivided attention then telephoned Henry Hambley, of Hambley, Lawrence and Radcliffe, my lawyers, and asked if he could give me five minutes in the afternoon. Another box ticked. Now I was free to concentrate on the main event.

I started to write.

Telling myself the story as I knew it seemed to clarify the chain of events. Questions that hadn't occurred before jumped out at me. I made notes in the margin, spawning more notes. I'd been at it a couple of hours when I dug the list of Ian's effects from the in-tray. It was short, nothing significant there. The envelope from the Lomond Inn lay beside it; it had never been opened. I remembered the bill being more than I expected. In hotels and restaurants I always checked because mistakes were common. Another sign of how distracted I'd been.

The Inn hadn't over-charged: there were three items, everything in order; the room, Ian's bar charges, he'd been drinking heavily, and two telephone calls to the same number, a number I recognised, I had it stored in my mobile. It was Fiona's.

The calls to Spain were made in the days before they caught him. The woman at the Inn said she thought Ian was waiting for someone. Now I knew who.

My fingers brushed against the fax Andrew had gone the extra mile to get. I smoothed the crumpled sheets, smudged and distorted, almost unreadable. Almost, but not quite.

Emil Rocha stared from the page, defiant and sullen. Not the kind of face you would forget. Rocha was the same age as me. That was where the similarity ended. His eyes were empty and unforgiving. Now I added cold and old. His early record was remarkable for its brevity: the only convictions were as a teenager, stealing from tourists in coastal resorts. Emil Rocha had risen. The second page was a list of what might have been, littered with suspected of…believed to be involved in… thought to be behind, but lacking concrete proof. The Spaniard was immensely rich, and clever. He always had an alibi. Whoever had up-dated his file had a sense of humour; descriptions of him as a businessman dripped irony.

I was looking at Ian Selkirk's boss and Jimmy Rafferty's supplier.

Double crossing him was the worst idea my friend ever had. Rocha had the resources to keep searching forever if necessary. Robbing him meant looking over your shoulder for the rest of your life. Five million. Ten million. No amount of money was worth it.

It wasn't hidden. Far from it. It sat in the centre of the first line, and I would've seen it if my head hadn't been somewhere else.

Emil Rocha. Full name: Emil Sebastian Rocha.

Fiona had told me he was a building contractor, an important part of her operation. Possible. Rocha would use legitimate enterprises to launder cash and mask the true nature of his empire. I studied the black and white image of the man Ian had worked for, knowing I was seeing a killer.

Fiona talked about Sebastian, referred to him as her partner. What I was thinking horrified me. In my mind it had always been Ian and Fiona and Charlie. The gang of three. Old friends are the best friends and all that crap. But it hadn't been like that. I was the third wheel. A glorified hanger-on. At the time I couldn't understand why they allowed me into their club. They were the friends.

And she was the leader.

In Glasgow and in Thailand, Fiona Ramsay was the only one who could influence Ian; he mocked or ignored everyone else. My mistake – I'd made so many – was to believe her when she told me how uncontrollable he'd become. I saw what she wanted me to see, heard what she wanted me to hear. Now the truth was clear, not just about Spain, about how it had always really been.

Ian hadn't stolen Rocha's money. They had stolen it.

Twenty-four hours ago I had cut Patrick Logue off, certain there were no facts to review. Now I was drowning in them, choking on their bitterness.

I wanted to be sick. The stress of the last five weeks, the hopes the fears, the dreams and the nightmare were finally more than my body and mind could stand, and I broke. Facing what I had uncovered was one of the most painful experiences of my life. I was devastated. My hands gripped the chair so tight the skin stretched white against the bone beneath. It took minutes before anger arrived; when it did it was like a storm raging inside me.

Everything was a lie; the rekindling of our affair had been a sham, a matter of convenience; the hotel hopping was because she was afraid they were closing in. I was useful cover. Round about then it must've occurred to her just how useful I might be. In Skye it was Fiona who urged me to get involved, betting I'd find out what Ian had done with the money. Jimmy Rafferty didn't fill me with dope and throw me in the loch for the same reason; he could have killed me anytime, instead he gave me a chance to lead him to it. The bastards had been using me.

The guy in the car at Daldowie crematorium wasn't interested in Charlie Cameron – it was Fiona he was following. I happened to be the fool who went to the city mortuary on the wrong day.

That brought other realisations. If Ian and Fiona were on Rocha's payroll, what was her relationship with him? It hurt to think about it. And where was she?

The cute text:
NITE NITE
SLEEP TIGHT
DONT LET THE BED BUGS BITE
The reassuring message:
SAFE FOR NOW
And the last communication:
THINK THEYRE ON TO ME
WHAT HAVE U FOUND OUT
FI x

None of it was real. She was playing me, turning the screw, forcing me to try harder to get her what she wanted. Our conversations about our new life together were a smokescreen to lure me in. It hadn't been difficult. I'd been in love with the Moti Mahal Fiona, the Thailand girl. If she ever existed. My old friend hadn't been my friend at all. It was a heartbreaker.

Patrick knocked on the door and looked in. 'Just checkin' you're where you're supposed to be.'

I pulled myself together and put on a front. 'One way in and out.'

'What you doin'?'

'Knocking some ideas around.'

'Ideas are good, Charlie. I like when you have ideas. Tells me you're on the ball.'

'Not all good, Patrick. Be better off without some of them.'

He seemed satisfied. 'By the by, couldn't find anybody who hires boats. Not popular, the residents don't encourage it.'

I made a noise that meant I understood. Truth was I didn't care anymore. I needed a drink but all I had was an empty whisky bottle, the one Pat Logue made a hole in the day he offered to work with me. I buzzed the bar. 'Large gin and tonic, Jackie. Make it a triple, will you?'

Her surprise travelled down the line. 'Is this one of your jokes, Charlie? Sorry, I'm not in the mood.'

'Gin. Extra large. Please don't give me a hard time.'

She brought it herself. I wasn't known for drinking alcohol in the morning; something had to be wrong. She leaned her arms on the desk and stared into my face. 'Want to talk about it?'

Jackie meant well.

'No.'

'Is it Fiona?'

I took a mouthful of gin, it tasted strong and fresh.

'Has that bitch dumped you?'

Which part of no didn't she understand?

'I really can't discuss it, Jackie.'

She wasn't listening. 'I never liked her. There was something…'

'Jackie. I appreciate the support, it just isn't the time, so…' I gestured to the door, '…if you wouldn't mind.'

'Sure, Charlie. Whatever you want. You know where I am if you change your mind.'

When she'd gone I took out my mobile. I wanted to look Fiona in the eye and hear her tell me it was a mistake. My fingers trembled as I wrote.

NEED TO SEE U

TELL ME WHERE U ARE

But there was no mistake. I stared at the words until they blurred and pushed the rest of the gin away. I needed a clear head. This might be the moment to bring DI Platt into the picture; then again it was all supposition. Circumstantial. Hours before he died Ian Selkirk had called Fiona. So what? I was the only one who understood the dynamics of their relationship, and why I was sure he hadn't planned it himself. Ian was the front man, she was the brains, always had been. The Sebastian connection was a feeling in my gut rather than proof positive. Spain was teeming with guys called Sebastian, it needn't be Emil Rocha. Except I knew it was.

Back at the beginning I had ruled out running – that way it would never end – and although a future with Fiona Ramsay couldn't be, I still had a lot of living to do. She was out there, watching how it developed, believing I would solve the puzzle and deliver somebody else's money to her.

In her dreams.

She was with Rafferty and Rocha on the other side of the fence. I was on my own, just as I'd always been. That was fine by me.

At three I quit NYB and walked to West Regent Street and the office of Hambley, Lawrence and Radcliffe. As far as I could guess no one followed. Henry was waiting. I told him what I needed. He was an old dog, long in the tooth, a raised eyebrow was as close as he came to questioning me. My instructions were exact. In less than thirty minutes my new will, witnessed by him and one of the partners, was resting in his files.

Later in the flat I lifted the phone to order South Indian garlic chicken, rice and pakora then changed my mind and dialled a pizza place instead. On my way to bed I wondered if my shadow was still around. He was, the collar of his coat pulled up against the cold night air.

I was still important to somebody.

***

Kevin Rafferty said, 'He went to the bank then to his lawyer. And he sent the text. Coincidence? Get real, Sean.'

Sean shook his head. 'Cameron isn't part of it. Either he's on to us or he's on to her. Firing his car should've produced a reaction. His behaviour hasn't changed, he's been to gay bars and Celtic Park. Him and the other guy went back to Luss. They just stood on the pier and talked. He's as much in the dark as we are. We do nothing.'

Kevin rounded on his brother. 'Suddenly it speaks. Who put you in charge? And you're wrong as usual. He's involved. We've tried it your way, Sean.' He turned to his father. 'Cameron's seven days are up. Say the word, Jimmy.'

Jimmy Rafferty might not have heard. He stared out of the window at the manicured lawn running fifty yards to the wall surrounding the house, a far cry from the slum where he'd been dragged up on the edge of poverty by alcoholic parents. The situation they were in couldn't have happened when he was younger. Emil Rocha was a powerful ally. Better to have kept it that way. The patriarch couldn't remember which son had suggested the double cross – probably Kevin – Sean never offered much. It was a bad idea. A terrible idea. They already owned the east end. No need to take chances. On a better day he would've recognised the dangers outweighed the gains. Instead he'd listened and now it had gone wrong.

Poor judgement. Weakness. His. This Cameron character was the last card.

Sean had been impressed with the show Rocha had put on for their benefit. Jimmy saw beyond it. Despite his wealth, at heart Emil Rocha was a peasant, somebody Rafferty understood, a man cut from the same block. Both were patient. They could wait, and their anger never dimmed. Still there was something he couldn't put his finger on. If the circumstances were reversed how long would it be before he tired of waiting?

Jimmy knew the answer and it bothered him. The money, the woman; they should have heard from Rocha before now. So why hadn't they?

The old man's left arm shook. He threw the hated stick to the floor. Kevin asked again. 'Tell us what to do about Cameron.'

The patriarch dredged strength from some final reserve. He turned and faced his boys.

'Time's up,' he said. 'Lift the fucker.'

Chapter 35

I lay for a while with my eyes closed, listening to the sound of birds and the growl of a passing car with an exhaust problem. Sunlight flooded the room. It was strange to know that in a matter of hours I could be dead. As Patrick Logue might say, I'd got a good day for it.

Since the beginning of the week my pal had sat like a sentinel at the bar, nursing his juice, popping his head round the office door every so often to make sure nothing bad had happened to me. Touching. At first. Until it became annoying. His logic escaped me: at night when I was most vulnerable he was nowhere to be seen. He hadn't slept in the flat since Friday. I guessed he was taking comfort from the storms of married life in a less demanding port.

I showered. When I shaved my hand was steady. The face in the mirror surprised me by the calmness in the eyes. No butterflies in the belly, no sign my life might be about to end painfully.

Cecelia McNeil had faith. I had little spiritual strength to draw on. Yet something coursed through me. I'd reached my breaking point in the office when the truth was revealed. And now, now I was all right.

What could Rafferty do to me worse than Fiona had already done?

It was difficult not to invest every action with special meaning; when I caught myself musing on whether I'd ever boil the kettle again I laughed; an over-developed sense of the dramatic wasn't needed. I took the envelope from my pocket and put it on the table where Mrs McCall was sure to see it – the least I could do for someone who had worked for me for half a decade without ever being asked their first name.

Cleveden Drive was quiet. The promise of sun had been an empty one, clouds blanketed the sky and it was cold. Not such a good day for it after all. I tugged at my coat collar, started the car and pulled away, wondering if it was the last time…

Get a grip, Charlie.

The Big Issue guy was back on the corner – early for him – better dressed than usual, wearing a new coat. I stayed well clear; another tirade was more than I could handle. Perhaps he sensed it because he left me alone. Jackie was busy behind the bar doing Roberto's old job. I probably wouldn't be clogging-up the energy much longer. My sense of the ridiculous was headed towards the macabre. Nerves. Patrick was in his usual spot with newspaper and juice, a reformed man. Like glue he'd said and he'd meant it. He looked me up and down, checking I was still in one piece, and went back to reading the football gossip.

I sat in the office and considered what I was going to do. The cases had petered out: I was unemployed. I couldn't just wait for Rafferty to come. Patrick Logue's opinion was that Jimmy Rafferty wasn't a man I could reason with. But hell, what was there to lose? The easiest way was to tell one of his heavies I wanted to speak to his boss. I'd seen no sign of anyone following me, but they would be around. Downstairs Patrick wasn't on his barstool. He'd be against what I planned and would stop me if he could.

I spoke to Jackie. 'Where is he?'

'Gone to the toilet I think.'

All that orange juice.

In Scotland you can have four seasons in a morning; this was one of those days. Rain was falling, heavy enough to leave puddles. I turned towards Cochrane Street. The Big Issue seller saw me and screamed. He charged at me. I couldn't make out what he was saying. He was a frightening sight: hair matted against his cheeks, eyes wild, waving his arms and yelling.

He shot past into two men behind me. Rafferty's men. I hadn't seen them. The three of them went down. Across the street a black car mounted the kerb and screeched to a halt. The doors flew open. My jaw fell. The feeling of unreality, of not quite believing I was in danger, cracked like glass and fell away. Adrenaline kicked in and I ran.

The lights at the City Chambers were green; traffic was moving. I dodged between a bus and a car, stumbled and almost got hit by a Renault. The driver was a woman; there was a baby in the back seat. The horror on that lady's face was something I wouldn't forget; one second she was smiling, the next a man jumped in front of her and disappeared under her wheels. Momentum rolled me off the road on to the pavement. She wasn't so lucky. She braked, too late to save me if I'd been in the way. The crash of metal against metal told me she'd have some explaining to do. And her husband wouldn't believe she wasn't to blame.

I raced through George Square. The steady drizzle meant there were few people around; those who were paid no attention. I assumed Rafferty's thugs had recovered and weren't far behind. My heart hammered; my throat and lungs were beginning to burn; better for me if I had listened to Gary. Someone called my name. Surely they didn't expect me to stop? I kept going. Queen Street station offered alternative exits. Perhaps I could lose them in Buchanan Street. I'd never know because a better option arrived. The station concourse was busy. I burst through the doors and made a decision. Ahead of me a guard was closing the gate. Without thinking I vaulted the barrier, landed clean and sprinted for the last carriage. The door shut with me half in and half out, pressing against my shoulders before releasing me from its grip. I fell inside and heard it swoosh behind me.

I lay exhausted, shaking, close to passing out; gulping air into my tortured lungs, expecting Rafferty's men to arrive and drag me away. It didn't happen. Nothing happened. The train juddered to life and crawled out of Glasgow with me trembling on the cold floor.

I was safe. For the moment.

A voice, soft with concern, was the first thing I heard. The first thing I saw was a tartan scarf. 'Are you all right, son?' A man in his sixties peered at me through thick spectacles. 'Only just made it, eh?'

I gathered myself together.

'Was my wife that saw you. Says you burst on like this was the last train out of hell.' He smiled. 'Let me help you.' He took my arm and hauled me to my feet. 'Yeah,' he said, 'you're okay. Sit down. Get your breath back.'

I thanked him. 'Must be something awful important to put a rush on like that. A girl, I'm thinking.'

It was simpler to agree with him. 'I'm already late. Can't keep her waiting any longer.'

'Especially if she's a looker. Felt the same myself when I was your age. Slower now. But I still get there.' He winked and went back to his seat. His wife added her smile. I moved through the carriages until I was nearer the front. The train was half-full; people read or rested their arms on their backpacks or stared at the Campsie Hills; the tourist season was beginning. I didn't need to ask where we were going, I knew.

I had eluded Jimmy Rafferty's men, but for how long? The Glasgow/Edinburgh service ran every twenty minutes, they'd be on the next train. Rafferty would have connections in the east, by the time we drew into Waverley, they'd be in position.

Out of the frying pan.

With one advantage: they hadn't actually seen me; they would be working from a description. I could change my appearance and gain a little time. Once I was clear of the station losing myself in the crowds that haunted Scotland's capital wouldn't be difficult.

Falkirk High was the first stop. The train slowed. I considered getting off, but then I would be in the middle of nowhere, a sitting duck. Edinburgh gave me a hiding place until I figured out what to do.

I called Patrick. No service. None of the people coming on resembled Rafferty's thugs; that thought brought me comfort. We stopped a couple of times. As we approached Edinburgh Haymarket my fears returned. Haymarket was minutes from where our journey ended. I expected company and I wasn't disappointed.

Two solidly built men with the permanent frown of the not very bright scowled their way on to the last carriage. Their knuckles didn't drag on the ground but I'd bet their grandfathers' had. Starting in the middle and splitting their efforts would've made better sense considering how close we were to Waverley.

I approached the man who had spoken to me at the start.

'Excuse me, can I buy your scarf?'

He fingered it. 'What do you want with my old scarf?'

'Call it a peace offering.' My turn to wink.

His wife nudged him and gave young love her support. 'Go on, Alec. Give him it.'

He took it off and handed it to me. 'MacDonald,' he said. 'Alec MacDonald. You're not a Campbell by any chance?'

'Cameron.'

'That's okay. Wouldn't give it to a Campbell. Cameron's fine. Not related to the whisky people, are you?'

'Wish I had their money.'

'You'd only find more expensive ways to be unhappy. That scarf's a lucky scarf. Was wearing it the last time we beat England.'

'As old as that?'

Leave them laughing, Patrick said. I edged forward, through the carriages. On the way I ditched the coat and put on Alec MacDonald's scarf. It didn't make a big difference, it was the best I could do.

A voice announced: 'Waverley station! This service terminates here!'

I looked over my shoulder for Dumb and Dumber. A woman with a push-chair was right behind me. I helped her down the stairs and walked beside her. The sullen child looked up at me; a boy. I leaned in and talked gibberish to him until we were clear of the platform, then I was off again, dodging past strangers, no clue where I was going or what to do when I got there.

If I got there.

The coat was no loss; it was a much better day in the east than in Glasgow. I took the Waverley steps two at a time. Princes Street basked in the late morning sun. My eyes darted right and left, trying to discover who was interested in me. I remembered there was another exit from the station – the idiots from the train might come that way. The human traffic swallowed me. I hoped it would be enough. At North Bridge Street I checked again and saw no one suspicious. From there on I forced myself to walk. For a second I considered booking into the Carlton hotel and calling DI Platt. I resisted and tried Patrick's number again – it was engaged.

Cockburn Street rose in front of me, veering right, climbing towards High Street and the Royal Mile. Halfway up I looked down the cobbled road, searching for my pursuers. No one was after me. My reflection in a bookshop window took me by surprise. I was still wearing the scarf. The man on the train said it was lucky. I needed all the luck I could get. The scarf stayed. At the top I hid in a Starbucks, ordered a latte and stood by the window, watching. I didn't have to wait long. Somehow the heavies who boarded at Haymarket had guessed where I was going. It hardly seemed possible. They were big guys, over-weight. Cockburn Street was steep, too much for one of them. He bent over, hands on his knees, shoulders heaving, shaking his head when his pal urged him on. I stood away from the glass.

They headed down the Mile to John Knox's house and Holyrood Palace. That made my decision easy; Edinburgh Castle had over a million visitors a year. Today I would be one of them.

I was doing all right, but where did it end? If they missed me now there was always tomorrow. I picked up the pace. At Castlehill a woman crossed the street, facing away from me. Her hair was long; black curls cascaded down her print dress. She shrugged them away, it was Fiona. Everything I'd learned – the lies, the deceit – was forgotten. I called to her.

'Fiona! Fi..!'

The cry died in my throat. She turned. It wasn't her.

I was remembering another Fiona, the girl I'd fallen in love with. She didn't exist, she never had.

Pat Logue got it wrong. I should've gone to Rafferty at the start, told him how it was; explained. Patrick had been intimidated by the gangster's reputation, his fear had infected me. My failure to act had brought me to this, being chased through Edinburgh, hunted for something I knew nothing about.

After Castlehill, high on the plug of an extinct volcano, grey and magnificent, the castle towered to the sky. I saw people on the battlements, tiny figures, flashes of colour in a sea of stone. In the warm spring light, with a blue sky that went on forever, it was the most impressive thing. This wasn't the time to appreciate it, I had my own drama going on. I'd been here once, on a school trip; short trousers and larking about; sticking our heads into the mouth of the big gun. Not a care in the world, unlike today.

The Esplanade opened broad and flat with the castle at one end, the entrance at the other, and grandstands down both sides. People from all over the world came for the Tattoo every year in August. They'd fill those seats night after night. I crossed the bridge at the far end – wanting to run, willing myself to stroll – and joined the queue for tickets. The place was thick with tourists. I searched the faces for Rafferty's men. Talking to the gangster seemed a ridiculous notion now; he would have what he was after or he would kill me. It was that simple.

The queue moved quickly. In minutes I was at the ascent to the Lower Ward. Granite rose on either side, cold in the midday sun. I followed a couple of teenage lovers, whispering in French, unaware of anyone but each other. A battery of gun barrels poked like black fingers above me, if I kept going I'd be where they were. Hurrying would mark me as different from those studying guide books and maps. Hiding in plain sight was all the hope I had because I'd made a mistake, perhaps a fatal mistake. I'd chosen the higher ground thinking I'd be safe.

Far from it. The castle guaranteed crowds, that was its advantage, but it was a dead-end. Some instinct ordered me to look back at just that moment and I saw them at the gatehouse. Not the fools I'd lost in High Street. These two were new; their expressions and the way they carried themselves told me all I needed.

I was trapped, as much a prisoner as any who had enjoyed the hospitality of the dungeons. And there was no escape.

They hadn't spotted me, not yet. I couldn't stay here, sooner or later I'd have to leave, when I did they'd be waiting.

A lady with a red umbrella leading a party of about twenty walked by. The umbrella was open, a focal point so the group knew where she was. At the height of the season there would be more visitors and many more umbrellas. I tagged on; a few steps placed me near the centre. She pointed to a line of light artillery on her left.

'Here on the Middle Ward is the Argyle battery,' she said. 'The One O'Clock Gun stands alone. It is fired every day except Sunday. The original purpose was to give an accurate time check to ships in Leith harbour. Not necessary nowadays, but the tradition survives. At midnight every thirty first of December they use the gun to announce the start of a new year – the signal for a quarter of a million people to party on Princes Street.'

She glanced at her watch. 'We're early, we'll come back in time to see the district gunner do his stuff.'

An excited murmur passed through the group. Americans love history. The guide smiled, an old hand who knew how to tease the most from the tour. The party turned left. She told us we'd arrived at the Upper Ward and went into another spiel. Her voice droned on. I switched off.

Thirty yards down the hill a guy with a scar from ear to chin was coming towards me. It was Kevin Rafferty. He looked straight at me and away. I'll never know why he didn't see me. I'd been about to abandon the cover the tourist group gave; that changed my mind. I followed them into the chapel, squeezing my way to the front. The chapel was small; it was a crush. That suited. The more bodies between me and them the better, except now I really was trapped. The guide was in full flow. I didn't hear a word she said. My heart was a banging drum. Cold sweat dried on the back of my neck. My mobile rang – it startled me. The tourists glared, I was spoiling the moment. It was Patrick Logue.

'Where are you?'

'Edinburgh.'

'I know that, where in Edinburgh?'

'The Castle.'

'Stay with it, Charlie. We're comin'.'

'For Christ's sake make it quick.'

The party filed out of St Margaret's. I was last to leave. If they were there it was over, Rafferty would have me. Even if I could give him what he wanted, death would follow.

The sunshine hurt my eyes. Our guide gestured to a curved line of guns. I heard the words Half Moon battery. She started back the way we'd come with the Americans trailing her red umbrella. The decision wasn't mine any longer, the group couldn't protect me now. I quickened my pace, not certain whether my enemy was ahead or behind, and moved to the parapet next to Crown Square. Far below in the Grassmarket, people and traffic went about their business.

When I looked back scarface was watching, his ruined skin stretched white along the slash. I darted to my right. Laughter, raw and rasping, from deep in his throat followed me. His gaze went beyond me to his partner, inviting him to share in the joke. I'd had the whole of Edinburgh to choose from. If only I'd gone another way, doubled back, or jumped in a taxi.

Crown Square was all that remained. There was nowhere else.

The Square was the centrepiece of the castle and the only real memory I had of that wasted school trip. The crown jewels were kept here, and the Stone of Destiny; one of my countless disagreements with my father had been over where the Stone should rest. Patriotism meant nothing now. The Square was busier than any other area I'd been in. Apart from two narrow passages between the buildings there was no way out. Easy meat.

I edged into the centre space. They didn't rush, why would they? Kevin Rafferty strolled into the Square, enjoying himself. His mate covered the only other exit. Tour guides rattled out facts about the precious Honours of the Kingdom, Mary Queen of Scots and the controversial Stone. Rafferty flexed his fingers, bared uneven teeth and came towards me.

He shook his head, feigning regret. I tensed, expecting them to attack. Kevin was having too much fun for it to be over just yet. Another tour group led by a yellow umbrella gathered in the space between us. Nobody noticed the drama. Rafferty toyed with me.

'Gave you plenty of chances, Charlie, plenty of chances, can't say we didn't. My father was sure you knew what that thieving bastard did with the money. I'd have brought you in for a chat a month ago. Sean said no. Jimmy said…'

A tremendous boom interrupted his soliloquy. Everybody ducked their heads, caught off balance. It was one o'clock, the ships in Leith harbour were getting their time check; the break I needed, I crashed through the tourists, through the gap at the corner and raced down the slope. Ahead, a troop of soldiers going towards the Esplanade marched with flawless precision, their buttons glinting in the sun; cameras and camcorders captured the show. I walked in-step beside them past the gatehouse out to the grandstands.

For a moment I actually believed I'd got away. I ran.

Right into Jimmy Rafferty.

He was standing in front of me leaning on a walking stick, older than in the picture on the steps of the High Court – I guessed in his seventies; his hair was white and had thinned. In spite of the sunshine he wore a long black winter coat.

And he wasn't alone.

Two men were at his side; neither acknowledged me although only days before, one of them had been charming the ladies and arguing for Fair Trade coffee growers in NYB. He was part of it. His eyes were cold, colder even than Jimmy Rafferty, and there was a resemblance to somebody I couldn't place.

Since Ash Wednesday my life had been turned upside down. Like living a bad dream. Surreal. Now, seeing him here, it went beyond that. It was crazy. Insane. Nothing was as it seemed; a mystery I was never going to solve.

Kevin Rafferty came up behind me. 'Have to admit he's got balls, Jimmy. Got to give him that.'

'Balls are ten a penny, Kevin. Who'd know that better than you?'

He spoke to me. 'You're a big disappointment, Charlie. I really thought you could pull it off. The reports said you were smart. Got a lot of respect for smart people. Your father for instance, he's an old bastard but he's a smart old bastard. Can't imagine he rates you. Thought you were having us at it at first. Realised you didn't have a Scooby. Kevin was keen to meet you; he's a boy people tell their secrets to. I said no. Give Charlie the full measure. Give Charlie a chance. If he knows where the money is he'll lead us to it, if not he'll find it for us. Respect see. Intelligence deserves respect.'

They watched me the way a boy watches a bee in a jar, curious, without pity. To my left the city of Edinburgh rolled away as far as Cramond Shore and the Firth of Forth, and in the distance the bridges spanning the water to the Kingdom of Fife shimmered in the haze. An epic view, one to remember for the rest of your life. Not very long in my case.

I looked for security. No sign. If I had parked in somebody's space they'd be all over me. Jimmy Rafferty said, 'Saw you were making heavy weather of it. Gave you a wee incentive. Show him, Sean.'

Kevin's brother put his hand in his pocket, took out a mobile and stabbed at it. My phone burst to life with the cheery jingle Fiona had put on it before she went to Spain. 'Take it, Charlie, he said. 'Might be important.'

I read the message. Rafferty spoke to his sons as if I wasn't there. 'Mr Cameron finally gets it.'

Two words on the screen.

GUESS WHO?

Kevin Rafferty smiled; this was too easy.

He said, 'Good try, Charlie. It was fun, for a while, wasn't it? Playing the detective, thinking you were a step ahead.'

He slapped my face because he could.

'You've caused a lot of trouble, mate. Now we'll do what we should've done at the start. Selkirk was a clown. The woman was the clever one. Whole fucking thing was her idea.'

His face was inches from mine. I smelled cheap wine. Over his shoulder Scotland's capital city sparkled. 'Nothing like doing a clever woman, is there?'

I snapped and butted him with all the force I had. He was so confident I caught him off-guard. Blood exploded from his nose. He was going down when I hit him again; the second blow knocked him backwards. His head cracked against the ground.

A party of Japanese were yammering away, cameras clicking, oblivious. Jimmy Rafferty pulled a gun from his pocket. 'You fuckin' bastard! You bastard! Kevin wanted to sort you out early doors. I wouldn't let him. She said Selkirk told you. The last thing she said. Why I let you be.'

He spat and aimed the gun at me. His hand trembled. 'Never trust a woman, eh, Charlie?'

That was when Roberto shot him in the temple.

A silencer muffled the sound but not the horror. Two more bullets shared between them made certain the Raffertys would never get up. And I remembered where I'd seen those eyes: on a crumpled fax in my office. Emil Rocha's cold stare. Sebastian.

Sean Rafferty came forward, he'd played no part. His father and brother were dead yet he seemed calm. Roberto spoke to him. 'My uncle is a forgiving man. It wouldn't be wise to disappoint him again.'

'I won't.'

Sean looked down at Jimmy. '"Those who know don't speak." Got that from you.'

To Roberto he said, 'Tell Emil the east end is under new management, thanks to him.'

He turned and faded into the crowd.

Roberto paused, unhurried. 'You were unlucky, Charlie. Got caught up in something that wasn't your concern. Rafferty's job was to find the thief and the woman. Sebastian's woman. He had other ideas. Selkirk would've told us everything if the idiots hadn't killed him too soon. By the time I arrived in Scotland she had vanished and you were involved.'

'Jimmy told us he didn't know where they were. He lied. Kevin killed her, just like Selkirk. That wasn't what Sebastian hired them to do. For weeks they've been denying it, hoping you would take them to the money.'

'Why come to NYB?'

'In case she came back. The Raffertys had lost, Sean realised that and offered a new arrangement. He owns Glasgow now.'

'And Sebastian owns him. That's what this has all been about?'

'For Sebastian, yes. She was his. The money was nothing, except to that piece of crap on the ground.'

'But she deceived him. She deceived me.'

'She was still his woman. How she should be punished was for my uncle to decide. Say goodbye to Jackie for me. And go somewhere else for your holidays, Spain's out. Understand?'

Tyres screeched. Car doors slammed. Uniformed police were running towards me. Andrew Geddes got there first, Pat Logue behind him.

There was no sign of Roberto.

Detective Inspector Platt bent over Jimmy Rafferty, feeling for a pulse he wouldn't find. I said, 'Cut it a bit fine, didn't you?'

Andrew placed a hand on my shoulder. 'Knew you had it under control, Charlie. Is it over?'

'It's over.'

'So now I can get some sleep instead of freezing my balls off in Cleveden Drive.'

'That was you?'

'Patrick told me they'd given you one more week. We took it in turns to be your guardian angel. I drew the short straw. Night shift.'

'You sneaked by me at NYB,' Pat Logue said. 'Chased you across George Square with Rafferty's goons. I shouted to you. You didn't hear me.'

'I heard, I assumed it was them.'

'Andrew got a hold of DI Platt. We had no idea if you'd get off somewhere. As a place to hide Edinburgh was a better bet. We caught the next train, twenty minutes after you. Quickest way. The others took the motorway, made good time as well. Andrew phoned ahead. They missed you at Waverley.'

Patrick tapped the tartan scarf. 'Easy to see why. You're a master of disguise, Charlie.'

Platt didn't ask after my health. He said, 'Jimmy and Kevin Rafferty are dead. Who killed them?' I let his question go unanswered. 'I'm taking you to the station. Looking forward to hearing your version.'

Andrew stepped in. 'He'll travel with me, Detective Inspector. Charlie's the victim here, let's remember that. He isn't suspected of any crime, or is there something I'm missing?'

Policemen were already cordoning-off the scene. At the gatehouse two interview points had been set up, everyone leaving had to give their name, address and proof of identity. Some unlucky coppers had their work cut out. All for nothing: Emil Rocha's nephew had already walked right past them.

The drive from Edinburgh to Glasgow seemed to last for days. From the front seat Andrew leaned over and spoke to me. 'Platt's agreed to interview you when you've recovered, and I want you to listen this time. Don't fuck him about. He hasn't got the result he wanted. He still isn't happy. And he doesn't like you, Charlie.'

Patrick said, 'Good guys two, bad guys nil. What more does he want?'

'He has three bodies, Ian Selkirk and the Raffertys, but the drug money is still out there.'

'Four. Fiona's dead.'

'Sorry, Charlie.'

Andrew carried on. 'What happened wasn't down to Platt. Not much Nigel can take credit for. It was Charlie who brought it into the open. Just watch yourself, that's all.'

At Newhouse a sign said GLASGOW 12 MILES. The city filled the horizon. The sun had made it through; it was a fine afternoon. I closed my eyes. When I opened them I was home. They let me go without a word and drove away. There was nothing to say.

Chapter 36

I ran the shower as hot as I could stand it and stayed under for twenty minutes.

To Jimmy Rafferty, it had all been about money. Sean Rafferty was the exception; he saw an opportunity to take over. DI Platt needed to find it to salvage his career, and I guessed Ian needed it because Fiona said so.

As for Fiona? She just wanted it.

It changed everything for all of them. That's what money does.

Like my father with Perry Sommerville I had learned that old friends or new friends, people were just people. And some of them lied.

I unplugged the phone and turned off my mobile. The world would have to wait. It would be there when I was ready. I went to bed, pulled the clothes over my head and slept. The car with the dodgy exhaust woke me. I went to the lavatory, then to the fridge, poured a glass of milk and back to bed. That routine or something like it survived for three days. As for Patrick, I had a feeling he didn't live here anymore. On the fourth day I threw on a t-shirt and jeans and lay on the sofa. I didn't play music or read, I just lay there. No thoughts, no emotions; I was numb. When night came I welcomed the darkness.

And so it went on.

One morning I was startled by a hammering on the door. For a moment I imagined the Raffertys had come for me, then the memory of Edinburgh Castle flooded in. I wouldn't have answered except whoever it was kept on.

A woman shouted through the letterbox. 'Charlie! Charlie!' It was Jackie.

I opened the door a fraction. 'What do you want?'

She didn't hesitate. 'You,' she said. 'Let me in.'

The first thing she did was hug me, tight, for a long time. After that she opened the windows and camped in the kitchen. I heard the splash and sizzle of bacon and eggs. She set it in front of me. 'Eat it,' she said. 'Eat it all. Then get dressed, we're going.'

'Going where, Jackie?'

'To the land of the living, Charlie.'

Jackie asked no questions on the drive, knowing I'd tell her when it felt right. I said, 'What day is it, I've lost track?'

'Monday. Missed a stonking weekend. A hundred and five covers Friday and Saturday. Seventy odd last night, and downstairs was rammed.'

To please her I pretended to be interested. 'Good.'

'Alex says if he stuck a tenner to it he could pay the VAT.'

She dropped me on Cochrane Street. 'Mail's on your desk,' she said. 'See you soon.'

The Big Issue guy wasn't around. I wanted to thank him. NYB was mid-morning empty; a new barman had taken Roberto's place; I hoped his uncle was a carpet fitter in Paisley. The mail was where Jackie said, Cecelia McNeil's latest epistle on top. After what I'd been through it seemed like the most natural thing in the world, I took a strange kind of comfort from it.

Dear Mr Cameron,

I've had some good fortune. I've sold the house. The buyer is anxious to take possession quickly so I'll be moving out in a matter of weeks. I still haven't received an invoice. I can't go without paying you. It wouldn't be right. Please let me know the amount. And have a happy Easter.

Yours, Cecelia McNeil.

They say there's always somebody worse off than yourself. Mrs McNeil had lost a son and a husband yet she was starting again, putting her unhappiness aside. It was an example I could learn from.

The jungle drums were working overtime. Andrew stuck his head round the door.

'Glad you're here Charlie. Talk later. Give Platt a ring and finish it. Our Nigel's moving on. He can't hurt you now.'

I did as he asked. DI Platt wasn't there. I left a message. Patrick Logue was next. A flying visit, same as Andrew. He held his well known curiosity in check. I noticed he'd had a haircut. 'All right, mate?'

I pointed to his head.

'Yeah,' he said, 'if they catch the guy who did it he'll get sixty days. Got an interview on Wednesday. First impressions and all that.'

'What's the job?'

'Security.'

'Where?'

'House of Fraser.'

I wanted to laugh. 'Cutting out the middle man?'

'Just coincidence. Steppin' into the mainstream. Gail wants us to buy a house. That takes a steady pay.'

'Gail? Thought it was over with you?'

'Not quite. We're in the middle of full and frank discussions.'

'Does she want you back?'

'She's thinkin' about it.'

He left without asking anything about Edinburgh. Patrick was changing.

Detective Inspector Platt was the final visitor of the day. Jackie buzzed and told me he was on his way up. His recent success hadn't improved his disposition; his heart wasn't in it. He was almost civil, and most of what I told him he already knew. Towards the end his bitterness bubbled to the surface.

'You won't have me on your back much longer, I'm leaving Scotland.'

'Going where?'

'Haven't decided. Back down south.'

'But you brought Jimmy Rafferty down.'

'Did I? A couple of dead gangsters don't get many brownie points these days. What I managed were four murders. Your old chums and the Raffertys, a hit man running around the capital, and five million pounds of drug money unaccounted for.'

He was a difficult person to feel sorry for yet I did. I said, 'You were wrong about me. My connection with Ian Selkirk was ancient history.'

He scorned my innocence. 'I despise people like you. Your life is based on who you know, and how you can use that knowledge.'

'You're confusing me with my father.'

'Am I? If Selkirk had told you where the money was, what would you have done? Turned it over to the police? I doubt it.'

He was right to doubt it. Turned it over? Yes. To Jimmy Rafferty.

'You couldn't have resisted. You'd have disappeared with your girlfriend. Oh I forgot, she wasn't your girlfriend, was she? Need to be more choosy next time, Charlie.'

Detective Inspector Platt was a nasty bastard. And a sore winner. He stood. 'I may have to speak to you again, so…'

'Don't leave town?'

His jaw line twitched, the rodent eyes narrowed. 'Something like that.'

Later that night I tried the TV. Great picture, surround sound, a marvel of technology. Pity I couldn't find anything worth watching.

On Tuesday I followed Pat's example and got my hair cut, went to the supermarket and paid a few bills. Whenever Fiona Ramsay came into my head I fought the thoughts away; nothing good lay down that road. My mother phoned with news. Perry was dead, and yes, it was for the best, and no, my father hadn't gone to visit him. I kept my opinion to myself. More importantly, she was feeling better and that was all that mattered.

Patrick Logue was on a high on Wednesday afternoon – he hadn't got the job.

'Over qualified. That's what they said.'

'How's Gail taking it?'

'Gutted. She'll get over it once it sinks in her husband is over qualified.'

He rolled his shoulders. 'I'm happy the way things are. I do okay.' He put his hand in his pocket. 'What're you up to on Sunday?'

'Easter Sunday. No plans. You?'

He drew out a green and white ticket. 'Old Firm are playin' at Celtic Park. Scottish Cup quarter final. Biggest game of the season. Fancy giving it one last go?'

***

At first I didn't understand what he was saying. Patrick was Mr Fix-it.

Celtic and Rangers. One ticket. 'Stephen McNeil will be there. If not, he isn't in the country. Last chance. Time we got the break of the ball.'

'How did you manage it?'

He tapped the side of his nose. 'A magician never reveals his tricks.'

'Full house, we'll need another man.'

'Got just the guy, could use the money too.'

'Who ?'

He smiled a sly smile. 'Wait and see, Charlie. Don't want to spoil the surprise.'

I toyed with the idea of calling Cecelia McNeil and telling her. In the end I didn't.

We met at ten at NYB. Kick-off was twelve-thirty. Pat Logue was on time and he looked fresh for a Sunday. I reckoned he hadn't been drinking the night before. Sometime during the week he'd taken his clothes out of the flat, and though he hadn't said, it was obvious he didn't need bed and board any longer. Liam and young Patrick talked to each other and their father. I was still the invisible man. At ten to eleven I said, 'Where's your guy, Patrick. Have to go without him in another five minutes.'

He peered through the window. 'He'll be here. Stand on me. Solid gold. Know what I'm talkin'?'

Pat the Lad again. Negotiations with his wife must be going well. 'That's him,' he said. 'Let's head.'

Outside I didn't see anybody except the Big Issue seller. 'Where?'

'There. Tom. You'll like him, he's all right. Don't mention the Burns thing, he's embarrassed about it.'

My first reaction was dismay, then I remembered him charging Jimmy Rafferty's heavies, giving me the advantage I needed. Tom was wearing his nice coat. It dawned on me why I liked it so much; it was mine, the one that had hung behind the office door, clogging up the energy. I thanked him for helping me.

Patrick chimed in. 'He knows the score, Charlie. Had to buy him a phone. Doesn't have one. It's on the bill along with the ticket. Arm and a leg, by the way.'

'Fine, fine.'

We drove down High Street and left towards Glasgow Cross. Along London Road police were everywhere. Patrick, Tom and the boys jumped out, I drove on, retracing the route I'd taken when Motherwell were the visitors. The best clue to finding where Stephen McNeil lived was the credit card he'd used in Shettleston. People use the shops closest to their home. If that was true, McNeil was in the east. At a match as big as this a vehicle was a liability; close to the ground on foot was better. When the Old Firm played at Celtic Park the east end became the Rangers end. He'd come this way.

If he was here.

I went through the lights into the housing scheme and parked. Three small boys ran to me – the biggest one handled the deal. 'Watch your car, Mister?'

'Watch it? What for?'

'Case something happens to it.'

'Something already did.'

'It can get worse.'

'Yeah, like what?

'Spontaneous combustion?'

This young man had a future. I said, 'How much?'

'Fiver.'

I didn't quibble and gave them a medium photograph of the queen. They took it and ran.

Celtic against Rangers claimed to be the oldest club football match in the world and football was the least of it. This was a meeting of enemies. In too many minds the game represented division; religious and historical enmity. A clash of beliefs. Ninety minutes of organised antagonism that often ended in violence.

I made my way through fans in red, white and blue, singing their songs, men shoulder to shoulder with their sons. I wasn't a football supporter but even so I felt the tension, the sense of approaching battle and the atmosphere. Dangerous and dark. Jackie would call it energy. I had another word. I was witnessing a ritual, an initiation ceremony, the baptism of the next generation into the faith of the fathers.

The young were being taught to hate.

I didn't get it. I wouldn't bring any boy of mine within a mile of it.

Patrick and the others were eating burgers outside the main stand. Green and white were the colours now. We huddled in a circle. I was next to Tom. It was hard not to think of him as the Big Issue guy. Out of the blue he apologised. 'Sorry,' he said. 'About Burns, I mean.'

'What was that about?'

'That accent. Then you ignored me, I took offence. Thought you were just another superior Tory bastard judging me.'

'Got me confused with my father.'

'So Patrick tells me. Sorry, Charlie.'

'Why Robert Burns?'

'Equality. He was a socialist, so am I. Anyway, I was wrong.'

Mystery solved.

People hurried to join the queues, their eyes on fire with anticipation and anxiety; men old enough to know better, gangs of boys, well dressed business types, even priests. So much for the spirit of the Saviour risen.

Four girls in Celtic tops giggled by. Ginger hair and freckles, surrounded on all sides by testosterone. Out of date pop music drifted from the stadium over the stalls in the car park selling shirts and posters. Programme sellers shouted a linguistic shorthand I didn't understand. Touts with tickets asked for silly money. When the kick-off came the gold dust in their hands would fade to worthless scraps of paper.

Some fans were drunk. Carlsberg for breakfast, Buckfast wine for lunch.

The Glasgow police excelled on occasions like this, but then they'd had plenty of practice; this was no ordinary meeting; trouble was always expected and rarely disappointed.

Celtic Park was a cauldron, electrifying, like the last moments before the Stones blasted into Brown Sugar and took the audience to another place. Was there really any chance of finding Stephen McNeil in this crazy circus, or was it a sad attempt to succeed for Cecelia McNeil and salvage something of myself? I'd have the answer soon.

Patrick organised his sons. 'Remember, this is Celtic and Rangers. Sixty thousand rabid fans. Don't noise anybody up. If you get separated, no heroics. I've promised your mother you'll be fine.'

The boys would trawl for Stephen McNeil's car and be in position when the game ended. Tom would stay outside the exit and follow McNeil. Pat Logue was point-man, seated in the same section; he'd let us know if our target was here. I would float.

Pat said, 'Here's hopin', Charlie.'

'Here's hoping. And thanks, Patrick.'

'No sweat. Wait 'til you see how much I paid for the ticket. Might not be thankin' me then.'

Jackie Mallon and Pat Logue between them had brought me back, otherwise I would still be staring at the walls in Cleveden Drive.

I was involved again, exactly what I needed. Edinburgh Castle and Jimmy Rafferty were in the past. Eventually even Fiona Ramsay wouldn't hurt so much. I hadn't thought about her. Not once. My mind was focussed on the task. For today at least I was alive.

The text arrived before the game even started. From Patrick.

HES HERE

The second message came at the break.

ON HIS OWN

When Celtic scored I could've sworn the ground shook under my feet. Then the singing really got going. I pictured Pat Logue in the middle of it, completely at home, one eye on Stephen McNeil, the other on the pitch. At two ten a third text told me we'd finally got that little bit of luck Andrew Geddes spoke about. The mobile buzzed. I read the word and felt my chest tighten.

LEAVING

I was outside the main stand, a few fans keen to miss the mayhem at the finish were already there. Stephen McNeil walked right past me with Patrick and Tom behind. I couldn't miss him. He hadn't aged much from the photograph of him and Christopher. I studied the man who had broken Cecelia McNeil's heart a second time, wondering what kind of human being could leave his wife to bury their boy alone. He wore a t-shirt, faded blue jeans, and a green and white scarf round his neck. He seemed ordinary. But no ordinary person could have done what he had done. The crowd roared. He quickened his pace; the scarf came off and was stuffed in his pocket. Stephen McNeil started to run. He was five yards ahead of Patrick when the wave broke over us.

One minute we had him, the next he disappeared.

A torrent of bodies washed through the gates, mad glee on their faces. Excited fans collided with each other, pushing and shoving. A youth fell full length. In seconds he would be trampled. His friend pulled him to his feet. He got up, laughed, and ran on. It was impossible to choose a direction; the volume of people carried us like a tide further and further from Stephen McNeil. A guy, head shaved, wearing a gold earring, barged into Patrick almost knocking him down. It was bedlam, much worse than I imagined. The mobiles were useless. My plan had been a pipedream.

We were lifted and thrown together. Patrick shouted 'Where is he? Where's McNeil?'

My reply was swallowed by the noise. He stabbed an arm in the air. 'There! There, Charlie!'

I saw him. Then he was gone.

The human avalanche subsided as quickly as it began. The crush had taken us across the car park to the Rangers end. We'd been only an arm's length apart, but at the height of the exodus it may as well have been miles. I was exhausted. Pat Logue wheezed like an old man.

'Can't believe it,' he said. 'We had him. He was there.'

Failure was becoming my default position. We stood to the side in the aftermath, shaken, deflated and out of ideas. My phone buzzed.

SPRINGFIELD ROAD

HURRY

It was from Tom.

He was standing on the corner on the other side of the street. When we got to him he pointed. 'Alhambra bar. Just ordered a pint.'

We waited outside a fish and chip shop for McNeil to reappear. Rangers fans anxious to put distance between themselves and the defeat ran on by. He wasn't long. The boys hadn't found his car because Stephen McNeil was on foot. He crossed at a set of traffic lights. A mile further on he turned off Shettleston Road, not far from the Tesco where he'd used his credit card. We kept our distance, from him and each other. It was still possible to suss we were there and change his plans. He didn't.

I was nearest when he ducked into a tenement building. I raced to stay with him. The close smelled of cigarette smoke and cat piss. I crept up the wide stone stairs in time to see a door on the first floor shut. Patrick and the Big Issue guy, I'd never get used to calling him Tom, were at my shoulder. Pat Logue said it for me.

'219C. We've found him, Charlie. We've fuckin' found him.'

Chapter 37

Cecelia McNeil was wearing a blue overall and yellow plastic gloves. Her hair was tied back, two clasps held it in place. The look was severe but that wasn't what struck me. She had aged. Deep lines ran from the edges of her mouth and her eyelids were hooded. An aura of defeat covered her like a cloak. 'Mr Cameron.' She was surprised to see me. 'I wasn't expecting you. It's a holiday.'

Easter Monday was a family holiday. This lady had no family. 'Can I come in, I have some news?'

In the living room boxes sat on top of each other, a few already sealed with thick brown tape, others only half filled. Most of the furniture had been removed and the wallpaper seemed more faded than I remembered. 'I'm almost ready,' she said. 'Another day or two should do it. How rude of me. Do you want tea? Can't offer you much, I'm afraid, I'm running everything down.'

'I'm fine.'

'What's the news? Has Stephen gone south?'

'No, Mrs McNeil, we've found him.'

I thought she was going to fall; she staggered and grabbed the sofa. I caught her arm and helped her sit. 'Would you like a glass of water?'

'No. No. It's shock, that's all.'

Her body shook and the dam broke. She covered her face with her hands. Tears trickled through her slender fingers. She made no sound. I held her hand until it stopped. She pulled a handkerchief from her sleeve and blew her nose.

'I'm so sorry, Mr Cameron. That wasn't what I expected after all this time.'

It had been forty seven days. She looked like someone wakened from a dream trying to work out where they were. The chaos in the room puzzled her.

I went to the kitchen and brought her water. 'You're a kind man, Mr Cameron. That first day in your office I knew, I knew you'd find him. And you have.'

I told her the street and the number. She didn't write it down or ask questions.

'I still haven't had your bill. Tell me how much it is and I'll pay you now.'

'That isn't necessary. Really it isn't.'

'No, I insist. The labourer is worthy of his hire.'

I could argue. 'I'll figure it out and send you an invoice. The important thing is you can talk to Stephen. Persuade him Christopher's death wasn't his fault.'

She brightened. 'Yes. Yes, you're right. I'll have to alter my plans.'

I left her at the door happier than I'd seen her. It dawned on me I had a lot to do with it. From here on it was between her and her husband.

NYB was jumping. The forecourt of the Italian Centre was a suntrap. Under the Martini umbrellas people drank coffee and chatted. It might have been Paris or Rome except it was Glasgow on a sunny day. Fine by me.

Jackie was in her element, she stuck an elbow in my ribs and nodded at the entrance.

'Red Door. Toad God. "Oh ye of little faith", Charlie.'

It was hard to disagree. 'Mr Strang left a couple of books. Put one on your desk in case you need any more convincing.'

Patrick wasn't around. It wouldn't be a surprise if Gail had him up a ladder painting the kitchen ceiling. I settled down to read about Feng Shui, the ancient art of Chinese blah, blah, blah...'

Tuesday came and went. Mrs McCall was especially nice to me since her windfall and Tom didn't hound me when I passed. I made sure I always had coins; I liked it better this way. A memorial service for Peregrine Sommerville was being held next month. The great and the good would be there. My father was head of the organising committee and, as Perry's oldest friend, he would give a eulogy. My parents lived in a strange world. I was glad I wasn't part of it.

And I finished Mr Strang's book.

On Thursday I got a call from Andrew. He sounded grim. 'I'm in the east end,' he gave me the address, 'there's something you should see.'

A feeling of foreboding gripped me. I drove on Duke Street, an almost straight line all the way to Shettleston. Police cars were parked outside, officers barred the entrance to the close keeping the crowd of chattering neighbours at bay. I asked for DS Geddes and Andrew came down. He took me upstairs and stopped. 'Can't let you in, Charlie, it's a crime scene. Just look. Sure you're ready?' I nodded. 'No you're not,' he said. 'Couldn't ever be ready for this.'

The flat was larger than I thought it would be. The lights were on, cordite mixed with metal in the air and a shotgun lay against the skirting. The walls were washed in blood, pools had dried dark brown and black, even on the ceiling. And the television – the only new piece of furniture – hadn't escaped, bits stuck to the screen.

Cecelia McNeil was on the floor at a crazy angle, eyes open wide, staring, her body almost halved in two. An aluminium rod, a bore brush, a silicone cloth and a can of gun oil lay close by. Across the room a man slumped in an armchair, the white shirt he was wearing no longer white. It was crimson. Stephen McNeil was unrecognisable. Most of his face was missing. DS Geddes stood at my shoulder.

'He killed her, Charlie. Her husband killed her. Must've been cleaning his gun when she arrived. It's over there. Nobody heard a row – just the shots. I remembered you had an interest, that's why I phoned.'

I tried to speak and couldn't. Her husband's mental state had concerned her from the start. When I found Christopher's father

I sealed her death warrant. It was a hellish scene; the demons that tortured Stephen McNeil had done their work well.

I didn't stay.

My father had tried to order my life as his had been ordered in my early teens. In his opinion, like Pat Logue, I could've been anything; instead I'd chosen to be nothing. Today I struggled to disagree. Both cases had ended badly, poorer for my involvement. If I hadn't come across Ian Selkirk at the mortuary. If I'd let the investigation peter out at Celtic Park after the Motherwell game.

If, if, if.

Maybe it was time for a re-think.

I didn't arrive at the office until noon on Friday. My services weren't in demand. The usual assortment of junk mail and utility bills waited for me; the envelope was at the bottom of the pile. I touched it and my fingers trembled. It was from her. She'd been alive on Easter Monday and dead by the Thursday. In between Cecelia McNeil had written to me. Her letters were always full of thanks, this one would be the same. A cheque for more than I would've asked for fell on the desk. The familiar penmanship was there, clean and clear. As ever the tone was polite. Gracious. Not one of the succinct notes I was used to receiving, this one ran to paragraph after paragraph.

Dear Mr Cameron,

The news you brought yesterday was beyond my wildest dreams. I'm sure you realised I'd lost hope. I'm so grateful. But I have a confession. I've lied to you.

In your office I told you Stephen had been the perfect father. That wasn't the truth. He kept his real self hidden until after we were married. Or perhaps it was always there and I was blind. I wanted a partner, what I got was a master. A man who made every decision, whose word was law. I guessed early on he met other women, he made so little effort to keep it from me. I ought to have left him then, and I would have, but the church doesn't recognise divorce, without it I was trapped. I went to mass, put my faith in the Almighty, and carried on.

When Christopher was born I prayed it would change him, and it did.

Stephen became a tyrant.

My boy wasn't like his father, he was reserved and sensitive. Stephen forced him to be what he could never be. Football and fishing and the rest of it. Christopher hated those things. So many nights he cried himself to sleep dreading the next time his father would get out the guns or the rods or the scarves. One day he rebelled, teenagers do, he refused to take part. Stephen shouted and threatened and sulked, it made no difference. I said Christopher neglected his piano practice, that wasn't true either, his father wouldn't let him play at home. He considered the kind of music he played unmanly. I sent my son to lessons with George Lang, secretly at first. His father was furious, when he found out, he beat me.

But my son had talent so I held my ground.

Relations between them deteriorated, they hardly spoke to each other. The incident with the car, when Christopher left the scene of an accident really happened, and my husband acted as any father would. He could understand it, you see.

I knew my child. I already knew who he was. After Christopher told us he was gay his father taunted him, baited him. Some of the things he said I couldn't repeat. Then my son fell in love with George. Stephen saw them kissing in George's car one night. From then on he hounded him, abused him physically and verbally. It never let up. Stephen had become his own father. Worse. Christopher lost weight, became ill. And still it didn't stop. Eventually he couldn't take it anymore and went to the garage.

The church preaches that suicide is a mortal sin and homosexuality an abomination. I asked God to help me, help our family. He didn't, he let my son die.

For better or worse, in sickness and in health. Just words? Not to me.

The information you gave me was all I needed. I'm going to see Stephen now and be free of him forever. 'Till death us do part'. I intend to kill him. Then I'll join Christopher.

I'm sorry, Mr Cameron, you've been so good. Good people deserve better. Don't blame yourself and please don't think too badly of me.
Yours, Cecelia McNeil.

I was stunned. And very, very sad.

It was around nine when I left NYB. Patrick and Gail Logue were at the bar. Seeing them together was rare. Patrick was wearing a suit. Gail smiled. Normal service had resumed and they were happy. Now wasn't the time to tell him. Maybe I wouldn't tell him. I put on a face and went into my act. 'Gail. Don't see you too often. How are you?'

Her husband passed a drink to her, blew the top off a lager and answered. 'We're fine. Never better.' He raised the glass. 'First today.'

For once it probably was. I ran my finger under his lapel. 'Nice suit. Whose is it?'

He put an arm round his wife. 'Celebrating, Charlie. Our anniversary. Out on the razzle. A few jars then off for some traditional Scottish grub. Chicken tikka masala and Irn Bru.'

A light went on in my head. I shook his hand and kissed Gail Logue on the cheek.

'Enjoy yourselves,' I said. 'You've made my night.

Chapter 38

Those who know don't speak. Those who speak don't know.

My senses filled with cumin and ginger and cardamom. An old man with bushy white hair leaned on the cloakroom counter. His eyes danced when he saw me. It was Mr Rani.

He pressed my hands in his and shouted to his family. Videk appeared from the kitchen, grinning from ear to ear. Geeta waved. We sat at a table. He asked about Ian and I told him. Mr Rani didn't deserve a lie. Anjali, his wife, had died; his other son, Salman, was married and living in Manchester. Geeta brought a plate of pakora; she was older too and smiled less. Business was good he said. Life was good.

'Did you ever go back to Kerala?'

'No,' he said, 'it wouldn't do. I have my memories.' He tapped his forehead. 'They live in here. Going back would spoil it.'

I told him why I was there. He called his son and whispered in his ear. Videk brought it to us, a cardboard box taped shut with DRUGS in large letters on the side. Ian. Always the joker. He laid it at my feet. I didn't rush to leave. Speaking to Mr Rani was more important. Patrick had taught me that. We agreed it had been too long and I promised to come back soon. I believed I would.

At the flat a Stanley knife sliced through the layers of tape. Inside were two identical attaché cases. Not even locked. I'd never seen that much money before, not many people have. Who hasn't dreamed of finding a bag of cash and speculated on what they would do? I was no different. Emil Rocha had written it off, he didn't need it. I knew people who did. That night I slept like a baby and woke refreshed for the first time in a long time.

On Cochrane Street, Tom was selling the Big Issue. I handed him the bundle and walked away, picturing the look on his face when he counted it. Stephen McNeil set the bar at fifteen thousand, a nice round figure to begin a new life. Gail Logue wanted to buy a house; the deposit was a start. Patrick would be a hero. Jackie deserved something, just enough to keep her in Jimmy Choo's for a while. I didn't want to step on the Toad God's toes.

Detective Inspector Nigel Platt was last on the list. Platt would rather not have shared the same planet as Archie Cameron's 'son and heir'. The feeling was mutual. He was surprised to hear from me again and complained about the meeting place, a drive out of the city; it didn't suit him. Good.

I walked to the pier in a steady drizzle. I didn't care. My mind was back at the beginning with three kids who thought they were the coolest thing in the world. It hadn't always been bad; Ian, the free spirit, outrageous and so funny. And Fiona: I loved her then and a part of me still did.

The loch was calm, empty of traffic, very different from the day the youngsters impressed each other diving into its cold water. Off to my right the jagged spikes that snared Ian Selkirk's dead body pointed to clouds and Ben Lomond in the distance. It was easy to suppose the reason I was here began with Cecelia McNeil. Really it started long before with a guy struggling like a salmon against the tide, determined to get where he needed to go, seeing his girlfriend's lovely face through the bar crowd, and my hand outstretched to pull him home.

Thanks mate, what you drinking?

What I found at the city mortuary took it out of my hands; the choices were no longer mine, but I preferred my memories the way they'd been even if they weren't the truth, no doubt about that. Mr Rani was right: the past is what you want it to be. I wouldn't go there too often but when I did I'd find old friends, and they'd be the best friends.

DI Platt scowled his way down Pier Road. He was done with Scotland. Every hurried step said he couldn't wait to get away. 'This better be good, Charlie,' he said, graceless to the end. 'I've a train to catch.'

His black eyes widened when he saw the cases at my feet. The photographs of the queen softened his attitude, though even when fortune favoured him he still looked like a rodent with attitude. 'Want to tell me where it was?'

Those who know don't speak

'No. Make up a story. Just leave me out.'

He smiled at some secret joke. 'I suppose you think this makes us even?'

'Not at all, Inspector, I didn't do anything to you. You owe me. Don't forget it.'

I left him running a hand through the neat piles of notes, realising what he had and what it could mean to his future. He called to me, trying to sound casual and failing.

'Is it five million?'

I kept on going. I didn't look back.

'Yeah,' I said. 'Give or take.'

THE END